Praise for

FACELESS

"*Faceless* is gorgeous and wrenching, full of gigantic questions and even more gigantic answers about love, identity, and appearance. I couldn't put it down. Alyssa Sheinmel's writing is so true, her characters so real, that they live on long after the last page is turned."
—*New York Times* bestselling author Luanne Rice

"[Sheinmel's] depiction of a disfigured adolescent girl, already searching for herself and now suddenly forced to accept this new enormity, is compelling . . . absorbing." —*Kirkus Reviews*

"Fascinating . . . Maisie's struggle is certainly one that not many teens will have to face, but teens will identify with her struggle to accept that her old life is gone forever. The anger and grief that she feels is palpable and vividly expressed." —*VOYA*

"A fascinating human portrait of a unique medical procedure, this work paints a complex picture of a young life impacted by a mammoth change." —*School Library Journal*

"Compelling . . . Maisie's emotional torment is authentically conveyed." —*The Bulletin of the Center for Children's Books*

"Sheinmel's prose is accessible to a wide range of readers who, for whatever reason, find themselves struggling with differences. A touching reminder that real change is rarely skin deep."
—*Booklist Online*

FACELESS

ALYSSA SHEINMEL

POINT

PART I

SUMMER

ONE

Step, breath. Step, breath. *typography*

My best friend, Serena, doesn't understand why I run. She said once that of all the different forms of working out, she thought running seemed like the absolute worst. The most punishing. Of course, Serena does yoga.

Step, breath. Step, breath.

As far as I'm concerned, nothing feels better than a run, especially on a morning like this. It's early; the fog is still hanging heavy over the bay. I have the town almost to myself—just me and the dog walkers and the deliverymen, all of us making our way through the thick morning air. It's almost May, but at this hour, it's barely in the fifties. Perfect running weather. I alternate each step with an exhalation. My breath clouds the air in front of me and I race right through it.

Step, breath. Step, breath.

The funny thing about running is that everything hurts. Not just the obvious parts: calves and quads, ankles and glutes. No, my stomach hurts, every muscle straining to help me make the next step, especially when I'm going uphill, like I am now. My shoulders hurt, aching in the joints from which I swing my arms to propel myself forward. I always do whatever I can to keep from focusing on the pain. When I was studying for my SATs, I used this time to test myself on vocabulary words. Before that, I listened to music as loud as I could, like I thought I could drown the pain out. Right now, I'm going over—moment for moment, word for word—the events of last night. When Chirag finally asked me to junior prom.

If I'm honest, maybe that's why I'm out here this morning instead of sleeping in like the rest of the world. Why should I sleep when it's so much more fun to be awake, thinking about what happened last night?

Step, breath. Step, breath.

It's not like I didn't think he was going to ask me. We've been going out since January; of *course* he was going to ask me. But I didn't know *how* he was going to ask me, and I certainly didn't think he was going to show up on my doorstep at nine o'clock on a Tuesday night with a dozen red roses and a sign that read: *Maisie Winters, I love you. Will you go to prom with me?*

We'd never said *I love you* before.

I didn't let him inside. I stepped out onto the porch, shut the door tight behind me, and opened my mouth to say *I love you, too.* But the sound of my parents fighting, audible even through the closed door, stopped me.

We heard my father's shouts, loud and clear. Something about the dishes he'd left in the sink for days.

"Why didn't you just put them in the dishwasher if they bothered you so much?"

"Because it's not my *job* to clean up after you. And I wanted to see just how long you'd let them sit there before you realized you'd left a mess for me to clean up."

"So the dishes were some kind of test I didn't know I was taking?"

"Yes, a test you failed—"

I don't think they even care what they're fighting about anymore. I think they just fight because they've forgotten that there's any other way to communicate. But anyway, the sound of their shouts kind of put a damper on the whole love thing. So I didn't say *I love you* back. Instead, I pushed Chirag down the front steps and toward his car in our driveway. I'd done this at least a dozen times before—dragged him away from our house during one of my parents' many epic battles. Undoubtedly, Chirag knew why he was being pushed backward so rapidly that we nearly fell down the front-porch stairs, but he was sensitive enough not to mention it. Instead he grinned, because with every step I repeated the word *Yes. Yes, yes, yes,* I'll go to prom with you.

When he left, I worried that maybe I'd done the wrong thing. Maybe I should have said *I love you, too* before he drove away. But then, he didn't actually *say* he loved me, so maybe I wasn't *supposed* to say it back. Maybe it doesn't technically, officially *count* until it's said out loud. Maybe there's some strict etiquette about *I love yous* that I don't know because it's never happened to me before. Late last night, I actually considered putting it in a note of my own, just so that we'd be perfectly even.

Now I blink, brushing some sweat from my eyelids, and picture his liquid brown eyes staring at me, crinkling at the edges as his lips widen into a smile. We're polar opposites, physically at least. I have red hair and blue eyes and pale skin dotted with too many freckles. He has caramel skin without a single blemish. To Chirag, my freckles are exotic. He once told me he thought they were sexy, like hundreds of tiny tattoos.

We're going out tonight. Maybe I'll say it then. If he says it first, then I'll definitely say it. I practice the words now, saying them aloud softly in between heaving breaths: *I love you, too. I love you, too. I love you, too.* I break into a sprint, panting. Each word is an effort. This is the last hill before I'll turn back and start running home. I just have to make it around one more curve. Sweat trickles down my neck, beneath my ponytail, getting caught somewhere in my sweatshirt.

I found the dress I want to wear to prom in a magazine over a month ago. It's green and silky and practically backless. It even has a matching headpiece, the same shade of green, for me to pin my long hair around. It's expensive, but I think I can convince my mom. It's the least she can do after last night. Typical of my parents to ruin one of the most important moments of my life with their fighting. But I'll have to work up the nerve to wear the headpiece to the dance anyway. With my red hair, a green sort-of hat could look like I'm dressed up as a Christmas elf or a leprechaun or something. I showed Serena a picture of the dress the other night and she thought that I could totally pull it off, but I'm not convinced yet.

I turn around and start the trek home. This is the easiest part of my run; mostly downhill and with the promise of a hot shower and breakfast once I make it back. I don't notice the first few raindrops; they mix in with my sweat. But as the rain increases, it becomes impossible to ignore. Serena would say that I should've looked at the forecast before I decided to run this morning. Serena wouldn't understand that I rolled out of bed hours before my alarm went off, got dressed in the dark, and jogged out the front door without even looking at myself in the mirror, let alone at a weather report.

I'm keeping this run short, just in case Chirag wants to run together after school later. When we run together, it always turns into a competition, a dozen tiny races along the way. Who can get to the end of this street faster? Who can make it up the hill first? Who can jump highest over the tree stump on my corner? I won't mind a second workout today. I never miss an excuse to spend more time with him—or anything at all that keeps me out of the house, and away from my parents' fighting, just a little bit longer.

Only a few blocks left; I can see the tree stump from here. It was an enormous oak once, but it was struck by lightning years ago. Its branches crashed through the windows of the nearest house; the trunk fell flat across the street and caused some kind of massive car accident. No one ever bothered getting rid of the stump, though. Apparently, its roots were so deep that digging it up would have been really expensive. They'd have had to cut off the plumbing to half the neighborhood. At least that's what my father told me. Maybe he was just trying to scare me from going outside in a thunderstorm, like I am right now.

The rain turns icy cold, snaking its way under my sweatshirt and into my sneakers. I shiver. The first crack of thunder makes me jump. I break into a sprint; I can almost see our house from here. Anyway, I shouldn't be such a baby, scared of a little thunder and lightning. When I was younger, I'd crawl into my parents' bed during thunderstorms, settle myself right in between them. I couldn't do that now if I wanted to. My father started sleeping in the den months ago.

Lightning streaks across the sky, breaking up the fog, drenching my neighborhood in light. For a split second, everything is completely clear, as bright as if it were the middle of the day and not six in the morning. It takes me a second to realize that I've stopped running, that I'm standing still.

Another crack of lightning, closer now, and I spin around in the direction of the sound. Behind me, a tree has been hit, just a few yards away from the tree stump. Who ever said that lightning didn't strike twice in the same place? A blackened branch hangs on to the tree's trunk by just a few fibers of wood, draped down over the electrical wires, or phone wires, or whatever they are, dancing in the wind, setting off sparks that look almost like fireworks.

I should get moving, go on home, take off these soaked clothes and sit on top of the radiator until I'm warm. But for some reason, I find myself rooted in this spot, staring at the embers flying down. It's strange to see sparks even as the rain grows stronger, stranger still when they ignite into flames. There is an audible *whoosh* as the fire travels up the branch of the tree, a crisp sort of crackling as the leaves begin to burn, filling the air with tiny pieces of white ash. I taste smoke in the back of my throat, so thick and heavy that I think I might retch.

I press my hands to my face when the branch finally snaps from the tree, dragging the wires to the ground with an enormous crash every bit as loud as the thunder.

Another flash of lightning illuminates the sky, but my neighborhood is already saturated with light from the fire and the sparks coming off the wires. When they hit the wet ground, they sizzle.

I close my eyes and listen: The sizzles sound almost like whispers.

Hiss, hiss, hisssssssssss.

TWO

I t feels like swimming. No, I wasn't swimming. I was running.

Step, breath. Step, breath.

"She's moving!" someone shouts. My father's voice. But what's he doing here, on my run? We haven't run together in years. He can't keep up with me anymore.

Step, breath. Step, breath.

Slowly, I become aware that I'm not standing. That my feet aren't pounding the pavement but flailing around, trapped under tightly tucked covers. The sensation of swimming had nothing at all to do with water, but swimming up into consciousness after a long, deep sleep.

"Hurry, please!" My mother's voice this time. "She's moving!"

Why are they shouting like it's some kind of miracle that I'm moving? I move every minute of every day. I even move in my sleep— I toss and turn, one of those people who can't stay in the same position all night.

A deep voice that I don't recognize says my name once, twice. He shines a bright light in my eyes. "Dilated," he murmurs. Louder: "She's going to drift in and out of consciousness for the next hour or so. Don't be surprised if she's a little fuzzy for a while."

It takes me a second to realize that the man with the deep voice isn't talking *to* me, but *about* me. I open my mouth to speak, but sleep sneaks up on me again, swallowing my questions before they have a chance to escape.

This happens at least three more times that I can remember—I move, my parents shout, the man with the deep voice shines a light in my eyes and I fall back to sleep—but the fourth time, my eyes finally stay open.

The skin surrounding my eyes is wrapped up in something thick and bulky so that I have tunnel vision: I can see only what's directly in front of me, and since I'm lying on my back, all I can see is the ceiling, painted a sticky sort of light blue that someone probably thought looked like the sky.

I try to speak, but my voice is nothing more than the thinnest of croaks, as though I haven't had anything to drink for weeks. My throat feels like it's made of sandpaper and my lips feel like there are dozens of tiny needles pricking them over and over.

"Mom?" I whisper. I try to clear my throat, lick my lips, swallow, but everything is dry. My lips are cracked and when I stick my tongue out to lick them, I feel something foreign on my face.

I think it's bandages. I think I'm in the hospital.

"Mom?" I croak. I try to roll over but my left side feels like it weighs a thousand pounds. I *can't* roll over.

"I'm here, honey." My mother's voice sounds soft and soothing, nothing like it sounded when she shouted for help earlier. I try to lift my head to see her face, but I can't actually turn my neck. My head feels like it's encased in plaster. Maybe it is. I begin to sweat, a string of panic twisting its way through my rib cage. *What happened to me?*

My mother must position herself so that her face is directly above mine, because finally I can see her hovering above me. The string of panic tightens when I see the expression on her face. I've never seen her look so frightened. She looks about ten years older than she did the last time I saw her.

My god, this must be bad. My heart starts beating hard, so fast that a nearby machine begins to wail.

"Sweetheart," she says, trying to reach for me, but I shake my head. Or I try to shake my head. I can't move my neck. Oh god, I'm paralyzed. Oh god, I broke my spine and I'll never run again. I'm going to be one of those people who sit in a wheelchair and move it forward by blowing into a tube.

No. *Get a grip, Maisie.* I was able to move my legs before. They *saw* me moving my legs. I kick them now, just to make sure I can. I exhale deeply, my throat still parched, but my heart begins to slow. The machine resumes its steady beep. Listening carefully, I guess that it must be right next to the bed, just above me on the right.

"Water," I croak. It's hard to make words from beneath whatever it is that's wrapped around my face. The word comes out sounding like *wa-wa*, but my mother must understand because she nods, then disappears. She doesn't go far; she's just moving to get a cup of water from my bedside table, but that's outside of my field of vision.

"Is it okay?" my mother asks.

Another female voice answers, "Just a little."

"Who's that?" I ask. I wish I could see. I wish I could sit up. I wish I could *move.*

"One of your nurses," Mom says. "Anna."

Then Mom reappears. She holds a cup to my mouth and I use a straw to drink, even though it hurts my lips. I hold it with my teeth instead. Water has never tasted so good. I could drink ten, twenty, thirty glasses of water. I swish the water around in my mouth, wetting all the places that feel so dry.

"Not too much, sweetie," my mother says, pulling the cup away, her face back to its place above mine. What's wrong with me that *water* is dangerous?

Footsteps; someone coming into the room.

"Give her a chance, Sue," says another voice. My father's this time. "She hasn't had anything to drink for nearly a month."

It's hard to drink lying so flat and water goes down the wrong tube. I cough—or anyway, I try to cough, but it's hard when you're as immobilized as I am. What does he mean, I haven't had anything to drink for nearly a month? I must have misheard him. Every sound is muffled through whatever it is that's wrapped around my head.

"What happened to me?" Even after the water, my voice sounds strange. I can barely move my mouth: *Wha happa ta ma?*

"You're in the hospital," Dad says, not answering my question. I can't see his face but it sounds like he's standing at the foot of my bed. There's room for only one person in my limited field of vision and it's still my mother.

He adds, "The burn unit of the hospital. Do you remember your accident?"

I keep forgetting that I can't shake my head. The burn unit. The panic string in my chest tightens. A burn unit is not a good place to be.

"You were running," Dad prompts. It's strange to hear his voice, feel his presence in the room, without seeing his face. "There was a storm."

"Lightning," I say, remembering. The words come out muffled, as if my mouth were stuffed with gauze. "I was struck by lightning?"

My question is met with silence at first. Another time, another place, that question would be a joke. No one is actually struck by lightning, right? I mean, I know somewhere, someway, people are. But it's really really rare, right? Nervous sweat drips down my neck, seeping into my bandages. Finally, my mother says, "She can't see you shaking your head, Graham."

"There was a fire," Dad answers finally. There's something weird in his voice, like he can barely stand saying the word *fire* out loud. Mom leaves my side for a moment; I hear her shoes clicking on the floor as she crosses the room. Is she going to hug my father? I can't remember the last time I saw them so much as shake hands.

Whatever's wrong with me, it must be really bad if she's comforting him.

My heart starts to pound again. I beg it not to go so fast that the machine starts screeching again, concentrating the same way I do when I run and I'm trying to save up my energy for the final sprint. But my will isn't strong enough to overcome my body, at least not this time, because the machine starts to wail. I hear footsteps and the sound stops—the nurse, Anna, must have turned off the machine.

"Dad, please. What's wrong with me?" My question sounds absurd: *Wha wron wit ma?* I repeat the question, struggling to make the words sound clear. They'll never tell me if I sound like a toddler.

It *can't* be that bad. I'm not the kind of person really bad things happen to. Not particularly good things, either. I'm just a normal girl. I'm not the most popular, but I'm not the biggest nerd either. I have a boyfriend, but it's not like he's the captain of the football team and I'm homecoming queen. I've had the same best friend since first grade. My parents fight, but everyone's parents fight. I'm just *normal*.

And it can't be that bad because I'm not in any pain. Nothing hurts. I try lifting my right arm; it feels fine. But when I try to lift my left arm, I discover that something is holding it in place.

Finally, Mom says, "The doctor will be here in just a second. Your father went to ask for him the minute you woke up."

"Why can't I move my left arm?"

"It's all wrapped up in bandages, baby. You suffered second-degree burns on your left arm and torso."

I exhale. Second-degree burns. *That's not so bad,* I think. Can't people get second-degree burns from just staying in the sun too long? I'm going to be okay. The string of panic loosens; my heart slows. I take a deep breath.

Footsteps again. Then a face I've never seen before is hovering above mine. But when he speaks I recognize his voice. He's the one who said I'd be a little fuzzy for a while.

"Second-degree burns aren't that bad, right?" I ask immediately.

He ignores my question. Or maybe he didn't understand it. How will I get answers if I can't make myself be heard? Beneath my bandages, I feel hot. I fight the urge to yank at them like a too-tight collar.

"Maisie, my name is Dr. Cohen. I've been handling your case since you were brought in."

Something about the way he says *since you were brought in* gives away the fact that I've been here a long time. My father's words come back to me.

"What did my dad mean when he said that I hadn't had anything to drink for nearly a month?" It takes me a while to ask such a long question. I have to hold each word in my mouth before it can get out.

Dr. Cohen blinks, hesitating. He looks away for a second, to my parents maybe. He nods. His dark brown eyes remind me of Chirag's, though his aren't quite so deep, not quite so liquidy. In the right light, Chirag's eyes look like cups of black coffee.

"You've been getting all the fluids you need from your IV," Dr. Cohen says. He sounds positively cheerful about it, as though getting fluids from a needle is a much more convenient way to stay hydrated than, say, drinking.

"Have I been in a coma or something?" I ask slowly.

"Something like that," Dr. Cohen says. "Though not a coma like you'd think of it."

What is that supposed to mean, I think but do not say. I've never actually thought of a coma one way or another before.

"We induced your coma," he says carefully.

Suddenly, I wish it was my mother's face and not Dr. Cohen's that I was looking at, no matter how frightened she looks. In fact, for the first time in a long time—maybe for the first time ever—I wish I were sitting on my mother's lap, wish she was rocking me back and forth and saying things like *It's gonna be okay, baby* and *Nothing to worry about, just a scratch or two.*

"Why?" I ask finally.

"With your injuries—Maisie, you were burned very badly." His face is serious, his mouth settling into a perfectly straight line in between sentences. "Your injuries were so severe that we thought it would be best to keep you in a coma until we could manage your pain. Your body needed the time to recover."

That doesn't sound so bad. I must be almost fixed, then, if they've decided it's time for me to wake up. I must have slept through the worst of it.

"For how long?" I ask.

"A few weeks," Dr. Cohen answers.

A few weeks? A few *weeks*! I know I shouldn't be surprised—Dad said it had almost been a month—but seriously, who do these doctors think they are, the bad fairy in *Sleeping Beauty*?

I close my eyes, trying to imagine everything I must have missed. Prom, for starters. It was scheduled for three weeks before the end of the school year. Serena and I were going to get ready together. She was going to do my hair for me, since I never have the patience to do anything but pull it into a ponytail. She was going to be ready with her camera when Chirag picked me up, to catch a picture of what his face looked like when he first saw me in my dress. We weren't going to sit out a single dance all night.

Has the school year ended yet? Don't they know I can't miss my final exams? I have papers to write. Races to run. Am I going to have to repeat my junior year? How am I going to get into Berkeley with something like that on my record?

Summer school. I can go to summer school. Plenty of kids do. And the doctors will put a note on my file explaining that I wasn't a delinquent or something, I just had an accident.

"When can I go home?" I ask, though I say it too fast and it sounds like *Whe cah ah ga ho?* I say it again, slower this time.

Dr. Cohen blinks again. "Maisie, I'm afraid you're going to be with us for quite some time yet."

"But why? For a few second-degree burns?"

Even as I ask the question, I know that there's something more, something they haven't told me yet. Suddenly, I'm certain that something very bad has happened to me. I can hear it in the timbre of my mother's voice and I can see it in the rehearsed smile that's plastered on Dr. Cohen's face. The panic is setting in again. My heart is beating faster. Sweat pools at the nape of my neck.

They don't put you in a coma for a few second-degree burns.

My mother's voice rings out, clear as a bell: "Maisie. It wasn't just your left side that got burned."

THREE

I t was my face. Electrical burns to my face from the wires the tree branch brought down. They tell me the story, piece by piece. I don't remember anything after the sparks that looked like fireworks, so I listen as though I'm hearing about something that happened to someone else.

"The Smiths called 911," Dad says. The Smiths live three houses down from us.

"Evan Blake ran out with a fire extinguisher and tried to spray the flames away," Mom adds. Evan Blake lives in the house to the left of ours. He and Dad sometimes go fishing together. I wonder if my parents saw Evan running toward my burning body with the extinguisher or if they put the pieces together later, when they saw Evan standing there, red can in hand, my body covered in foam.

Mom says that by the time the ambulance showed up, the tree was smoldering and smoke was still rising from my body. I was unconscious; whether from smoke inhalation or from shock, they didn't know. They weren't sure I was going to survive, but by some miracle I pulled through.

Isn't that wonderful, Dr. Cohen says, by some *miracle*.

I thought doctors didn't believe in miracles. I thought they were scientists. Chirag isn't even a doctor yet—he wants to be someday—but he would never call what happened to me a *miracle*. Instead, he would explain the science behind my survival.

I wish Chirag were here instead of Dr. Cohen. Unlike Dr. Cohen, Chirag would never tell me I should be thankful. I want not just the Chirag of right now—the high school track star who would hold my hand and kiss my knuckles—but I also want Chirag as he'll be twenty years from now, the man with all the medical expertise required to explain my condition. I close my eyes and picture Chirag in a long white coat when Dr. Cohen says again, "Do you know just how lucky you are?"

A few hours after I wake up, the pain sets in. Apparently, whatever drugs they'd given me to ease the transition are wearing off.

I gasp when I feel it. I might not remember what it felt like to burn—maybe my body went into shock immediately so that I didn't actually *feel* it at all—but it can't have been worse than this.

I didn't know pain like this existed. Dr. Cohen says that the body can't actually remember pain. It's what allows women to have more than one child, he adds with a wry smile. I wouldn't have laughed at such a lame joke under even the best of circumstances, and at the moment it's hard to imagine that I'll ever laugh again.

Anyway, I don't believe him. *He's* never been in pain like this. *He* doesn't know what he's talking about. I will never forget this: the sensation on my side, like a million needles are digging in all at once; my left hand, screaming in protest when I try to move it even the slightest bit. Tears blur my vision, but it hurts too much to cry. Crying doesn't seem like *enough* for what I'm feeling. My god, if this is what they woke me up to feel, what must it have been like when they put me into the coma?

I hear Dr. Cohen ordering morphine, hear the click of a needle being fitted into my IV. I always thought only old people, dying people, got morphine. But apparently they give it to people like me, too.

And then, as suddenly as it came, the pain stops. I gasp again, this time with relief.

The world is strange enough with such a limited field of vision—filled with voices that I don't recognize, no faces to attach them to—but over the next few days, I discover that it's even weirder through the hazy veil of painkillers. It feels like I'm walking through cotton. Not that I'm walking through anything at all: I haven't left my bed since I woke up.

The first time a nurse comes in to rub salve onto the second-degree burns on my left arm and my side, I don't even realize what's happening until she's pulled back the already meager covers and exposed my broken body for the world to see. Since I can't see anything but what's directly above me, I don't know if my parents are in the room. I wonder how many times they've seen me undressed since all this happened, how many people have seen me naked. I wonder exactly what's left for them to see.

I'm mortified. I was the kind of girl who hated changing in the locker room in front of my friends and teammates. And those were people who knew me well, people who were exposing themselves, too.

I'm aware of the nurse's touch, but it feels far away, like something that happened hours ago. A chill runs up my spine and I try to shudder, but my body won't cooperate.

I always thought salve was supposed to be soothing, but it's actually something that aches and burns and stings. With my right hand, I squeeze the button that's supposed to send morphine down my IV and into my veins, but I don't think there's a painkiller on the planet strong enough to make this go away. I try to concentrate hard on something else, just like I do when I run. While they change my bandages, I close my eyes and imagine that I didn't miss the prom after all; I picture myself in my dress, slow-dancing with Chirag. Every day, I pick a different song, and in my imagination, it plays on an endless loop until the pain subsides. I imagine that it's Chirag's arms around me instead of the nurses'. When they rub the salve into my burns, I imagine that it's Chirag running his hands up and down my back. When it stings so much that I have to grit my teeth to keep from shouting, I imagine that Chirag's mouth is pressed against mine in a long, sweet kiss. My lips, apparently, received only first-degree burns that had mostly healed by the time they woke me from the coma. Beyond being terribly chapped from so much time without drinking water or gliding on lip balm, they're fine.

Physical therapists come into my room to move my limbs around so that I don't get bedsores and my joints don't stiffen. Doctors come into my room when they think I'm sleeping, a gaggle of students trailing behind them. I listen as they drone on about my *special* case.

I don't feel *special*. I feel trapped. I want to disconnect all these tubes and wires, to jump out of this bed, slip on my sneakers, sprint into the hallway, down the stairs, and out the door. When I sleep, I dream of running around the track behind our school, of winning every race I enter, of beating Chirag when we race to the tree stump. In my dreams, I feel the wind on my face.

It's when I sleep that they change the mask. They never go near my face when I'm awake.

Apparently, electrical fires burn hotter and faster than regular fires. Apparently, they're able to blaze even in the rain. They tell me the fire was so hot it burned blue. And eventually, they tell me that the burns on the left side of my face are not second degree. When I ask if they're third-degree burns they say no, but they don't call them fourth-degree burns either. I tell myself that they can't be that bad because my face actually doesn't hurt as much as my side.

Every day, I ask someone—a doctor, a nurse, my parents—*When will I get these bandages off my face? When will I be healed?* I never get a straight answer, and every time someone avoids the question, the string of panic around my rib cage tightens, until I think that the real miracle is the fact that my ribs haven't split in two. I ask if Serena and Chirag have visited, but they say only immediate family is allowed. I'm still not out of the woods. My mother promises to call and tell them that I miss them. My words are still so muffled that they wouldn't be able to understand me if I called myself. Anyway, cell phones aren't allowed in this part of the hospital.

It's my father who finally tells me the truth. I wake up in the middle of the night and for once, there's only one person in the room with me, instead of an army of doctors and interns and who knows who else. I recognize the sound of his breathing. I can hear the scratch of his pencil against paper so I know he's not asleep. He's probably doing a crossword puzzle.

"Daddy?" I say into the darkness.

"I'm here, sweetheart," he answers. His chair squeaks against the linoleum. He's pulling it to sit along my right side. He takes my hand in his. His palms are hot and clammy, like he's nervous about something. He stays sitting down instead of standing with his face above mine, so I can't see him.

For what feels like the millionth time, I ask, "When will these bandages come off? When will I be healed?" I've gotten much better at speaking with this mask on, but the words still come slowly.

Dad doesn't say anything for so long that I think he might have fallen asleep. But finally, he says, "Your face won't ever heal."

That doesn't make any sense. Everything heals eventually, right? If my face isn't going to heal, then what am I doing here, in the hospital? My seventh-grade science teacher taught us about *if, then* statements, and I always liked how undeniably logical they were. So I ask my father the most undeniably logical question:

"If I'm never going to heal, then I'm dying, right?" The words struggle to make their way around the lump in my throat.

"No, sweetheart. It's just these burns—"

"I know," I say, the words coming out stiffly from beneath my bandages. "I've heard it a dozen times already. They're so severe. More severe than the burns on my side. Do I need a skin graft, is that it?" We read about them in biology class my freshman year. In cases of third-degree burns, they take the undamaged skin from one part of your body and stretch it over the burned part.

My father squeezes my hand in his. "Your face is more than just burned. It's—" He pauses. Takes a deep breath. When he speaks, his voice is shaking. "Part of it is destroyed."

Destroyed. The word sounds out of place here, in a hospital. *Destroyed* is what happens to villages in the path of tsunamis. To buildings when bombs drop. To ships that sink to the bottom of the sea. *Destroyed* isn't something that happens to a thing as small as a single person's face.

Dad continues, "Your nose, your left cheek, most of your chin. The tissue was killed in the fire."

Destroyed. Killed. It's like I've never heard the words before. I have no idea what he means. How can parts of a person's face die?

"The dead skin, the muscle, the bone—the doctors had to remove it." That must have been when they put me into the coma. They wouldn't have been able to manage the pain any other way. "Now your face is wrapped in a special kind of antiseptic gauze, a kind of temporary substitute—"

"Part of my face is *gone*?" I interrupt. How is that possible? What exactly is the gauze wrapped around?

My father doesn't say anything. His breathing is ragged. He's crying. I don't think I've ever seen my father cry. Of course, I'm still not seeing it. I'm just hearing it.

Electrical fires burn hotter and faster than regular fires. How strange to think that as the fire grew hotter, it turned blue. Blue is the color of the cold bay, the cool afternoon sky, the color of freezing lips and fingertips. I can't imagine a hot kind of blue.

I think it might be easier to make sense of what my father's saying if I could just remember what it was like to catch fire, but my mind is blank. Maybe I'd already lost consciousness by the time it happened. Or maybe that's something your brain does for you; induces a sort of selective amnesia so that you can't remember the most terrifying moment of your life. But I wish I could remember *something*. Because right now, nothing my father is saying sounds true. None of it sounds like something that happened to *me*.

"My face—my nose, my cheek, my chin—they just *melted* off in the fire, is that what you're saying?" I close my eyes and try to imagine it, an enormous jagged C curving around the left side of my face. It looks like something from a movie, a fairy tale, a horror story.

"Yes," he says hoarsely. "Kind of." The chair squeaks against the linoleum again. He's standing up. "I'll get you a tissue."

"What for?"

"You're crying." I felt the lump in my throat, but I didn't feel tears, and I guess I didn't feel my nose running because I no longer have a nose to run.

Oh god. I no longer have a *nose*. The lump in my throat rises until I think it will choke me.

Now he does come into my line of sight, carefully pressing a tissue into my eyes. I didn't feel the tears sneaking beneath my bandages to stream down my face, and I don't feel the pressure of his touch now.

"Why don't I feel anything?"

"The tissue is dead, baby. You *can't feel* anything."

I guess that explains why my face hurts less than my side. But I still don't understand. How can I not have a nose, two cheeks, a chin? That's not possible. There must be *something* left. There can't just be a big black hole where my nose used to be, can there?

Pink light begins streaming through the windows. Outside, the sun must be rising up through the fog.

It's not a lot of light, but it's enough. There won't be much to see, not with my face covered up the way it is, but I need to look. I don't think I'll believe it until I see it for myself. Not because I think Dad is lying—but because I literally can't conceive of it, can't wrap my mind around it.

"I need to see it," I beg softly. "Please."

My father nods, then disappears. For a second, I think he's leaving to get a doctor, a nurse, to insist they increase my morphine drip so that I'll fall back to sleep. Maybe he hopes that when I wake up, I won't remember any of this, or that I'll think it was just a dream. It seems like something out of a dream. A nightmare, really. Because in the real world, there's no such thing as a girl without a face.

Much to my surprise, Dad comes back with a mirror in his hand, the kind they put in the bathroom to help you put makeup on. I wait for him to put the mirror above my face so that I can see my reflection.

My head is wrapped in bandages, but I can see that where my nose should be protruding, it's flat as a pancake. My face kind of collapses just below my bottom lip—the gauze sinks inward where my chin used to be, like someone took an ax and sliced the bone right off, leaving nothing but empty space between my mouth and my neck.

The string of panic around my rib cage is tight, tighter than it's ever been before. I've never seen anything so ugly. I'm a freak, an alien, an extra from a sci-fi movie. I'm a monster who makes children cry, the cautionary tale parents tell.

A choked sort of gasp sticks in my throat as my eyes—the only features I can still recognize—fill with tears. What happens to a girl after she's been destroyed? Does she stay in the hospital forever, like an ogre from a folktale, locked away in a tower? Does she go back to school and get pointed at, gawked at, gossiped about? Does her boyfriend . . . oh my god, my boyfriend. Chirag can't see me like this. Chirag can't see me ever again. I can't believe I actually found it comforting to imagine he was sitting in a chair beside my bed, holding my hand all this time. Does Chirag even *know* about this?

What have my parents told him? I wish I'd never made Mom promise to call him. My heart is pounding so hard and so loud that I want to cover my ears.

Before my dad leaves, I ask him to put the mirror on the right side of my bed. I want it to be within arm's reach so that I can grab it anytime I need to remind myself that I was wrong:

There is such a thing as a girl without a face.

FOUR

I wake to the sound of footsteps, and a voice I don't recognize shouting, "Good morning!"

"The burn unit is no place to be chipper," I mumble, opening my eyes. I don't think whoever it is hears me. Or cares.

They've lowered my morphine. Everything is becoming a bit sharper around the edges.

"My name is Marnie," the voice continues, as though I greeted her with enthusiasm and have been awake for hours, just like she has. I can't believe I used to be a morning person. "I'm your physical therapist."

"I have a dozen physical therapists," I answer, thinking of the folks who come in and out of my room every day, standing at my bedside to move my limbs around, making sure that the muscles don't atrophy, that my skin doesn't freeze in place as it heals.

"Of course, Maisie, but I'm going to be working with you—Oh!" she says suddenly, cutting herself off.

"What's wrong?" I ask frantically.

"I just realized how similar our names are. Maisie. Marnie. Just one letter different."

"Two letters," I correct. Who the heck does this woman think she is? She has no right to come in here and talk to me with her bright voice and her upbeat tone.

Don't you know what happened to me? Can't you see what I look like?

I close my eyes. My mirror is within arm's reach, but I don't have to look. What I saw last night is imprinted on my brain. I try to swallow the lump in my throat, but I think it's taken up permanent residence.

I haven't seen Marnie's face yet, but I have a feeling I know exactly what *she* looks like. She probably has shiny blond hair in a high ponytail and tan skin and cheeks covered in blush and bubble-gum gloss on her lips. I bet she was a cheerleader in high school. Maybe she uses her old pom-poms to cheer her patients now. I wonder if I can ask to be assigned to someone less perky.

Then a stunningly beautiful African-American woman floats into my field of vision. Instead of flowing blond hair, she has an enormous Afro, and when she smiles, her teeth are bright white but just a little crooked, like she decided not to get braces because then she would've been too perfect.

"Let's get you sitting up, all right?"

"I don't think I can," I answer timidly. I haven't actually sat up since before my accident.

"You can," Marnie says firmly. "You'll just need a little help the first time."

As always, I wish I could shake my head. What's the point of all this? Who cares if I can sit up or not? A girl without a face doesn't need to be able to move around. I'll probably stay in bed for the rest of my life: the blinds drawn, the door locked. Hidden away from the whole wide world, like Rapunzel in her tower.

But Marnie doesn't seem to care that there's no point, because she steps closer and presses a button on the side of the bed, which begins to move. She leans down and circles me in her long arms, holding me steady as the bed folds beneath me, until I'm angled at about forty-five degrees instead of flat on my back. I can just see the wall in front of me. Instead of the sticky blue of the ceiling, it's white, and someone has taped pictures of me all over it. Me with my parents, me with Serena, me with Chirag. Who put them there, and why?

With one arm, Marnie pulls the covers back, exposing my bare legs. She keeps her other arm steady around me. "Now swing your legs over the side of the bed."

The string of panic circles its way around my chest. The gauze wrapped around my head feels like it's made of glass, like if I move too fast it will break, taking what's left of my face along with it.

"I'm not supposed to move," I say stubbornly. I don't *want* to move.

"If you weren't supposed to move, honey, I wouldn't be here."

"Maybe we should wait until my dad gets back."

"Your dad went home a few hours ago."

I can't believe it. He didn't want to be here when I woke up, after what he told me last night? But maybe he needed some time to recover from the conversation, too.

"Maybe we should talk to the doctors first."

"The doctors are the ones who told me to come work with you, silly," she counters.

"But my face—" I stop myself. Does she know exactly what's wrong with my face? There are so many people coming in and out of my room at all hours. It's hard to believe that every one of them knows all the details. I've only known for eight hours.

Then again, no one but me *needed* to be told. Everyone else can see it the instant they lay eyes on me. For the rest of my life, every single person who sees me will know. Strangers. Teachers. Serena. *Chirag.*

The lump in my throat rises again. I don't want to cry, not in front of this perky, beautiful woman who's probably never felt ugly a day in her life. What were they doing, assigning her to me? Did someone think it would be an interesting social experiment: *Let's see how the freak reacts when she has to work with the most beautiful woman in the world.*

"I know what I'm doing, Maisie," Marnie says, sounding for just an instant more solemn than chipper.

I can tell that Marnie is the kind of woman who doesn't take no for an answer. Who will stay here until I do everything she asks. I recognize it in her voice because I've always been that stubborn, too. So I say, "Okay." Maybe the sooner I give in, the sooner she'll leave.

"Come on, now, honey," Marnie orders. "Swing."

I know I can move my legs. The day I woke up from the coma, I was practically trying to sprint.

Marnie guides my torso, twisting it so that it follows my legs as I turn. I think about my stomach muscles, the way they worked when I ran. Even though it's been a long time, they should still be able to hold me up, right? The tight skin on my left side screams in protest.

"There!" Marnie says triumphantly. She drops her arms so that she's only holding my hands. My legs dangle over the side of the bed and I swing them back and forth like a little kid. "Good job, sweetheart."

"I don't think you know me well enough to call me sweetheart."

Marnie laughs. "Maybe not. But I will."

"You will?"

Marnie nods. "We'll be spending a lot of time together soon enough."

She drops my hands and bends down, disappearing briefly. I sway from side to side, light-headed. Perhaps *literally* light-headed. Who knows the weight of the pieces they removed? God, bad joke. But seriously, is there such a thing as a good joke at a time like this?

"Use your abdominals," Marnie commands. "I know you have them. Your parents told me you were an athlete." I can hear that she's moved off to the left, toward the door.

"You're not going to leave, are you?" I press my hands into the mattress, trying to steady myself. Seconds ago, I never wanted to see this woman again, and now I'm terrified of being left alone. When did I turn into such a wimp?

"No such luck," Marnie says, reappearing. She's holding a ball in her hand, the rubber kind my father keeps on his desk at the office, for squeezing when he's stressed-out.

"Are you a lefty or a righty?"

"Righty," I say.

"Well, that's lucky."

Stop calling me lucky, I think. I am so sick of being told I'm lucky. I'm pretty sure I'm the least lucky person I've ever met. After all, everyone else I've ever seen in my entire life hasn't been faceless.

32

Marnie takes my left hand from the bed and unwinds the bandages, exposing my skin. I try to gaze down at it but then I remember I can't tilt my neck, so I lift my hand into my field of vision. I used to have a dark brown freckle on the knuckle of my left pointer finger, but now there is just pink skin surrounded by jagged scars. The skin looks unfinished, like it belongs to a baby who should still be in utero, who isn't ready to be exposed to the light of the world.

It certainly doesn't look sexy, like Chirag used to say my freckles were.

Would it have been better or worse if it had been my hand that was lost, and my face that only suffered second-degree burns? The question reminds me of those miserable math problems in the SATs, the ones that look like they don't actually have an answer.

Marnie turns my hand so that my palm is facing upward in front of me and places the ball in the center of it. Immediately, the ball rolls off my skin and down to the floor.

Marnie laughs, bends down, retrieves the ball, and puts it back. It rolls off again.

"You have to squeeze it," she says, still laughing. I hate her for laughing, but I guess I should get used to the sound. The way I am now, she certainly won't be the last person to laugh at me.

This time, when she replaces the ball on my hand, I bend my fingers. I gasp, shocked by how much it hurts. It feels like I'm wearing a glove that's about ten sizes too small. It feels like if I keep bending my fingers, the glove will rip right down the middle. Like my skin will just crack open.

The ball falls to the ground. Marnie laughs and replaces it. She holds it in place. I grit my teeth the same way I do at the beginning of a race.

"Don't laugh at me." She lets go of the ball and I bend my fingers, holding my breath to steel myself for the pain. She wouldn't be telling me to do this if my skin were really going to rip apart, right? I bend some more, trying to concentrate not on the pain but on the rubber of the ball in the palm of my hand. My fingertips just barely graze the top of it before I can't hold it anymore. I relax my fingers, and the ball falls again.

Next, Marnie says I'm going to stand up. The mere thought sets my heart pounding once more. She reaches for my IV bag and hangs it onto a pole with wheels on it so that I'm no longer attached to the bed. She puts her arms around me, fitting her elbows beneath my armpits. I can feel the warmth of her skin and the bumps of her muscles through my flimsy hospital gown.

That's one of the many indignities I didn't know about before I was in here: the hospital gown. When you see people wearing them on television shows about hospitals, you don't know that the gowns are made of material just slightly thicker than paper, that they tie up the back, and that in real life they keep gowns untied for easy access. And the people on TV are surely wearing bras and underwear under their gowns; I haven't worn a bra or underwear since I've been here. I never imagined I would long for underwire. On TV, they never mention a word about catheters and—once they take the catheter away—bedpans, adult diapers, and the mats they place under the sheets on the bed in case you leak.

They certainly never mention just how many fluids a person can leak.

Now the tips of my toes hit the floor first. The linoleum is surprisingly warm beneath my bare feet. Marnie guides me off the bed, and slowly, gingerly, I lower my heels to the floor. The thick calluses on my heels from years of running are still there. Marnie backs away from me until her hands are on my elbows.

"Don't put all your weight on your right side," she warns, and I shift, feeling the pressure of my weight engage the muscles beneath the ruined skin on my left side, which feel so much weaker than they used to.

"Take a step, Maisie," Marnie says, like I'm a toddler who's learning to walk for the first time. I slide my right foot out in front of me and Marnie shakes her head, her curls bouncing back and forth. "Don't shuffle," she instructs. "Lift your foot off the ground."

I hesitate and press my toes into the floor. What difference does it make if I never walk again? It's not like a girl without a face has places she needs to go.

"I won't let you fall," Marnie says. "I promise."

I should have stepped with my left foot first. Then all the weight of my body would be my right side's responsibility.

"Good!" Marnie shouts as I lift my right foot, grinning so that I can see her crooked teeth.

I always thought that when people said they saw their life flashing before their eyes, it was just some kind of expression. I certainly never thought it was literal. But as Marnie slides her grip down my arms from my elbows to my hands, I close my eyes, and I swear, I can see my life flashing before me like a series of pictures.

My first race, which I finished dead last, the only freshman to make the team.

My next track meet, where I came in third.

The time I nearly dropped the baton on a relay. Now I can practically feel the hot metal of it in my hands.

The first time I won a race. My arms overhead, my ridiculous little victory dance.

Sophomore year, when Coach said she thought I might be able to get a scholarship.

Then I flash back further, even younger: eighth grade, when I raced Dad around the local reservoir and won. Third grade, running down the street to catch the neighbors' dog when she dug her way out from under their fence. Kindergarten, running around during recess, faster than all the boys, volunteering to be "it" when we played tag.

And then a sudden flash forward: running alongside Chirag through the fog and the mist on the track behind the school. Running barefoot with him in the woods. Running out of his reach when he tried to grab me, and laughing all the while.

My whole life, always, always running, as fast as my legs could carry me. Sweat dripping down my face, getting into my eyes and mouth. The taste of salt on my tongue.

I open my eyes. Shaking, holding on to Marnie's hands so tight my fingers ache, I take another step. Marnie cheers.

FIVE

At two in the morning, I wake to the sound of alarms wailing somewhere down the hall from my bed. I open my eyes: It's never really dark in here, but it doesn't matter how light it is because I can't crane my head to look at what's going on. I think it's a patient they brought in early yesterday morning. I heard the nurses talking about him: victim of a house fire. Third-degree burns. Fourteen years old. Even younger than I am.

But still, not quite as tragic. Because technically, third-degree burns aren't as bad as what I have.

But technicalities don't seem to matter now. Soon, the wail of the alarms from the machines by his bed are accompanied by shouts, things I've only ever heard in the movies: *Code blue* and *Stat*; *Don't let go* and *Breathe!*

I can hear it when the doctors stop yelling and the machine's wail turns into a beep, then fades into silence. I can hear it when they give up on him. I can hear it when he dies.

I wonder if all the other patients in the burn unit are listening the way I am. Do their nurses tell them they're lucky, too? In a few hours, will my morning nurse be standing above my bed murmuring about my good fortune, a sad look on her face because when she reported for duty at eight a.m., the nurse whose shift she was relieving told her that they'd lost a patient overnight?

But not the girl with the irreparable damage, the one whose burns are so bad there's nothing but empty space where her flesh and blood used to be. No, it was the teenage boy who maybe set fire to his house by sneaking a cigarette in his room, or burning a candle to make it romantic when his girlfriend came over. Maybe his house had shoddy wiring. Or maybe, just maybe, it was hit by lightning.

In the morning, my parents are fighting in the hallway. I haven't heard them fight since the night before my accident. That's what we've taken to calling it. My *accident*. Sometimes I think that three little syllables have never been burdened with so much meaning.

I close my eyes and imagine my father leaning against the nurses' station, as though the extra support can help him withstand the onslaught of my mother's argument. It's littered with flowers, at least half of which are for me. My parents' friends have been sending flowers throughout my stay here at the hospital. They don't know that there's no place for flowers in my highly sanitized room, so every single arrangement ends up decorating the nurses' station. I wonder if my parents' friends know what happened to me—the full extent of what happened to me. Do they know that Sue Winters's daughter, the straight-A student, the track star, doesn't have a nose? Do they realize that, without an actual nose, the apple of Graham's eye no longer has the sense of smell?

I can't taste anything either. Yesterday, when I was panting from the effort of our physical therapy, Marnie handed me a plastic cup to sip from. I thought I was drinking water until I saw that the liquid coming up the straw wasn't clear but golden: apple juice. I guess I haven't actually tasted anything since I woke up from the coma, but the loss didn't feel *official* until that moment.

The last time I wondered if something was official, it was Chirag telling me he loved me.

A couple days ago—the same day that I made it up to four steps without Marnie holding my hands, my left side feeling like it might rip in half the entire time—I talked to Chirag on the phone for the first time since my accident. He was on speakerphone, so his voice echoed across the burn unit for everyone to hear. We'd barely said hello when he asked about visiting. I could see Mom smiling—she was holding the phone for me—and for a split second, I thought she was about to surprise me by opening the door to reveal him waiting on the other side. That's the kind of terribly misguided surprise my mother would think I'd like. Like the time she bought me this really expensive purse that was like nothing I would ever wear. She ended up keeping it for herself.

Mom answered before I could: "I've already told you, Chirag. Maisie's in the burn unit. Family only."

I wished that I could take him off speaker and hold the phone close to my face, the way I used to when he'd call to say good night, which he did nearly every day since we started dating. But then I remembered I didn't have a face to hold the phone close to. And then I was relieved that the burn unit doesn't allow non–family members in.

Anyway, it would be weird to see Chirag without being able to smell him. He always smells delicious, like clean sheets and Ivory soap, plus a tiny hint of curry from his mother's constant cooking.

Although he's always telling me that the scent I think is curry is actually cumin. Not that it matters anymore.

"Maisie needs to rest now," Mom said, signaling the end of our phone call.

"I miss you, Maisie," Chirag said.

"Bye," I answered. I couldn't imagine saying *I miss you, too*, not when Mom could hear me.

Serena and I talked on the phone for the first time yesterday. She asked how I was and I said I didn't want to talk about it. So she told me about the summer classes she's taking at a college in the city and the new SAT words she learned. Her bright shiny voice rang through the room—the phone was on speaker again, of course.

I listened as she told me that last Sunday—not that I have any idea what day it is right now—a bunch of our friends went to the beach and Serena tried to surf for the first time, falling head over heels into the waves. She texted a picture to my mom's cell phone. I know Serena well enough to know that she thought she looked awful in the picture, dripping wet and squinting her eyes because the salt water made them sting. But all I could see was how beautiful my best friend looked, tan and toned in her bikini, not a single burn or scar marring her skin.

"The water was so cold I couldn't believe it," she said. She didn't know that I could stick the left side of my face into the ocean and not feel a thing. Maybe the waves would wash away whatever the doctors left behind.

I haven't been outside in two months. Too many germs, and anyway, what's the point? It's not like I can feel the sun on my face or smell the eucalyptus in the air. I may as well not even be in California. It's July; my favorite time of year, fall, isn't that far off. Soon, the days will get shorter and the nights longer. Serena always said I was such a nerd for loving the fall; only a dork like me would actually look forward to going back to school. But I know that Serena loves school just as much as I do. We were both going to apply to Berkeley this year. We've been talking about it since the sixth grade. We wanted to get an apartment together off-campus.

I wonder who she'll room with now that I live in the hospital.

Out in the hallway, my mother is having a hard time keeping her voice down. She keeps repeating the words *tempting fate* and *not enough time*.

Now Mom's voice rises, loud and clear: "It was enough of a miracle that she survived the accident in the first place. Her body has barely had any time to recover from the initial trauma. The doctors made it very clear that another surgery at this point would be risky."

Another surgery. What could they possibly want to do to me now? There isn't much of me left to do anything to.

My father counters. Sometimes their arguments remind me of an epic tennis match, just back and forth, with no end in sight. Although this one does sound different than their usual fights over nonsense. This actually sounds like they each kind of have a point. Since I'm still under eighteen, my parents have the authority to make all decisions regarding my treatment.

"We don't know when we'll have a chance like this again. I don't want Maisie to have to wait for years."

"I know," Mom agrees. "I know. But this is all happening so fast." Strange. Mom likes things to happen fast. She's usually the one pushing them forward. Pushing *me* forward. She continues, "Most patients are on the list for a long time. Normally, she'd have had a series of grafts before this was even an option."

"Grafts that the doctors would have to replace periodically— more surgeries and more surgeries and more surgeries. Sue, they showed us pictures of the kinds of reconstruction they can do with prosthetics—you know as well as I do that they don't look natural."

"But they've barely even begun her psychiatric evaluation. Usually they have more time to assess whether a recipient can handle—"

"You think anyone can really predict how Maisie—or anyone— can handle this?" Dad interrupts.

I didn't know I was being psychiatrically evaluated at all.

"She's going to be wearing someone else's—" Mom stops herself midsentence. "We don't know what kind of psychological impact that will have on her. She's only sixteen."

Nearly seventeen. It's my birthday in a few weeks.

"This is our chance to get our daughter back." Back? I didn't know he thought I was gone. A lump rises in my throat as Dad explains, "All the research I've done, every article I've read—every parent said the same thing—*I have my child back*—the instant they saw the results."

He continues, "She's young and she's strong. She'll never look the same no matter what we decide. And the sooner she gets this surgery, the sooner she might be able to feel something, smell something, *taste* something."

There's a surgery that might allow me to smell and taste and feel again? A surgery that will make my parents say *We have our daughter back?*

Seriously, what could Mom be thinking? This is a no-brainer if you ask me. I wish I could see out the door, try to catch my father's eye, but my bed isn't angled that way.

"I can't believe we're even arguing about this, Sue." My father is whispering, but somehow it sounds as loud as a shout. His voice is hoarse, like someone has rubbed his vocal cords with sandpaper. "This is a gift that luck has dropped in our laps. Maisie won't have to wait for years like everyone else."

Won't have to wait for what?

"*I* can't believe we're arguing about this," Mom answers, her voice growing more shrill with every word. "There are too many unanswered questions. She'll have to take pills for the rest of her life, and their side effects could make her sicker than she already is. She's supposed to go to college next year. The immunosuppressive regimen is impossible for most adults to maintain, let alone a college student. And you know what will happen if she—"

I wish I had my cell phone with me. I'd look up the word *immunosuppressive*.

"This surgery is Maisie's best chance to live a normal life again. Who are we to deny her that chance?"

My mother is crying. She isn't even trying to be quiet anymore. Her sobs are as steady and high-pitched as the beep from my heart monitor.

"This was never supposed to happen," she says with conviction, as though the injuries and illnesses that happened to everyone else in the hospital around us were predestined somehow, but mine was a fluke, an error, a cosmic mistake.

"Oh, Susie," Dad says. I haven't heard him call my mother Susie in as long as I can remember. He used to call her that all the time. But I guess it's hard to use a nickname on someone you're usually shouting at. Now my mother's sobs grow louder, and I can hear my father take a step. I try to picture him holding my mother close, rocking her back and forth until her tears subside. It's almost impossible to imagine, but I'm convinced that's what's going on out there.

Finally, my mother takes a deep breath and says, "I just don't know how many miracles one family is entitled to."

"We have to talk to Maisie, Sue. It's her body."

"You're right," Mom answers finally. "It should be her decision."

I close my eyes when I hear them turn and walk into the room. I want them to think that I've been sleeping all this time. I don't want them to know that I was listening, wondering what I'm about to get to decide.

SIX

Mom shakes me awake. Even though she's trying to be gentle, I can feel her fingernails through my thin gown.

"Sweetheart," she says, "we need you to wake up."

I flutter my eyelids, pretending that they've woken me from a deep sleep. "Why?" I ask innocently.

"We need you to help us make a decision, and we don't have much time."

I snap my eyes open wide. I don't want to miss my chance for whatever this is. I wonder why the timing is so important. Maybe there's some doctor they've flown in who's only available today. Or maybe there's some procedure that can only work *now*, exactly this many days after my accident. However many days it's been. I press the button that shifts the bed into an upright position. I'm not allowed to sit like this for too long because lying down flat is better for my injuries. But I feel like I need to be sitting up to have this conversation. "How much time do we have?"

As my bed lifts, Mom's face comes into my field of vision. She's been spending most of her days in here, with me, so her skin has taken on a sort of gray pallor from so many days without sunshine.

Mine is probably even paler. Then I remember: I don't have skin. At least, not in all the places I used to.

Instinctively, I reach for the mirror on my bed stand. My reminder. I don't hold it to my face but grip it like a security blanket.

"I'm not sure exactly," Mom answers, and she looks kind of frantic, so I release the mirror and take her hand in mine. She'll never let me do this—whatever *this* is—if she's too nervous. Why can't she be levelheaded under pressure, like my father, like me? I've always been more like him that way; I don't even break into a sweat before a track meet.

"Graham," she says, turning to my father, "how much time did they say we had?"

I can't see my dad, but I can hear that he's standing to my right, just behind my mother. "Let's not worry about that for now. Let's just weigh our options first."

The bed groans as my father sits on the edge of it. He rests his hand on my right leg and squeezes.

"Maisie, for a while now, the doctors have been saying that you're a candidate for a procedure called a face transplant."

"A face transplant?" I echo. Could that possibly be exactly what it sounds like? "What does that mean?"

"The same way they'd give a heart transplant to someone whose heart stopped working, or a kidney transplant to someone whose kidneys stopped working—"

"But that's different," I interrupt. "A kidney goes *inside* of you."

"Yes, it's different, but the idea is the same. When tissue dies, it needs to be replaced."

If I could shake my head, I would. A *face transplant*. It sounds like something out of a sci-fi movie. In fact, I'm pretty sure that if

Chirag were here, he could rattle off the names of at least six movies where something like a face transplant happens. He always knows random trivia like that.

My father continues, "The doctors say that with a transplant, you'll probably be able to smell and taste again, maybe even feel."

"How?"

My father clears his throat. "Well, right now you don't have a nose. You're missing some skin."

The implications take a second to sink in. He means that they're literally going to put someone else's nose and skin onto what's left of my face.

That's how I'll be able to smell—through someone else's nose.

That's how I'll be able to feel—with someone else's skin.

I seriously think I might throw up.

"Are you guys joking?" I ask finally. It'd be a ridiculous joke, a sick attempt to make whatever the *real* decision is a little easier. "I mean, seriously, who ever heard of a face transplant?"

"Not a *full* face transplant," Mom adds quickly, as though that changes everything. "It's just your nose, your cheeks, and your chin."

"Why both cheeks? My right cheek is okay, right?"

"Your right cheek was still damaged, though not as severely."

If I could nod, I would. I know that even though only the left side of my face was completely destroyed, the rest of my face still suffered burns. One of the doctors said that it had to do with the mercurial nature of electrical fires and I was tempted to congratulate him for using such a good SAT word. But I guess, for him, it's just a word.

Mom continues, "If your right cheek had survived intact, they might have tried to reconstruct your left, but given the damage—"

"Can't they at least try?"

"You'll keep your own forehead and your lips," she says, like it's some kind of bonus.

"Oh boy, I'll get to keep my own lips. Why didn't you lead with that? Now I feel so much better about giving up the rest of my face."

My mother sinks out of my field of vision, sliding her hand out from under mine. Usually if I talk to her like that, she scolds me for being rude. But now I hear her start to cry instead. Quietly, my father says, "Maisie, you aren't giving up the rest of your face. It's already gone." He pauses, clearing his throat. "The only alternative to this is a series of skin grafts and prosthetics that will need to be constantly repaired and replaced for the rest of your life. And with the grafts, you'll never regain any sensation; no smell, no taste. It'll just be like a mask over your—" He stops suddenly. I think he was going to say a mask over my face. But since I don't really have a face, it'd be more like a mask over nothing at all.

I take a deep breath through my mouth. In the hallway, Dad said that this was my chance to live a normal life again. But how normal could my life possibly be after something like this? "And with the transplant, will I look—normal?"

He doesn't say anything and for a few minutes, it feels like the only sound in the room is my mother's ragged breath.

Finally, Dad says, "You'll look more normal than you do right now."

That doesn't sound particularly promising. I mean, right now I barely look human.

"So no matter what, I'll be a freak?" I ask. Even though I can't feel my tears, there is a lump in my throat so that I know I'm crying.

"No matter what, you'll be our little girl," Dad answers.

Liar, I think. He doesn't know that I heard him when he was in the hallway: *This is our chance to get our daughter back.*

I swallow and trace circles on my hospital gown with the fingers of my weak left hand. "You said we don't have much time. What did you mean?"

Finally, Mom gets her sobbing under control so that she can answer me. "When they first told us this might be an option, they warned us that it could take a long time to find a donor. That's why we didn't tell you sooner. Your body needs time to recover. There didn't seem to be any reason to rush into telling you anything that might make this more stressful than it already is."

Why does my mother think that protecting me means withholding the truth from me?

"But?" I prompt.

"But a possible donor has become available, and we have to act fast, while the face is still viable."

"Become available? You mean someone died, right?"

"Yes," Mom answers. "Someone died."

So I won't just be walking around with someone else's face glued to my head. I'll be walking around with a dead person's face. I'll be a living, breathing ghost.

SEVEN

Dad stands abruptly, making the bed shake. "This is a big decision," he says. "We know you must have a lot of questions. The plastic surgeon has more answers than we do." I listen to his footsteps fade as he walks away to get the doctor.

I wish Chirag were here. If I'm levelheaded, like my dad, then Chirag is next-level-headed. He would approach this as a future physician; he would ask scientific, logical, smart questions about my health and my quality of life. He certainly wouldn't ask the one question that's currently playing on a loop inside my head: Will I ever be pretty again?

Pretty, Chirag would understand, is beside the point. The point is *healthy*. The point is *normal*. It makes me feel like a silly little girl that all I can think about is *pretty*. Even the word sounds silly and small, a shallow and immature concern.

The plastic surgeon's name is Dr. Boden, and before I can ask him anything, he launches into a grotesque explanation of my surgery, repeating the details my parents explained. Apparently, he's a really important doctor, one of only a handful of surgeons who can perform this operation.

Finally, I ask, "What did my parents mean when they said we had to do this while the face was still viable?"

"If we wait too long, the donor tissue will die."

For a second, I consider just letting the clock run out, going on without making a decision at all, until it's too late and it won't matter what I choose.

"There is a lot more to this than the procedure itself," Mom jumps in. "You'll have to take special sorts of pills for the rest of your life, even after your face heals. And they have all kinds of side effects."

"Why will I have to take them after I'm healed?"

"To keep your body from rejecting the alien tissue."

Alien tissue. Do they have to use words that make it sound like I won't be fully human?

"And if you don't want to do it," Mom adds, "that's fine. There are a lot of risks with this procedure, and no guarantees. They've only done a handful of these before. It might be better if we waited until another donor became available, gave your body more time—"

"But you said that could take years, right?"

Dr. Boden nods. "We can move forward with the skin grafts, try that for the next few years. We'll keep you on the transplant list and wait for another donor."

I never thought before how strange the notion of a transplant list is. The only lists I've ever really given much thought to were grocery lists and to-do lists, lists of homework assignments and lists of clothes I wanted to buy before school started. I never thought there was such a thing as a list of names, people waiting for new faces. People waiting for someone else to die. Maybe there's a group of doctors who meet in a narrow white room each day, deciding which of us gets which face. Who gets to be pretty, who will have freckles and whose skin will be alabaster smooth, whose nose will have a bump and whose cheeks will have dimples.

So this is what happens to a girl without a face. She's given a choice: remain faceless (skin grafts), or take someone else's face instead. But you better do it now, because there's a long list of people waiting.

I close my eyes and imagine that Chirag is standing beside the bed, holding my hand, his eyes narrowed the way they do when he concentrates. If he were here, he'd probably make a meticulous list of pros and cons, as though there is a correct and incorrect answer, like this decision is as straightforward as a math problem.

I bite my chapped lips and try to imagine the answer we'd find at the end of his list.

Surely we'd conclude that spending the rest of my life with someone else's face is better than spending it with no face at all.

So I tell them *yes*.

Everything moves really quickly after I announce my decision. The doctors come in and out and my parents sign what seem like a million consent forms. It gets so I can recognize their signatures from the sound their pens make against the rough paper. My bed is lowered so that it's flat again, and the nurses prep me for surgery. It takes about a dozen people to move me from this bed onto the one that they'll wheel into the OR, the bed where I'll sleep throughout the operation. And all the while, everyone keeps saying the same thing: I'm lucky.

A nurse tells me how lucky I am to have survived my accident. One of the doctors who'll be scrubbing into the surgery says that I'm lucky to have lost only my nose, cheek, and chin. My lips, mouth, and forehead are still intact. Lucky because there are only a few hospitals in the world where they do this kind of surgery and I'm in one of them.

A psychologist comes in to speak with me as they prepare me for the transplant. I've met with her a few times since waking from my coma, though I never guessed that she was evaluating me, like my mother said. I thought it was more like: *You've lost your face, so we want to make sure you're not thinking of strangling yourself with your IV tubes,* that kind of thing. But it turns out that usually, with a face transplant, candidates—that's what they call me, a candidate—are evaluated thoroughly, to determine whether they can handle the psychological impact of having another person's features staring back at them in the mirror. I have to say, I think my dad is right about this: How can they possibly know, before it happens, whether or not I can handle it? But apparently, they've been testing me for this procedure all along, making sure my body and my brain are strong enough for it.

What a waste all that effort would have been if I'd said no.

"You're a lucky girl," the shrink says before she leaves the room.

I can't help thinking that I would have been luckier not to have gone on a run that morning two months ago. My donor would have been luckier not to have died today. Maybe it's the doctors who are lucky—they get to perform this once-in-a-lifetime surgery. Someone whispers that fewer than thirty transplants have ever been performed. They seem practically excited.

Dr. Boden says that my donor was killed in a car accident. The family has chosen to remain anonymous. She's older than I am, and for a second, I kind of hope that she's much, much older. I hope that she lived a long and happy life before that car slammed into her.

But then I remember that I'm getting her face. What if she has wrinkles and sun spots, like my mom is always complaining about? What a freak I'll be, a wrinkled, sun-stained teenager with someone else's skin stapled onto my bones.

Then Dr. Boden says that she's only a few years older than I am; that's part of what makes her a suitable donor.

I'm relieved to hear that she was young. I know it's selfish, but I can't help it. The doctors continue to chatter: Face transplants aren't like kidney and heart transplants. We have to share more than a blood type. She also had to have coloring like mine. Someone says that her hair wasn't quite as red as mine; it was darker, more auburn.

I want to know something else about her. Something that has nothing to do with who she was relative to me.

"Where did she live?" I ask, and Dr. Boden shakes his head.

"I can't tell you that. Her family has asked for total anonymity."

Suddenly, even where she lived takes on a whole new significance, and the familiar string of panic weaves its way around my rib cage. "But what if I'm walking down the street one day and someone recognizes their dead daughter's nose, cheeks, chin?"

Another selfish concern. I thought I wanted to know something about her that had nothing to do with me. But I guess from now on, everything about her will have *something* to do with me.

Dr. Boden shakes his head. "They wouldn't be able to recognize her features on your face. And I promise, your donor didn't live anywhere near here."

"I thought you couldn't tell me that."

He nods. "I can't. But I do know that a team of my colleagues are on a plane right now to operate on her. If she lived close by, what would they need a plane for?"

"Okay," I say. Dr. Boden explains that once his colleagues reach my donor, they will begin the work of removing my donor's face, peeling back the skin like the peel coming off a banana. (I decide I will never eat a banana again.) Next, the face will be placed in a cooler full of ice, just like the kind you might take with you for a day at the beach, and flown to us here in San Francisco.

"By the time the face gets here," Dr. Boden continues, "we'll have begun your surgery." They will expose my nerves and arteries in order to join them with my donor's. "Like rewiring a lamp," he says, as though that will make it any clearer to me. He uses phrases I've never heard before: words like *microsurgery* and *craniofacial specialist* and *immunologist*. Apparently, there are more different kinds of doctors than I ever knew existed, and apparently, they're all going to be working on me today.

My parents take turns kissing my right hand as I'm wheeled past them toward the OR.

"We love you," my mother says, her voice strained. Just barely inside of my field of vision, I see Dad put his arm around her and she leans into him like she can't stand up on her own anymore. I'm tempted to close my eyes; I hate seeing how scared they look. But I force my eyes open even wider, just in case. Just in case this is the last time I'm ever going to see them. Just in case I'm going to end up like the boy from the middle of last night, the one who didn't live, no matter how hard the doctors begged him to.

In the OR, they begin by removing the gauze mask from my face. The lights in this room are blindingly bright if, like me, you can only stare at what's directly above you. I close my eyes.

"Maisie," one of the doctors says. The anesthesiologist. "I need you to count backward from one hundred."

"Why?"

"It's just part of how we put you to sleep. When you wake up, this will all be over."

He makes it sound so simple. They said this would be a long surgery, but I didn't think to ask just how long it would be. Six hours? Ten? Twenty-four? I guess it's too late to ask now.

"Okay," I say, taking a deep breath as though I'm about to dive underwater. I pretend that Chirag is here with me, holding my right hand. I imagine him leaning down to kiss my undamaged right knuckles. "One hundred, ninety-nine, ninety-eight . . ."

Then nothing.

EIGHT

Waking up from my surgery isn't all that different from waking up from a coma. Voices float around the room above me. I swim up from sleep once more, trying to make out what they're saying. I begin to open my eyes, but I can't see anything.

Oh my god, the surgery went terribly, terribly wrong. I'm blind. They blinded me.

The string of panic twists its way around my rib cage, tighter than it's ever been before, until I think it's going to pull me apart. I can't seem to articulate any of the questions flying around in my head so instead I say, "Give me back my eyes." My voice comes out sounding like I'm about one hundred years old. My throat feels like it's on fire.

"Give me back my eyes," I repeat, growing desperate. "Please," I plead. "I need my eyes." I try to lift my good arm—my right arm—from the bed to touch the place where my eyes used to be. But it's stuck beneath a tightly tucked sheet. I'm covered in blankets from the neck down.

A voice I recognize says, "Maisie, sweetheart. We need you to calm down. You're going to hurt yourself." It's one of the nurses who called me lucky before the surgery.

"Give me back my eyes," I say again.

"Should we sedate her?" the nurse asks as though I can't hear her.

A male voice answers, "No." He folds back the covers and pulls my right arm out, placing my hand between his. "Maisie," he says calmly, "it's Dr. Boden. Do you remember me?"

"Yes," I croak. "You're my plastic surgeon."

"That's right." He sounds pleased. "What's the last thing you remember?"

Who cares what the last thing I remember is? "What went wrong?" I ask, my tongue feeling paper-dry and thick in my mouth.

"Nothing went wrong," Dr. Boden answers calmly.

Nothing went wrong? *Nothing* went wrong? When they wheeled me into surgery, I could still see. I'm sure of it. I remember my parents' faces, their tight-set mouths, the tears brimming in their eyes.

"Maisie," Dr. Boden prompts. "The last thing you remember?"

"Ninety-eight," I answer, though I don't see why it matters. Mom was right. This surgery was tempting fate. We used up all of our luck when I survived the fire; there wasn't enough left over to get me through the surgery unscathed.

"Seriously, doctor," I beg. "What went wrong? What happened to my eyes?"

"Your eyes?" He sounds confused. Oh god, he doesn't even know that he blinded me?

"I can't see!" I try to shout, but my throat is too dry.

"Your eyes are just covered with some gauze. You can't feel it— your face is still numb. Here—" he says, and I hear the sound of a chair squeaking against the linoleum floor as he stands and leans over me. He gently unwraps one eye, and then the other. I blink as my eyes adjust to the light. He stands over me, where I can see him. He's smiling warmly. His honey-colored skin is just a little bit lighter than Chirag's.

"That's better, isn't it?"

I can't nod, but I take a deep breath. *Yes. That's much, much better.*

Dr. Boden offers me some water and I sip it through a straw carefully. "Where are my parents?"

"They're just outside. You're in the recovery room, and we wanted to wait until you'd woken up before letting them visit."

"I'm awake."

"I know. But I thought you and I might talk for a few minutes before they came in, if that's okay with you."

I like it that Dr. Boden is treating me like an adult, acknowledging that I'm old enough to ask questions without my parents by my side.

"How did the surgery go?"

He squeezes my hand between his. His palms are cool and his grip is firm. I guess he has to have good hands, to be a surgeon.

"It went wonderfully, Maisie. We're all so pleased with the results."

"I thought maybe something was wrong with my eyes," I say. The words come out slowly; it's as difficult to talk as it was when I first came out of the coma. My face feels completely immobile; I can move my lips, but not my chin or my cheeks.

"I'm sorry we scared you." He pauses. "Maisie, I'm a plastic surgeon. Other types of surgeons, they make you better by taking things away. Dr. Cohen, he had to remove all that charred muscle and bone two months ago." I shudder, trying not to imagine Dr. Cohen hacking away at my face. "But I make my patients better by putting things back. I would never have taken your eyes away."

He sounds like he's some kind of superhero, and I kind of hope he is. He continues, "We were able to completely replace your nose, cheeks and chin." How strange to think of body parts as interchangeable like that.

"Will they cremate her?" I ask suddenly.

Dr. Boden looks confused, like he thinks maybe I'm still a little stoned from all the anesthesia. "Who?"

"My donor."

"I don't know what the family is planning."

"I don't want them to have to see what's left of her." Maybe I am still foggy from the drugs. What a strange thing to say about people I've never met.

Dr. Boden smiles, his dark eyes narrowing warmly. "Don't worry," he tells me. "We're actually creating a replica of her face in case they opt for an open-casket funeral."

Wow, you've thought of everything. "You can do that?"

He nods. "We use silicone," he says. I don't know what's more grotesque—me wearing this woman's face for the rest of my life or the fact that she'll be buried wearing a mask of it, forever.

"Can I see it? The replica?"

Dr. Boden shakes his head. "I'm afraid not, Maisie. That would only confuse you."

I'm plenty confused already, but I don't think telling him that would help my case.

"Was I your first face transplant?"

He doesn't hesitate before answering, which makes me like him even more. "The truth is, only a very few of these surgeries have ever been done. But I was the number two surgeon on a full face transplant a few years ago. A thirty-hour surgery."

"The number two guy?"

"You never work alone on a procedure like this. I was one of three plastic surgeons in here with you today. We had a team of about twenty doctors."

"A team, huh?" Like this is a game or something. I wonder what the score would be. What inning we'd be in. When the shot clock ran out. "How did you all fit around my face?" I say, and Dr. Boden laughs. "The thirty-hour guy—did his face burn off, like mine?"

Dr. Boden shakes his head. *Show-off.* "Gunshot victim," he says matter-of-factly, like it's not a big deal that a bullet literally blew some guy's face off. "And I've led surgeries replacing noses, cheeks, or chins before."

"Just never all at once?"

"Right."

"Well, let's hope you had beginner's luck with me," I say, and Dr. Boden laughs again.

The nurse must have brought my parents in, because the next thing I hear is Mom's voice asking, "What's so funny?"

"An inside joke between Maisie and me," the doctor replies, squeezing my hand one last time before releasing it so that my mother can hold it instead. Unlike the doctor's hands, hers are hot and clammy, like she's been wringing them nonstop since my surgery began. Her face floats into my field of vision.

"How long was my surgery?"

"Sixteen hours," Dad's voice answers. I wouldn't be surprised if he had a stopwatch running the whole time, just so he could keep track. Sixteen hours sounds so short compared to the thirty of Dr. Boden's other transplant.

Mom offers me more water. "Look, sweetie," she says, "it's a bendy straw. You love bendy straws."

"Yeah, when I was five years old." All the straws in the hospital are bendy straws. I've been drinking from bendy straws for so long I can't remember what it's like to actually put my lips on a glass. I'm sick and tired of bendy straws.

"Can I have my mirror?" I ask, and my mother looks positively panic-stricken.

My father says, "It's in your room. They'll transfer you back there in a few hours. They want to keep a close eye on you here in the recovery room for a little while first."

I twist my right hand from my mother's grasp.

"Maisie, stop!" my mother gasps.

"I was just trying to touch my face. Dr. Boden, is it all right if I touch it?"

"Let me get you some gloves," he says, his voice even and calm. "You have to be sterile, otherwise you risk infecting the new tissue."

He slips a surgical glove over my right hand. I begin with something familiar: First I touch my lips. They're dry and chapped, but otherwise, they feel the same as they always have. Slowly, I walk my fingers toward the chin, like a little kid using tracing paper.

The chin is pointier than my old chin, thinner. My jawline is familiar but my new cheeks feel round, like a baby's. Up farther, to my forehead; even though I can't feel them, I know that my freckles are still there, above my eyebrows. I trace my fingers down over the bridge of the nose, which feels narrow and bony, harder than my nose used to feel.

"You look good," Mom says finally. "Great. You look great."

It's one of those hollow compliments she gives from time to time, like when I was in eighth grade and didn't get cast in the school play. She was absolutely shocked, insisting that I was such a great actress—this, despite the fact that I'd never acted a day in my life before the audition.

I just came out of a sixteen-hour surgery, getting a new nose sewn onto my skull. Or maybe stapled or glued, I don't even know.

How great can I possibly look?

I wish I could turn my head to see my dad's face, but I can't. I'm pretty sure he's disappointed. Because he hasn't said *We have our daughter back* like he thought he would.

NINE

I fall back asleep about a dozen times after that, the anesthesia working its way out of my body, just like it did when I came out of the coma. I'm out of recovery and settled into a new room—in the pediatric ward rather than the burn unit now—when they finally give me my mirror.

I lift it slowly. I feel like the wicked queen in *Snow White*, waiting for a mirror to deliver her fate. Though I'm certainly not expecting to be told that I'm the fairest of them all.

I thought I was prepared. I touched it in recovery, over and over, every time I woke up. It would be me, just with round cheeks and a narrow nose. But I never expected to see a monster staring back at me.

There are jagged lines running down my cheeks, hot pink, like I'm a toddler who played with her mother's lipstick and completely missed her mouth.

Another scar is visible when I tilt my head skyward, where they attached the new chin to what was left of my neck. My new cheekbones are as full as a chipmunk's. Dr. Boden slips a fresh glove over my left hand—my right hand is holding the mirror—and I gently touch my new cheeks, careful to avoid the pink lines. I can't feel a thing.

"It may take months for you to regain sensation," Dr. Boden supplies before I can ask. I'm not sure what would be stranger: Not being able to feel the stranger's features pasted onto my face, or being able to feel them.

"The swelling will go down," Dr. Boden adds, anticipating the next question I'd ask if I could. But I don't think I can. Technically, my mouth works just fine, but my own face has scared me into silence. I point to the lines on my cheeks.

"They won't always be so bright," Dr. Boden explains, his voice as calm as ever. "Right now, they're fresh, but they'll fade," he adds, as though scars are no different from produce or flowers or milk.

My parents certainly do not have their daughter back. I'm not sure who they have. I'm not sure *what* they have. I barely look human. I lower the mirror, my hand shaking. I'm not the evil queen in the fairy tale—I'm the monster who lives in the woods, keeping to the shadows so that no one will see her.

"We'll try again tomorrow," Dr. Boden says. "Your psychologist will be here. She'll work with you every day while you're here in the hospital."

Every day? I'm going to have to look at this horror every single day?

"It will get easier," Dr. Boden promises.

My mother walks into the room, a sandwich from the cafeteria in her hand. Not that I think she's been eating much lately. I don't imagine looking at her daughter—wrapped in bandages before and in someone else's skin now—is all that appetizing.

My mother is the kind of person who will send back steak at a restaurant if it wasn't cooked exactly the way she ordered it. Who'd send back a dress if it wasn't exactly the fit she'd been promised. Who'd make a painter repaint the entire house if the color wasn't exactly what she'd imagined.

I bet there's a part of her that's just dying to yell at Dr. Boden: *Maisie doesn't look anything like you said she would!* But you can't send back your daughter, no matter how badly they screwed up your order.

A few days later, a bad taste in my mouth wakes me from a hazy, painkiller-induced sleep. A bitter kind of metallic flavor sitting in the back of my throat. When I complain, the doctors literally cheer.

I can taste. Later, I'll learn that the bad taste was probably adrenaline, from fear, and I'll wonder whether it had been sitting in my throat, unnoticed, every day since I woke up from the coma.

Now Dr. Boden, Dr. Cohen, and a new doctor named Dr. Woo, an immune specialist, come into the room and tilt my bed so that I'm sitting up straight.

"We're here to discuss your medication," Dr. Woo begins.

"The nurses have been keeping a tight schedule," I say. All the pills look and feel alike to me. The doctors lean against the wall across from my bed. My parents are sitting in the only chairs in the room.

"Yes, but you can't count on the nurses forever," Dr. Boden says, a smile playing on the edges of his lips. "We're going to send you home in a few days."

Tiny beads of sweat spring at the nape of my neck. "Seriously?" My doctors look disappointed. I guess they were expecting something along the lines of *Hooray!* But I can't muster hooray, not even for Dr. Boden, whom I've come to like. Instead of excitement, I feel almost feverish.

With effort, I tilt my head to look at the ceiling, relishing the fact that I'm able to turn away at all. Since the surgery, without the plastery mask over my face, my field of vision isn't limited, and I can turn my head and look around normally. Which would be great if it wasn't for the fact that my new face weighs a million pounds. When I close my eyes, I imagine that my new features are sliding right off of me, the stitches that hold this nose and these cheeks and this chin to my face strained until they are about to snap. And I have a new pain to concentrate on: a literal pain in the neck. For the past few days, I've kept my head tilted downward slightly. Everyone probably thinks that I'm on the verge of nodding off.

Dr. Woo explains that she's here to make sure that my parents and I understand exactly what each and every pill is and how many I'll be taking each day.

I don't even care that I'm interrupting her when I say, "Why is this face so heavy?" Mom shoots me a Look with a capital L, annoyed that I'm not paying closer attention.

Dr. Boden jumps in with an answer. "The weight should be temporary, Maisie. The new tissue was transplanted onto your tissue bed, so it's not yet integrated into your nervous system."

"I don't see what that has to do with the fact that I can barely hold my neck straight."

"Right now, all the new parts feel, for lack of a better term, like a big flab of tissue hanging off your face."

I am so sick of hearing people say things like *for lack of a better term*. There's no way to make the details of my condition sound pretty, and everyone seems to think they should apologize for that fact. Dr. Boden continues, "Over time, as your own nerves grow into the tissue, you won't feel that heavy sensation anymore. All that new tissue will feel like part of you."

Why don't doctors understand that the science that's so interesting to them is pretty gross to everyone else? Except for Chirag. He loves that kind of stuff. Maybe that's why he decided to be a doctor in the first place.

"Dr. Woo," Mom suggests, an edge to her voice. Clearly she's irritated that I was too busy thinking about the heft of my new face to pay attention. "Maybe you should take it from the top?"

Take it from the top. Like this is all just a play we're rehearsing, not real life. I'm tempted to tell her that I didn't think I needed to pay attention. Not when she's scribbled down every word the doctors have said since I woke up from my surgery on one of her ugly yellow legal pads. I wish Chirag was the one taking notes across the room. Chirag would have a laptop balanced on his long legs, tip-tappily recording the doctors' instructions. He'd type up a schedule for me, the same way he did last semester for our SAT prep. He'd make it seem fun, like my health was an at-home science project, not another way for my mother to control me.

Instead, Mom's pencil against paper sounds like nails against a chalkboard to me. Maybe she thinks there will be a test later.

I mean, I guess that's what me coming home is. A test. Find out what happens when the girl without a face ventures into the real world with her new parts hanging off of her.

Dr. Woo starts again, explaining how my immune system is going to treat the new tissue—*the* new tissue, she says, not *my* new tissue. My doctors use a lot of very non-medical-sounding terms. They say that to my immune system, the new tissue is an *invader,* an *alien,* an *imposter.* The pills aren't *pills* but a *regimen.* Apparently, we're fighting some kind of epic battle here.

"But," Dr. Woo continues, "it's something of a delicate dance."

Am I the only one who thinks it's kind of funny that we just went from war talk to ballet?

"We don't want to weaken your immune system too much. As it is, on these pills you'll be more susceptible to a variety of infections—"

"Which is why," Dr. Cohen breaks in, "we'll also have you on antiviral and antibacterial medications."

"I don't have a virus," I say.

"They're prophylactic," Dr. Cohen explains. If Serena were here, she'd giggle at the word *prophylactic.* And if Serena were here, she'd distract me by standing behind my mom making funny faces. Though none of her faces would be nearly as funny-looking as mine. I sigh heavily, and Mom shoots me another Look.

"We're also going to put you on blood thinners to begin with," Dr. Boden explains, "to make sure your blood vessels don't clot off."

Dr. Woo says, "After you go home, you'll be coming in for regular blood tests. We'll start with once a week and then gradually taper off to once a month. Just so we can keep a close eye on your immune system."

I'm going to be poked and prodded for the rest of my life.

"And you should try to avoid people who are sick," Dr. Woo adds.

"That should be easy," I say. "I don't plan on leaving the house much."

"Maisie, don't be rude," Mom admonishes.

"Sue, this is all a lot to take in," Dad says, defending me. It's the first time he's spoken since the doctors came into my room. He looks at me and smiles gently. His smile brings out the deep, dark circles under his eyes. I don't think I've ever seen him look so tired.

My mother wants me to be the kind of strong and special patient you read about in books, the kind who doesn't get cranky even when she can barely move half her body, has lost her face to an electrical fire, and is in quite a lot of pain. Instead I'm the kind of person who says, "I think I've earned the right to be a little bit rude."

"Rude to the doctors who saved your life?"

"But now they all get to put my face transplant on their résumés," I joke, though no one laughs. I glance at Dr. Boden and see him struggling not to smile.

"I think we're getting off track," Dr. Boden says finally. "Why don't we let Dr. Woo keep going, and then each of you can ask all of your questions when she's finished. We'll go over this as many times as you need. Right now, nothing is more important than your immunosuppressive regimen."

Every day something else is the most important. First, it was pain management. Then it was Marnie's PT. Then the transplant. Then surgical recovery. Now immunosuppressive, a word I didn't know existed a few weeks ago.

Dr. Woo starts again. "One of the drugs you'll be taking is called CellCept. You'll be taking it twice a day. Normally you'd be required to take a pregnancy test before starting CellCept but since you've been here in the hospital for so long, we already know you're not pregnant."

Serena would be giggling so hard she'd be choking by now. My mother's face is bright red and Dad can't even look at me.

"As long as you're on CellCept," Dr. Woo continues, "you'll be required to take birth control, since it can lead to serious harm to an unborn baby."

Dr. Woo's face turns particularly stern. Come to think of it, why does *everyone* look so serious about this point in particular? Dad's smile has vanished and Dr. Boden can't even look at me.

Then I realize . . . they're telling me I can never get pregnant. I have to be on immunosuppressives for the rest of my life, and immunosuppressives cause birth defects. I mean, I'm in high school, everyone's priority is *not* getting pregnant. I know that having kids was a million years away, but it never occurred to me that I wouldn't at least have the option.

"Okay," I say, taking a deep breath. I can be levelheaded, even about this. If Chirag were here, he'd just add this new detail to the list, so I try to do the same. "Birth control. CellCept. Blood thinners. Antivirals and antibacterials. What else?"

"Now, we'll give you some literature about the side effects, but I must tell you, they are legion. The serious ones include: fever, chest pain, bloody or black stool—"

"But of course," Dr. Boden breaks in, "there are plenty of less serious side effects. Nausea, vomiting, stomach pain, anxiety—"

Those are the *mild* side effects?

"And of course, fatigue and insomnia."

"Wait, these pills are going to make me tired *and* keep me awake?" I ask, at the same time that Mom asks, "Will the side effects—will they lessen as Maisie's body acclimates to the medication?"

Dr. Woo waves her head from side to side noncommittally, ignoring my question to answer Mom's. "Her body may adjust. But of course, there may always be changes to her regimen, and as we update her doses, the side effects will vary."

Mom's pencil scratches endlessly against the surface of her pad. I close my eyes and try to imagine the rhythmic click of Chirag's fingers on the keyboard of his laptop.

"These are very powerful drugs, Maisie," Dr. Woo says. "We are weakening your immune system, and over time you're going to be more susceptible to certain types of cancer, diabetes, and of course any number of infections."

"Yippee," I say. Dr. Woo doesn't even crack a smile. I don't know why I keep trying to make jokes. Can you even call them jokes when no one laughs?

"This is all very serious, Maisie. I cannot emphasize enough how important it is that you take these drugs as directed by me and by the rest of your team."

"Don't worry, Dr. Woo," Mom interjects. "I'll make sure Maisie stays on schedule."

Dr. Boden says, "It might be best to keep Maisie in charge of her regimen. Give her a little bit of agency over her condition." I open my eyes and look at my plastic surgeon. When Mom isn't looking, he winks at me. Maybe he grew up with a controlling mother, too.

"Who are we kidding?" I say drily. "I'm not in charge of any of this." I glance at Mom, her hand hovering above her pad, ready to record the next doctor's order.

Just then, Marnie comes in. Apparently, it's time for physical therapy.

"Good afternoon, everyone," she says merrily. Dr. Woo gives her a stern look, but even Dr. Woo can't wipe the smile off of Marnie's cheerful face.

I notice that unlike Dr. Woo, Dr. Boden and Dr. Cohen and even my father are returning Marnie's smile. She doesn't seem to notice. I guess she's used to the way men react to her.

"Marnie," Dr. Boden says, "I'd say Maisie is one of your easier cases."

What are you talking about, easy? My case is one in a million, intricate and complicated. Dr. Boden said so himself a dozen times. "You wouldn't say it was easy if you knew what it felt like," I mutter. I've come to dread Marnie's entrance into my room every day. Come to hate the rubber ball she puts in the palm of my left hand with a passion usually reserved for the hatred of evil dictators and serial killers.

"Dr. Boden means that you're lucky you didn't need your jaw transplanted. I have to work for months teaching patients how to use their jaws again: to chew their food, to smile, to kiss."

Oh my god, would people please, please, please stop calling me lucky? And it's not like my mouth feels great or anything. I'm still speaking slowly, careful not to open my mouth too wide. For all I know, saying big words like *defenestrate* and *tintinnabulation* too quickly might mess up the work they just did.

"I think that's enough for today," Dr. Boden says finally. "Dr. Woo will be back in the morning to go over all this again."

"We're going over this again?" I moan.

"Maisie," Dr. Woo says, "we'll be going over your immunosuppressive regimen every day until you're released from the hospital."

A few days later, a group of nurses burst into my room singing "Happy Birthday." I hadn't even realized what day it was, but I guess that today, I'm seventeen. On Chirag's birthday back in March, we went out to dinner with a bunch of our classmates. Afterward, when everyone else had gone home, we made out in his car until our jaws ached. Gently, I touch my lips now, remembering how it felt to kiss him.

Marnie steps into the room, holding a chocolate cake with three candles, my parents hovering in the doorway behind her. "Why three?" I ask her.

"One for the past, one for the present, and one for the future," she says. "Though we can't light them in the hospital," she adds. "Could cause an explosion with all the oxygen tanks, that kind of thing." She grins, then holds out the cake in front of me like I'm supposed to make a wish anyway. I purse my lips and close my eyes. I imagine that I'm kissing Chirag, not blowing out the candles. I guess that's my wish.

Everyone cheers and I open my eyes. My mother cuts up the cake and offers me a piece. I gag when the buttercream frosting hits my tongue; I think it tastes sour but no one else seems to notice. Dad's already on his second piece. I put my plate down on the little table beside my bed, right on top of my hand mirror.

Just because I can taste again doesn't mean that things taste the way they did before. Maybe my donor hated buttercream.

Maybe she hated her birthday. Maybe I will hate mine from now on.

PART II

FALL

TEN

wake up screaming for the fifth night in a row. My mother is in my room so quickly that I wonder if she fell asleep at all tonight or just stayed up waiting for me to start shouting. My dad follows close behind, hovering in my doorway, looking groggy. Mom doesn't turn the lights on in my room, but light from the hallway spills in through my open door, silhouetting my father.

I've been home for almost a week now. There is no more plaster mask wrapped around my head, no more sterile gloves required before I can touch my face, just an army of ointments and pills. Dr. Boden said the scars on my skin—and on my donor's skin—would fade over time, though they'll never be invisible.

The only thing stranger than my new face is the fact that my parents are sleeping in the same bed again. I can practically feel their unified presence radiating concern from the other side of my bedroom wall.

My parents think that my nightmares are about the accident. They think that being just down the street from the scene of the crime is what's keeping me up at night. I don't tell them the truth. It's not *my* accident I dream of, but my donor's.

Of course, I don't know anything about my donor's accident except that it involved a car, so the dreams are different every night. I don't even know if she was the only person killed in the crash.

Some nights, she's driving, and someone else runs a red light and plows into her. I wake up with the sound of screeching brakes and twisting metal in my ears.

Some nights, she's walking down the street when a car whips around the corner out of nowhere and speeds up onto the sidewalk, throwing her into the air. She lands, backward and broken, several yards away in the parking lot of a fast food restaurant and slowly begins to bleed out.

Some nights, she's in the passenger seat beside her boyfriend or her husband. Maybe her kids are in the backseat. And I wake up to the sound of their screams.

My whole life, I made my dad kill the spiders and bugs that snuck into my room. Once, my dad caught a mouse in the kitchen and I cried because the poor thing was squeaking with pain and fear until Dad set him free in the backyard.

Now someone else died for my face and I'm supposed to be happy about it.

Dad thinks that maybe the nightmares are because I have to sleep on my back while my face continues to heal. "Ever since you were a little kid you always slept curled up on your left side. Maybe this is messing up your sleep patterns," he suggests with a shrug. He doesn't mention that I slept on my back the entire time I was at the hospital and my nightmares didn't start until they brought me home, nearly a month after the transplant, just a week before the first day of school. He doesn't mention that if I happen to shift onto my left side in my sleep, pain shoots viciously up my side, waking me up like some kind of cruel alarm.

"Oh, sweetheart." Mom picks my fluffy pink comforter off the floor and tucks it around me. I used to sleep with the blanket pulled up around my neck, but now I can't stand the weight of it. "You'll feel better in the morning," she says.

"Serena is coming over in the morning," I say quickly. Now that I'm home, I have my cell phone back; Serena and I arranged a visit over texts less than twelve hours ago.

"Are you sure that's a good idea?" I think she's worried Serena will hug me too tightly and smush my new nose or something. Or maybe she's worried that when Serena sees my new face, she'll turn tail and run away as fast as her legs can carry her.

"I do," I say firmly. I miss my friend. "I think it's important to try to do something normal," I add, because that's the kind of thing Mom would say. Not that I believe it, not even for a second: What could possibly be normal about Serena seeing my new face for the first time?

To my surprise, Mom smiles. "I'm so glad to hear you say that," she begins, "because I have a surprise for you."

"What?" I ask nervously.

"Chirag is coming over tomorrow, too."

My heart starts pounding, just like it did when the nightmare ripped me from sleep. Maybe I'm still dreaming. No; my subconscious wouldn't do this to me. Even in my worst nightmares, I've never dreamed about Chirag seeing me this way.

My mother never exactly encouraged Chirag to come over before. And when he did come over, she'd insist that we sit in the living room with the lights on. Maybe she hated the idea of her little girl having a boyfriend; hated that this was a part of my life she couldn't control. Dad was so much cooler about it than she was. But tonight, there's something almost wistful in her voice when she says Chirag's name, like she's worried that I'll never have another boyfriend again and she wants me to make the most of this one while I've got him.

I take a deep breath. "What do you mean, he's coming over, *too*? How did you know Serena was coming?"

"Her mother called me to make sure it was okay."

I shake my head. I love being able to shake my head again, for all the good it does me. Mom never listens. If she'd been listening, she'd have heard that even though I've talked about Serena coming over every day since I got home from the hospital, I've never asked for Chirag. Not once. No matter how much I wanted him to wrap his long arms around me and kiss the top of my head and tell me: *It's all right, it's all right, it's all right.* I miss the sound of his voice and the way he smells and the rough calluses on his thumbs rubbing the back of my hands. It's very strange that there is one person—the same person—whom I most want to see and most dread seeing.

I don't even pick up the phone when he calls. Because he would ask to come over, and I wouldn't know how to say no. But he *can't* see me this way. How can Mom not understand that? Once he sees me, he'll never want to wrap his arms around me again.

The last time I gave myself a good hard look was the day I left the hospital, with my therapist nodding her approval. I can still picture the hot-pink jagged scars on my cheeks; the mark where they'd attached the new chin; the cheeks, still comically full. The tip of my donor's nose was smaller than my old nose, almost aquiline. And she didn't have freckles; even beneath the swelling and the scars I could see that her complexion was pale, like mine, but milky white. I bet she was proud of her complexion. Maybe it was her special vanity. Maybe she wore sunscreen and hats even on cloudy days, just to be safe. My own freckles remained on my forehead but then stopped abruptly where my skin met my nose and cheeks.

I hate this face. It was easier to look at nothing than it is to look at a stranger's nose and cheeks and chin pasted onto me.

I should have listened more closely when they explained my options, the differences between the transplant and skin grafts. But I thought that Chirag seeing me with someone else's face would be better than him seeing me with no face at all.

"What time is Chirag coming?"

"Eleven, same as Serena," Mom replies.

I stiffen. In more than a decade of friendship, Serena has never been on time for anything. Which means that Chirag will see me first. I glance at my clock; he'll be here in less than eight hours. He'll be right on time. He's never late.

"I only wanted Serena."

Mom sighs. I used to have her chin, her nose, my dad's cheeks. I wonder if they feel like they're living with a stranger when they look at me now.

"Chirag has asked to visit every single day since you came out of the coma. You should have heard how thrilled he was when I finally said he could."

For some reason, all I can think about is the silence in my hospital room when Dr. Woo said I'd have to be on birth control. I wonder if my mother thinks that Chirag and I have had sex. Maybe that was why she never wanted to leave us alone in the house together.

The truth is, we hadn't actually come all that close. I never even told Serena that. Now I could kick myself for waiting. We should have done it months ago. I thought I had all the time in the world. Now I'll probably be a virgin forever.

"Fine," I say, leaning back against my pillows. They're arranged so that not only am I on my back, but I'm also practically sitting up. "But if I have some kind of panic attack when I see Chirag, it'll be all your fault." I imagine myself freaking out when he walks through the front door. My eyes rolling back into my head like someone possessed; my fingernails digging into the flesh of my new cheeks. Not that I'd be able to feel it, anyway.

"I'll risk it," Mom says, smiling. "Besides," she adds brightly as she gets up, "he's going to see you at school soon anyway." She makes it sound like a threat, like I'm a bratty little kid who wants summer to last longer instead of the girl who has, until now, always been excited for the new school year. She turns down the hallway to go back to her own room and Dad hesitates, then comes inside and kisses the top of my head, the only part of my head that's really kissable anymore.

Softly, he says, "Maybe you're having nightmares because you're scared to see your friends. Maybe your dreams will get better once you've gotten it over with. Like ripping off a Band-Aid."

He smiles before he switches off the lights in the hallway and my room goes dark. I listen to the sound of his footsteps fading away, the sound of their bedroom door clicking shut behind him. I never thought seeing Chirag would be something I'd want to get over with.

Alone in my room, I do what I've done every night since the nightmares began: I close my eyes and imagine myself dancing with Chirag, the same way I did when the pain overwhelmed me at the hospital. I imagine the soft green silk of my dress against my skin and I picture Chirag fixing one of the dress's skinny straps when it falls off my shoulder. It is the old Maisie dancing with Chirag, the girl who had only one scar: on the right side of her neck, just below her hairline, from the time when she was six and her best friend tried to do her hair and burned her with her mother's curling iron. I can still remember the sound the curling iron made when it touched my skin, a strange sort of steaming sizzle that sounded like someone gasping.

In my fantasy, Chirag presses his lips to that one single scar as we sway in time to the music.

ELEVEN

n the morning, I draft and delete a dozen text messages to Chirag. I start with explanations.

I should warn you: I don't look the way that I used to.

Did my mom tell you about the scars on my cheeks?

But I can't bear explaining, so I hit delete and try lying instead:

I'm not feeling so good today—not up for visitors.

The doctors said I can't have visitors so we're going to have to cancel. Something about germs. Too bad!

I don't know if my mom told you, but I have to wear a scarf across my face at all times. So you won't actually be able to see me.

And then, the biggest lie of all:

I don't want you to come over. Don't.

My finger hovers above the send button. It would be so easy to let the message go out into the ether. I close my eyes and imagine the sound his phone will make, alerting him that he has a new message. Other couples have pictures of the two of them together on their phones, selfies they took as they kissed or made funny faces. But Chirag's phone has a candid shot of me crossing the finish line at a track meet. My arms overhead, my smile wide, grinning from ear to ear.

I imagine him looking at that photo and smiling as he slides his finger across the screen. Then I picture that smile fading away when he discovers that I don't want to see him.

Would he know I was lying? Because I do want to see him, so badly it makes my stomach hurt. I just don't want him to see me. I wish the doctors really had given me a medical scarf to wear over my face. Gauze to wrap around my forehead and across my nose, like some kind of grotesque bride.

Delete. I toss my phone on the bed and start getting dressed.

I used to spend a ridiculous amount of time looking at myself in the mirror before Chirag came over. It was so stupid; it's not like he didn't see what I looked like every day at school. Not like he didn't see me a million times during a run, sweat dripping down my face and my hair in a messy ponytail. But still, when I knew he was coming over—which I always thought of as a date, even when we didn't actually go anywhere—I fretted and fussed in front of the mirror, trying this barrette and that blouse. I wanted to look pretty for my first real boyfriend, for the person who told me that I looked beautiful no matter what I was wearing.

He always said that he liked me best in jeans and a plain top and no makeup (though I never really wore any makeup unless Serena made me). So I pull out his favorite pair of jeans—dark blue and ripped just a little at the knee—and a plain white long-sleeved shirt. I don't know why I bother. It's not like he's going to be looking at anything but my face.

Would Chirag even recognize me if we bumped into each other on the street? He always said he loved my eyes, and they're the same at least. Maybe he'd know me by my eyes.

Or maybe he'd just know it was me because of the scars on my

85

face and running down the left side of my body. How many other girls in town have been burned like that?

The doorbell rings promptly at eleven. I let Mom answer it. She's home, even though it's a weekday. She's taking a leave of absence from her job to take care of me. Dad is back at work; it must be hard for him, going into the office each morning after another night interrupted by my screams, like the daughter they brought home from the hospital isn't a teenager but a newborn baby who still hasn't learned to sleep for more than a few hours at a time.

From my room, I can hear Mom saying *hello* brightly, like Chirag is a long-lost friend she's been waiting to see. I consider staying upstairs, but I guess my mom could just send him to my room to find me. Now that she doesn't have to worry about what we might be doing behind closed doors.

So I pad down our cool terra-cotta stairs in my bare feet, past all the old photos on the walls. This house is like a shrine to a face that no longer exists.

I should have worn shorts. My legs weren't burned at all. I squeeze my left hand into a fist, trying to ignore the way it still hurts. What if Chirag tries to hold my hand? Will he notice how tight the skin is? Will the ridges of my scars disgust him? I stuff my damaged hand into the pockets of my tight jeans, even though the denim scratches the tender skin.

Chirag is facing my mother, his back to the stairs, so I see the flowers before I see his face. Lilacs. I wonder where he got them this time of year. I'm pretty sure they usually bloom in the spring. The slim muscles in Chirag's back flex under his T-shirt as he tightens his grip on the bouquet, squares his shoulders. His caramel-colored skin peeks out from the borders of the shirt—at the neck, his arms, just above the waistband of his shorts—and I remember that it is always, always warm, every time I touch him. For a split second, my heart forgets about the way that I look and starts beating a little bit faster, excited to see him. He spins around before I reach the first floor.

I can tell that Chirag is trying very hard not to react to my face. He probably practiced in the car on the drive over: imagining what I would look like and trying to keep his face neutral, as if nothing had changed. Ever the scientist, he probably did research, Googling pictures of face transplants so he'd know what to expect. But now his dark skin looks positively ashen. His Adam's apple bobs up and down as he swallows: once, twice, three times.

I linger on the bottom step, tapping one foot against the terracotta floor. Chirag steps toward me, holding the flowers out in front of him. "For your birthday," he says.

"Thanks," I say, though I'm still standing too far away to take them from him. I don't make a move to come any closer.

"Those are Maisie's favorite." Mom takes the lilacs out of Chirag's arms. I want to tell her that of course Chirag knows they're my favorite. But I don't think they're my favorite anymore, because now the smell is making me queasy.

The flowers out of his hands, Chirag steps forward, his arms lifted slightly, like he wants to hug me. I shake my head, and he drops his arms immediately. He nods, letting me know that he understands.

It was always like that for us. A glance across a party could communicate everything: *I'm bored, let's get out of here.* Or: *Can you believe that outfit?* Or: *I know I look like I'm engrossed in this conversation, but really all I can think about is kissing you.*

"We should sit down," I say carefully, stepping toward the couch as Mom disappears through the swinging door that leads to our kitchen.

The living room is airy and bright, sun streaming in through the windows. I wait for Chirag to sit first, then I sit all the way across the couch, pulling my legs up in front of my chest and wrapping my arms around them. I used to sit right next to him. Maybe it would feel amazing to slide across the couch and rest my head on his chest and let his arms wrap around me. Maybe I would even cry and tell him how awful it's been, how much I've missed him, how scared I am, listen to the steady sound of his heartbeat against my cheek.

Instead, from my side of the couch, I stare at the features I know so well: his long arms and wide chest; his slim waist. I've always loved the way he looks. It'd be a lie to pretend that my feelings for him don't have something to do with how he looks. So how can I expect him to still love me when I looks so different? Sometimes I wonder if even my parents can love me the same.

"Serena should be here any minute," I offer. Serena can talk her way through the most awkward of situations.

"Good." Chirag rubs his hands against each other like he's cold. I shift, curling my legs underneath me. It's too hard to keep my scarred left hand in my pocket now that I'm sitting down so I cover it with my sleeve and then hide it beneath my undamaged right one for good measure.

Chirag seems determined not to stare at me, so I turn on the TV to give him a place to focus his gaze, even though it's the middle of the day and nothing's on. We haven't spoken in months and should have so much to catch up about, but instead we both pretend to be interested in a talk show about cheating husbands until Serena shows up, late as always, bounding through the front door without knocking.

Serena pounces on me and then bounces right back as though she's touched something hot. It's not that Serena can't read my signals every bit as well as Chirag can—it's that she chooses to ignore them. And I guess I love her for that, the same way I love Chirag for paying attention.

Serena's ebullience has remained unchanged since we met in kindergarten. She never seemed to develop that self-conscious streak that kicked in for the rest of us around middle school.

She sits down right smack between Chirag and me on the couch. Shyly—perhaps the only time I've ever seen her shy—she gazes at my face. The opposite of Chirag, she takes it all in, piece by piece by piece: my new nose and chin, my round cheeks. I keep my eyes on the TV, trying not to feel her staring, trying not to feel her disappointment that I don't look like the best friend she's had since she was five years old.

If it's this hard when people who love me look at me—though, in Chirag's case, the love is unofficial, and perhaps nonexistent at this point—what will it be like when everyone else who knew my old face—acquaintances, teachers, classmates—sees me for the first time?

Gently, Serena puts her arms around me and gives me the tiniest of squeezes. My mother comes in, arranging Chirag's flowers in a vase, which she sets on the coffee table in front of us.

"Those are so pretty," Serena says. "Chirag, did you bring them? Maisie, I should have brought you a present. I hated not being with you on your birthday."

If Chirag weren't here, I might ask Serena to tell me how I look. She'd be honest with me. My parents say that I look great and the doctors are mostly focused on how I'm healing. But I don't want her to say anything in front of Chirag, as though deep down I believe that if we don't point it out, he might not notice that I'm not pretty anymore.

"Thank god you're back," Serena says. "You should have seen how this poor boy pined for you—"

"Pined?" Chirag interrupts. He laughs but it sounds forced. "Are we in a gothic novel or something?"

"It's a legitimate expression," Serena insists, a giggle escaping from between her lips. "And the perfect one to describe you for months and months and months."

Not months and months and months, I think weakly. *Really, just summer. And some of the spring.* We missed prom. And my birthday. And in between, the Fourth of July. Chirag and I had planned to watch the fireworks together. He promised to take me up into the mountains behind the Golden Gate Bridge, to bundle me up with blankets and hold me close. My parents and I used to do that when I was little. But a few years ago, we stopped, and I've missed it ever since.

But of course, I was in the hospital on Independence Day. I wouldn't have even known it was Independence Day at all, if Marnie hadn't come in for PT that morning shouting *Happy Fourth of July!* instead of her usual chipper *Good morning!*

"Maisie," Serena adds now, turning toward me, "you are one lucky girl. Not many high school boys would be faithful for so long."

I almost groan: Even Serena is calling me lucky. I wish I could strike that word from the English language.

"Do you know how many girls wanted to go to prom with him?" Serena continues. I shake my head, happy for just a second that I can't blush. Something to do with the blood vessels beneath the skin, and the new skin that isn't fully integrated yet. If Chirag knew all the times I pictured us at prom together; all the dances I imagined we were dancing, the words I pretended we were whispering.

"You'll never believe what he did—"

"Serena," Chirag interrupts sharply. Serena turns to face him and he shakes his head firmly.

"What did he do?" I ask. Maybe he showed up with a dozen girls, six on either side of him. He could. All of the sophomores had crushes on him last year.

Serena shrugs awkwardly. Unlike me, she blushes bright pink. Biting her tongue has never come easily to my best friend, but I know that she's not going to say whatever it was she'd been about to share now that Chirag has asked her not to. Instead, she finally offers, "I have plenty of pictures. Wait till you see my dress."

As though prom weren't months ago, as though whatever dress Serena wore isn't shoved into the back of her closet, never to be worn again. Right now, she's wearing a peach T-shirt so sheer that I can see the bathing suit underneath and short denim shorts that show off her legs. Serena's mother is from Ecuador and her father is almost as pale as I am; the result is breathtaking. Right now, her normally golden skin is a few shades darker than usual, the result of spending summer in the sunshine, instead of inside a hospital. Her thick dark hair is pulled back into a messy bun at the nape of her neck.

"Are you wearing a bathing suit?" I ask, eyeing her T-shirt.

"I wasn't sure if you'd want to go to the pool later. Your mom said you'd been so cooped up since you got home."

Our school, Highlands High, has a pool that students are allowed to use in the summer. Right now, it'll be packed with kids desperate to soak up as much sun as possible before school starts.

Last year, Serena and I spent half the summer in that pool, even though I had to get out of the water every hour to reapply sunscreen so my pale skin wouldn't burn.

Showing up in a bathing suit isn't Serena being insensitive. I think she wanted to be prepared for whatever scenario I might throw at her today. But before I can say anything, my mother says, "That's a nice idea, Serena, but Maisie is on medication that makes her very susceptible to melanoma, so she's been avoiding the sun this summer."

I could laugh at the idea that the immunosuppressive medication is the reason why I haven't been spending a lot of time outdoors lately. It's not like I'll ever look halfway decent in a bathing suit with these scars on my left side. I'll probably never wear a bathing suit again.

I'll just add it to the list of things I'll probably never do. I glance at Chirag. He gives me a tiny smile, and then he winks, standing up.

"I guess you guys have a lot of catching up to do," he says. "I don't want to get in the way of your girl talk." A few months ago, I would have made fun of him for sounding like a middle-aged bachelor instead of a teenager. Now I just look up at him and nod. I'm not comfortable with him here, and he knows it.

"You're leaving?" my mother says.

"Yeah. But I'll be back tomorrow. I want to take Maisie out to dinner for her birthday." He looks at me, his eyes asking if it's okay. I nod quickly, forgetting for a split second that everything is different now, feeling for just an instant that this is a normal invitation: My boyfriend wants to take me out to dinner to celebrate my recent birthday. But just as quickly, I remember why he missed my birthday to begin with. We used to hold hands under the table at restaurants.

Now I keep my left hand hidden beneath my right, hoping Chirag hasn't noticed the missing freckle on my knuckle, the one that he used to kiss.

"Eight o'clock?" he asks.

Again, Mom doesn't give me a chance to answer before she speaks. "That's a bit late. Maisie's on a strict regimen of pills now." Since I've been home, Mom has adopted the doctors' war-ish lexicon, like she wants to make sure I don't forget that we're engaged in battle. "And she takes her evening pills at eight o'clock."

"How about six-thirty instead?"

You only want to spend ninety minutes with me? I think but do not say. After all, ninety minutes is a long time to spend looking at this face across from you at a restaurant.

"Perfect," Mom says, clapping her hands as though she's the one being taken out by her boyfriend. Maybe Chirag will kiss *her* good-bye.

I don't stand up. Chirag can't hug me when I'm sitting down, with Serena between us. But he surprises me by bending down, and before I can duck out of his reach, he gently kisses the top of my head. For a second, he's close enough that I can smell him, and I'm relieved that my new nose still loves his scent, even if it doesn't love lilacs. He lingers, pressing his nose into my hair. Maybe he missed the way I smelled, too.

I hold my breath until I hear the front door close behind him, like I'm trying to hang on to him. But really, I'm trying not to cry. Because that was a perfectly sweet kiss. But it was exactly the way my father kissed me after my nightmare last night.

What did I expect? That he'd French-kiss me in front of Serena and my mother and the people on TV? That he'd take me into his arms and say, "Don't worry, I still love you" even though he never actually said he loved me out loud before?

And what would I have done if he had? Maybe my face doesn't know how to kiss the way it used to. Marnie said I didn't need that kind of physical therapy, but what if she was wrong?

TWELVE

Here's the thing about not being able to feel most of your face: It is very, very strange. Stranger maybe than not having a face at all. I meet with Marnie at the hospital twice a week, and lately she's teaching me how to breathe in through my nose. I can't feel the air moving in and out of it. I can smile, but I can't feel my cheekbones rising when I do.

And, I've started walking into things. Losing my balance. The doctors say it's a side effect of the CellCept, but I think it's a response to the unfamiliar physical sensation—or lack of physical sensation. After all, this new face doesn't weigh what my old face did, though it doesn't feel as heavy as it did when I was in the hospital. Guess that means my nerves are reintegrating, or whatever Dr. Boden said they had to do.

When Chirag picks me up promptly at six-thirty, I've already done the math in my head: Whatever restaurant Chirag is taking me to, it's probably about a fifteen-minute drive away, right? And we'd have to leave in time to be back here by eight p.m. And knowing Chirag, he'll want to leave some extra time for the drive back—he's not a fan of cutting it close—so we'll leave the restaurant by about seven-thirty. Which means he'll only have to sit across from this face for forty-five minutes. In the car, he can stare straight ahead, eyes focused on traffic, hands placed firmly at ten o'clock and two o'clock, just like they teach you in drivers' ed.

Not that Chirag ever used to drive like that. We used to hold hands in the car, our arms tangled across the gearshift. He glanced over at me at every stop sign, every red light. A traffic jam was just an excuse to spend more time together.

Tonight, I tuck my left hand under my legs the instant I sit down in the passenger seat. I stare straight ahead. Chirag does the same, and I wonder if it's because he's following my lead or because he doesn't want to look at me any more than I want him to.

I never knew how much effort it took to avoid reflective surfaces, but I'm becoming something of an expert at it. The key is concentration; let your guard down and you'll catch a glimpse of yourself in a rearview mirror, in the tinted windows of a passing car or the sunglasses on your boyfriend's face. (Fat chance; I haven't even looked at him once since he picked me up.) I'm so focused on reflective surfaces that I can barely hold up my end of the conversation. I answer each of Chirag's questions monosyllabically. Chirag must take my semi-silence to mean that I'm scared he's going to ask me something about my accident or the surgery, so he sticks to safe topics like whether I'm taking AP physics this year (I'm not), or the traffic in downtown Tiburon (not so bad tonight), or—after one particularly desperate silence—what nice weather we've been having (quite nice).

In addition to avoiding my own reflection, I'm thinking about the fact that we should have said *I love you* sooner. Or anyway, I should have said it. I knew that I loved him long before he held up that sign for me. I should have said it while I had the chance.

I can't say it now. Not looking like this. It wouldn't be fair to ask him to say *I love you, too,* not to this face. And thinking about the silence that would follow if I did say it makes me want to jump out of this moving car. With my luck, I'd probably survive the leap, too. I'd just have another set of scars to add to the ones I already have.

So the words that I haven't said hang between us, taking up all the empty space that used to be taken up by our intertwined arms and hands and fingers. I close my eyes and imagine a blinking neon sign hanging down from the rearview mirror: *You are not holding hands,* it blinks in an ugly yellow scrawl. *You are not saying I love you.* Blink, blink. *You are not touching each other.* Blink, blink. *You may never touch each other again.*

Blink. Blink.

I wonder if my donor had a boyfriend. I wonder if they got to say *I love you* before she died. I wonder if he's moved on, or if he's still mourning her, staring at a picture of her before he goes to bed every night, longing to kiss a face that doesn't exist anymore.

To fill the silence, I finally decide to bring up a topic that I've always been able to spend hours talking about. It used to embarrass me, but right now it seems the least awkward of the subjects I have to choose from. At least it has nothing to do with *us,* with Chirag or me.

"So my parents are sleeping in the same room again."

Chirag slows down gently as we approach a red light. Did my mother tell him that my donor died in a car accident? It sounds like such a reasonable way to get hurt. So much more likely than being struck by lightning. Though I guess, technically, *I* wasn't struck by lightning. The tree was.

The tree is completely gone. There's not even a stump left. It must have been young enough that its roots didn't interfere with the pipelines.

"Wow," Chirag says once we're at a full and complete stop. "How long has it been since that happened?"

"At least six months, that I know of. Though it's not like I know exactly when they started sharing a room again. I just got home from the hospital and there it was."

"Weird," Chirag says, and I nod. For most kids, it'd probably be weirder if their parents *weren't* sleeping in the same room, but Chirag knows that in my house, it's weirder the other way around.

I try to picture just how it happened. Maybe it began the very day of my accident. Maybe they were so traumatized that they couldn't stand the idea of sleeping alone. But the day of my accident, they were probably at the hospital, waiting to see if I'd make it through the night. And then maybe by the time they got back home, they were too exhausted to remember to sleep in separate rooms and just fell asleep in the nearest available bed. But I don't think they ever actually left me alone when I was in the hospital—even when I was in the coma—I think they took turns sitting by my bed every night. So maybe it wasn't until my first night home that they found themselves sharing a room again.

"I wonder how it happened," Chirag says, and I have to remind my left hand to stay firmly tucked under my leg instead of reaching out to squeeze Chirag's right one because he knew exactly what I was thinking.

"So where are you taking me tonight, anyway?" I ask.

"I thought we'd go to Bay Leaf," Chirag answers.

"Seriously?" Bay Leaf is my favorite restaurant. I'm pretty sure I've asked Chirag to take me there on every date we've ever gone on. "You never want to go out for Indian food. I thought no one's cooking could stand up to your mom's."

"Well, no one's cooking can." I accidentally insulted Chirag's mother months ago when I noticed a handful of bay leaves on her kitchen counter and said, "Bay leaves. Like the restaurant."

Now I say, "So you're taking me to Bay Leaf, you're just resigned not to enjoy it." The blinking neon light disappears from my imagination.

"Hey," Chirag says, "it's a special occasion."

"At least now I know what I have to do to get you to take me to Bay Leaf," I deadpan as we pull into the restaurant's parking lot. "What do I get if I lose a limb next time?"

Chirag is silent and my hands—well, my right hand—goes clammy. Just like that, the neon light is back: *What were you thinking?* it blinks over and over again, this time accompanied by a loud buzzing. Apparently, cracking a joke was a bad idea. Chirag is taking me to Bay Leaf because he feels sorry for me. And there's nothing funny about that.

THIRTEEN

The instant Chirag pulls into a spot, I open my door and get out of the car. Chirag hasn't even turned off the motor yet. I'm so intent on walking away from him that I don't remember that Bay Leaf has a dark, reflective window on its front door.

The pink scars on my cheeks are so bright that from far away, you might think I was bleeding. The hollows beneath my eyes are so deep that I look like a heroin addict, an insomniac, a ghoul. Which I guess I kind of am: What's more ghoulish than wearing a dead girl's flesh on your face?

No wonder I can't sleep. I'm haunting myself.

I never really liked how I looked when I smiled. My nose went down when my lips went up. I had a dimple in my left cheek that I thought made me look like a five-year-old, though my mother always said that by the time I reached middle age, the dimple would make me look older because it would just look like a wrinkle. I think she was trying to make me cherish looking young when I could, but it just made me hate the dimple more.

I smile into Bay Leaf's front door, just the tiniest bit, just for a split second, just long enough for me to see that even though I still have the same mouth, my smile looks nothing like it did before. *This* nose stays perfectly still when I smile. And *these* cheeks are dimple-free.

"Hey," Chirag says, catching up with me. "Guess you're still turning everything into a race, huh?" He smiles, like that's the reason I hurried out of the car.

Chirag pulls the restaurant door open. How nice it must be, to be able to open a mirrored door like it's no big deal at all. How delightful to catch a glimpse of yourself in the glass, and the only differences you notice are whether the wind has messed up your hair or whether that pimple you've been battling has finally disappeared.

"Let's get something to eat," Chirag says, and he holds his arm out as though he's about to take my hand—my right hand—and pull me into the restaurant. I duck past him, out of his reach. My right hand is unscarred, but if I let him hold it, he might try to take my left hand one day.

I still remember the very first time I ever spoke to Chirag, almost a whole year before we started dating. We were in the same sophomore English class, debating *For Whom the Bell Tolls*. After class, he came up to me and apologized for getting so heated about it. He sounded so serious and solemn, genuinely sorry that he'd gotten worked up. And all the while, I was thinking, *that's* what he calls heated? He'd never even raised his voice. Instead, he just made a smart, thoughtful argument that I happened to disagree with. It made me wonder what fights looked like in his house.

"No problem," I told him. "Hemingway has that effect on men, right? Everything is life or death."

"Even deciding what to drink," Chirag agreed, and he smiled, showing his bright white teeth.

It was then that I noticed that his skin was the color of caramel, and for the first time, I wondered what it might taste like. I had a crush on him after that, even as I kissed the occasional other boy at a party or giggled with Serena when she made lists of which of the boys at our school she thought would make the best boyfriend.

Serena's list was made up of mostly super-tan surfers and super-fit football players, and I don't think it occurred to her that I might like a different type of guy than she did. She didn't put Chirag on the list, and I didn't tell her that I wished she would. I liked him too much to laugh about it during study hall.

Our first date—we didn't actually call it our first date at the time, but later we both agreed that it was when our relationship officially began—wasn't exactly the sort of scenario that invited hand-holding. It was in January of our junior year, the height of the rainy season, after last period on a Wednesday when we were the only two people on the track behind school. It wasn't actually raining at the time, but the sky was threatening to open up any second, and our coaches had canceled practice. After a few laps, we found ourselves running in step and we discovered that we were listening to the same song. Soon, we both took out our earbuds so that we could talk, although we were totally out of breath.

During lunch the very next day, Chirag invited me to eat with him on the bleachers even though it was drizzling. As the rain shifted from a drizzle to a downpour, Chirag stood up, grabbed our food in one hand and grabbed me with the other and we ran inside. My hand fit into his so easily and perfectly that I wondered how I'd ever walked with it just hanging on its own by my side before. I'd never held a boy's hand before. I'd held my parents' hands, and Serena and I held hands all the time in middle school. *This* was something else entirely. *This* was like my hand had finally found its way home.

It bothers me now that I can't remember whether Chirag was holding my left hand or my right. I try to picture us running down the metal bleachers and across the track to get inside, but I can't remember which side of him I was standing on. Halfway there, he dropped my hand and we turned it into a race: who could get into the building faster. I won, though I think it was mostly because Chirag was holding our lunches under his jacket, trying to keep our food from getting soaked.

He probably didn't even want to hold my hand today, not really. He doesn't know this girl whose parents sleep in the same bed, who no longer likes the taste of buttercream or the smell of lilacs; this girl who laughs at her own rude jokes and hasn't gone for a run in over three months.

If it were me, I wouldn't want to hold hands with a stranger.

FOURTEEN

The maître d' seats us at a table right smack in the center of the dining room. Everyone in the restaurant has a perfect view of me. Like I'm on display.

I haven't actually been to a restaurant since the accident. Now I wonder if it's rude of me: Will seeing me make all the other patrons lose their appetites? Maybe freaks like me shouldn't be allowed to eat in public.

Chirag says, "No one's looking."

I nod. That's the second time tonight that Chirag knew what I was thinking without my having to say a word. A few months ago, I would have texted Serena under the table, excited to share proof that I'd found the perfect boyfriend.

But nothing is like it was a few months ago. The last time we came to this restaurant, it was with a huge group of friends. I didn't insist on sitting next to Chirag—I didn't want to be clingy—but halfway through the meal, Chirag came to sit next to me and ate off my plate, insisting that his mother's cooking was better even as he gobbled up every last morsel. After the waiters cleared our table, I leaned against Chirag and continued a conversation with the girl sitting on my other side as he talked to someone across the table. It was all so easy. Later, Chirag told me what a cool girlfriend I'd been.

But it's impossible to be a cool girlfriend when you're uncomfortable in your own skin. Actually, in someone else's skin. I shudder, wishing for a second I could take it off like a shirt that doesn't fit, a dress that hangs all wrong. Then the other patrons in this restaurant would really have something to stare at.

Chirag continues, "They probably think you had plastic surgery or something."

Quietly, I say, "I *did* have plastic surgery."

"Not that kind of plastic surgery. You know, the regular kind. The kind people do just for fun. You know, famous people. Or women with very low self-esteem."

"And men," I interject, feeling for a second like I used to, challenging my boyfriend.

Chirag nods. "And men."

"So I should feel comforted that all these strangers probably think that I have very low self-esteem, not that I was in a terrible accident?"

"It sucks either way, I know." Chirag puts his hands in the center of the table and presses his palms against the surface, like he can't quite figure out how to reach for me. I put my own hands in my lap, bend my legs under my chair. Following my lead, Chirag moves his hands back to his side of the table.

The waiter stops at our table and asks what we'll be having tonight. Chirag orders a ton of stuff, remembering all my favorites.

"I'm really not that hungry," I interrupt.

"Screw that," Chirag says, rattling off a few more dishes. When the waiter disappears, he adds, "We're celebrating." I raise my eyebrows, and Chirag shakes his head. "Don't say that we don't have anything to celebrate."

I bite my lip, preparing for yet another person to tell me what a lucky girl I am: You survived, you found a donor so quickly, you ended up in one of the handful of hospitals where they have the ability to do this surgery. But instead, he says, "I have to make up for missing your birthday."

I nod, the tiniest of smiles playing on the edges of my lips. He's trying so hard. I continue sitting on my hands, determined not to reach out to him, even with my good one.

The food comes, and it's delicious. "At least I still like Indian food," I say without thinking, heaping my fork with rice and masala sauce.

"What do you mean?"

I tighten my grip on my fork. "Nothing. It's not important."

But Chirag figures it out anyway. "Do things taste different to you now?"

"Some things," I answer. I don't look at him, focusing on the food in front of me instead. I really am like a creature from one of his movies, someone a mad scientist took apart and then put back together again, not quite the same as she was before. "I'm sorry," I add quickly. "I shouldn't have said anything. It's gross." If I could blush, I'd be bright pink right now.

"It's not gross," Chirag says. "It's cool."

"Cool?" I echo, like the word has lost all meaning.

Chirag shakes his head quickly. "I didn't mean, like, that it wasn't a big deal. You know what I meant, right?"

I don't.

106

"Just that it's interesting," Chirag explains. "You know, the science of it."

I sort of half nod, reminding myself that teenage boys think lots of gross things are fascinating. Every day at school, some guy is daring some other guy to touch something gross, smell something gross, eat something gross.

Maybe the boys at school will start daring each other to touch me next.

But Chirag's never been like that. He's going to be a doctor someday. Maybe that's why he thinks this is cool, and why he can sit across from me now and eat without gagging. Maybe he thinks he has to get used to looking at things that would nauseate other people.

Maybe I'm good practice.

"Does everyone know about me?" I ask. "At school?"

He nods.

"Serena never could keep her mouth shut," I say through gritted teeth, suddenly angry at her, though I'm not sure entirely why. It's not as though my classmates wouldn't have found out anyway. What did I think they'd do when I walked into the building looking like this?

"It's not her fault," Chirag counters. "You were absent for so long that they held a special assembly on the last day of school. Telling everyone about your—" He pauses, not sure what to call it.

"My accident," I supply. "That's what we've been calling it." Before, when I said *we*, I usually meant me, Chirag, and Serena. Now I mean my parents, the doctors, the nurses, and me.

"Your accident." Chirag says the word slowly, like he's never heard of it before. "They told everyone about your accident."

107

I nod. Special assemblies are for when a student or a teacher passes away. Sometimes they're when the school has guest speakers come to tell us about the exciting possibilities that wait for us after we graduate. Or sometimes they're just so that the college advisor can remind us how important our test scores are, while simultaneously recommending that we all keep our stress levels down.

Chirag continues, "There were rumors all over the school about where you were—why you'd missed so much school. There was a story on the news about a girl who'd been burned, but no one knew for sure if it was you other than Serena and me. The administration just wanted to set the record straight." He adds, "They asked your parents' permission," as though that makes it better.

I shake my head. "But I hadn't had my surgery by then," I protest.

"They sent letters home to the parents a couple weeks ago. Once it was definite that you'd be coming back to school this year."

Like I'm a problem that the administration thought they had to warn the parents about.

"They would've found out eventually, May," Chirag says gently. I haven't heard him call me by that nickname in so long and it makes me feel warm. "Doesn't it make it a little better knowing that you won't have to be the one to explain it to them?"

"I'm not sure," I answer. I mean, I certainly don't want to have to explain it. I don't want to think about it at all, let alone talk about it. But I'm not sure what's worse: strangers looking at me because they have no idea what happened to me, or the kids I've gone to school with for the past three years looking because they know *exactly* what happened to me.

"Chi-Dog!" shouts a voice from behind us. Eric Anderson appears at our table, his tall body casting a shadow over our plates. He's on the boys' track team with Chirag. His girlfriend, Erica, stands beside him. It was always a joke around school: Eric and Erica. I doubt anyone will even mention their similar names this year. Not when there are more interesting things to laugh at. Things like me.

"Eric." Chirag stands up to do that handshake-slash-hug that boys do. Eric leans in close to Chirag and whispers loud enough for me to hear, "You're such a good guy, dog." He pats Chirag's back like he's trying to be reassuring.

"Say hi to Maisie," Chirag says, leaning away from Eric and gesturing to me.

"Maisie, man. Look at you." I want to point out that it looks like Eric can barely stomach looking at me, but I keep my mouth shut and slouch in my chair like a little kid whose feet don't touch the floor.

"How are you?" Erica says, her voice so saccharine sweet that I want to gag.

With forced cheer, I answer, "Fine, thanks. How are you?"

Erica cocks her head to the side and smiles; Eric does the exact same thing, though he'd never really struck me as a cock-your-head-to-the-side kind of guy.

I excuse myself and get up to go to the bathroom.

I don't actually go inside the bathroom. Public restrooms are dangerous because you never know exactly where the reflective surfaces will be. A mirror could be waiting for you the instant you open the door, or it could be around the next corner.

Dr. Boden once told me that face transplant patients tend to recover more quickly than hand or leg recipients. There's a theory that it's because we don't have to see our faces as often as we see our limbs. So my avoiding mirrors is practically doctor's orders.

Before, I would have held Eric and Erica's gaze. Maybe I would have said something, made Eric and Erica ashamed of staring. Now I hover by the bathroom door and wait a few minutes, hoping that Eric and Erica will be gone by the time I get back to our table, pretending that my heart isn't beating so fast.

I don't bother sitting down. I tell Chirag that I'd like to go home, and I don't wait for him before I head for the door. We didn't finish our food, I know, but it doesn't matter because I'm not hungry anymore. From now on, the taste and smell of Indian food will remind me of this night. I'll need a new favorite restaurant.

Chirag doesn't try to convince me to stay. He doesn't offer hollow comfort like my mother would, doesn't insist that our celebration isn't over yet.

I don't remember what it feels like to want to celebrate anything at all.

As we drive up the hills that will take me home, I stare at my lap. It's not safe to look anywhere else. The streets in my neighborhood are so densely tree-lined that if I turn to look out the window, chances are I'll catch my reflection thanks to the shadows the trees cast on the glass. Years ago, they literally carved our street out of a forest. The houses on our block barely have backyards since they're built into the hill. We'd have a view of the Golden Gate Bridge from our front porch if not for the redwoods across the street. My parents used to hate the idea of me running here; there aren't any sidewalks and the streets wind and curve their way around the neighborhood, in between the trees. They were scared I'd get hit by a passing car. Before, I probably would have found that ironic.

I know this route so well that I don't have to look out the windows to know when we're passing the winding streets that lead the way to my house, when we're climbing the steep hills where Chirag and I raced each other after school. Carefully, I shoot a glance in Chirag's direction: Did he think that, once I got home, we'd go back to running together like we used to?

I did. All that physical therapy with Marnie, strengthening the muscles that slept while I was in the coma, stretching that skin that shrank when it burned—all that time, even on the days when I couldn't walk without holding Marnie's hands, I believed that running was the endgame. But yesterday during PT, Marnie told me that I'd have to avoid rigorous exercise.

I shouldn't have been surprised.

"For how long?" I asked, but she wouldn't give me a solid answer. The words she didn't say floated in the room between us: *Maybe forever.*

When I was in tenth grade, I sprained my ankle and I couldn't run for four weeks. I thought I would go crazy. I took a yoga class with Serena and literally stomped out—hurting my ankle all over again—halfway through. How could anyone get any satisfaction from moving so slowly?

"I can't run with you," I tell Chirag now. "I'm going to have to quit the team."

"I know," he answers. He doesn't even sound sad about it, about this huge part of our relationship that's over.

"You do? Who told you?"

"I mean, I guessed as much a while back."

"Oh. Of course." *With your rational scientific brain, it was probably obvious. The most logical conclusion. You wouldn't have asked Marnie for how long; you would have known all along that you had to give it up.* Maybe that's why he doesn't sound sad. Unlike me, he's had some time to get used to the idea.

"At least you got that over with," Chirag says suddenly.

"Got what over with?" I ask.

"Seeing someone from school. It wasn't *that* bad, right?"

"Wasn't that bad? They stared at me like I was an animal in a cage."

"I know," Chirag agrees. "But you can't blame them for staring."

"I can't?"

"I mean, it was rude, but they couldn't help it. It's human nature. We're interested in things we don't understand. It's why we rubber-neck at car accidents, why carnivals had literal freak shows a hundred years ago."

Is that supposed to make me feel better, I think but do not say, *the idea that people are* rubbernecking *at me?* It's the kind of reasonable explanation that made me fall for Chirag in the first place—no screaming, no shouting, just perfect, indisputable logic. I loved when he'd end an argument in the lunchroom by using history and science to explain why Serena had gray eyes or why I had freckles. Why his parents were overbearing, or why teenagers are more likely to be impulsive than adults. Maybe, if I were a few years older, I'd never have made the impulsive decision to go running that morning.

"What did Eric mean when he said you're such a good guy?"

Chirag shrugs. "Eric's a jerk. Everyone knows he's a jerk."

I shake my head. Why would Chirag say Eric is a jerk for calling him a good person?

Then it hits me. It's so obvious that I can't quite believe it took me this long to figure it out.

Chirag pulls into my driveway, and I unclick my seat belt and open my door before he's even put the car in park. I move quickly, so that we can avoid the whole *should we or shouldn't we hug or kiss good night* moment. When I close the door and wave good-bye, I'm careful to avert my eyes from my reflection in the rearview mirror. Chirag shifts into reverse and drives away. I watch his taillights fade away into the fog.

Chirag is a good guy, because a lesser man would have broken up with a freak like me.

FIFTEEN

If my parents notice that my night out with Chirag was unusually short, they don't say so. Instead, they leave me alone in my room, where I sit with the door closed until my mother knocks at eight o'clock sharp to remind me it's time to take my evening pills. I guess it's a good thing Chirag and I didn't linger at dinner. I might have missed a dose by a few minutes.

"Dr. Boden said that I should be in charge of my medicine," I remind my mother as she enters my room with a glass of water filled to the brim, but she ignores me. She stands silently as I take pill after pill, like she's watching an unruly patient in a mental hospital. What will she do next year, when I'm living in a dorm?

I take the big ones first, to get them over with. I hold the water glass in my right hand—I'm scared I would drop it if I used my left. I've never had trouble swallowing pills—when I was little, I used to swallow chewable Tylenol, just to show that I could—but then, I never had to take this many before.

I'm on my third pill when I decide that I know which is worse: The kids I've gone to school with for the past three years looking at me was definitely worse than strangers who don't know what happened to me. Eric and Erica stared like I was a jigsaw puzzle whose parts needed to be rearranged.

And all the king's horses and all the king's men couldn't put Humpty Dumpty together again.

On my fifth pill, I decide that there is no chance, no way whatsoever, that I can handle seeing dozens, hundreds, of faces just like Eric's and Erica's on the first day of school in just a few days. And it's not a matter of needing more time. I will *never* be able to handle all those people: their sympathy and their horror, their sadness and their disgust.

The final pill gone, I take a long swig of water and say, "I think you should homeschool me."

"What?" Mom asks, her back to me. She's too busy counting pills to have heard me.

"I think you should homeschool me," I repeat. "Dad!" I shout, because I think he's more likely to take my side. When he comes to my door, I say, "I'd like to be homeschooled."

He doesn't respond, but at least he doesn't ask why. *Why* is painfully obvious to anyone in my eye-line. Finally, Mom says, "I don't think that's such a good idea."

"Why not?" My voice is high-pitched, like a child's.

"You love school," my mother answers, and I look at her, incredulous. Does she really think that anything is the way that it used to be?

"It's going to be awful." I hate myself for having a lump in my throat, for the tears in my eyes that threaten to overflow. I don't want to be a crying, whining little girl. I want to make a compelling argument for homeschool that they can't deny. Chirag would be better at this, with his scientific explanations. I wish he were here to make the argument for me.

I sink onto my bed. "Everyone is going to stare at me. They're going to ask questions. They're going to treat me like I'm made of glass."

"Well, what's the matter with that?" Mom says. "They *should* be careful around you."

I look at her like she's speaking a foreign language. She may as well be, for all that we understand each other. Dad sinks onto the bed beside me, but Mom stays standing over us. She never used to seem this tall. Dad glances up at her, and for a second, I think he's going to give in, but Mom shakes her head slightly, her eyes narrow and certain.

"Honey," Dad begins slowly, "your mother and I discussed this."

Mom adds, "It's part of why we allowed them to do the transplant in the first place. So you'd have a more normal life."

"What do you mean *allowed* them to do the transplant?" I protest. "That was *my* decision. And if I'm grown-up enough to decide whether or not to put a stranger's parts onto my face, I'm grown-up enough to decide that I should be homeschooled."

"You don't sound very grown-up now," Mom counters.

"Are you kidding me?" I shout. "You think that my not wanting to go to school is some show of *immaturity* on my part? You can't *imagine* what it will be like. You will *never* understand."

"The adult thing to do would be to face it, head-on."

"Pun intended?" I mumble angrily.

"Look," Dad interjects, resting his hand on my own—on my left hand, my bad one. Painfully, my fingers curl into a fist beneath his touch. "I know this is difficult, and I know we can't understand. But the reason we chose the transplant—all of us, together—was so that you'd have a chance at a normal life. Finishing high school with the rest of your class is something you have the chance to do *because* the surgery was a success."

He strokes my hand, his skin impossibly ordinary over my scars. Despite all the arguments my parents have—used to have—I always got the idea that Dad hated fighting. He just wanted to keep the peace. Maybe every single one of their fights was my mother's fault. I think back to the fight they were having the night before my accident: *She* was the one who left the dishes in the sink, a test for him to pass or fail, like he was an unruly student instead of her husband.

"I will *never* have a normal life," I growl, jerking my hand away. "Don't you get that by now? I will never *look* normal, and I will never *be* normal. I will never go to the beach with my friends. I will never get asked on a date because some guy thinks I'm pretty. I will never *not* be stared at. I can't even sleep through the night!"

Mom nods heavily. "Right now, all of that is true. But we don't know if it will be true forever. A few years ago, they wouldn't have been able to do your surgery at all. So who knows what they'll be able to do a few years from now?"

"So my best hope is that someday I might have to have *another* surgery? Someday I might have to go through all of this *again*?" The lump in my throat is choking me.

"That's not what I meant."

"I know exactly what you meant," I answer. What she meant is that she agrees: I look awful. Every time she said I looked great, she was lying. The truth is that she's hoping they'll come up with some better technology someday. A chance for her daughter to be pretty again.

Dad puts his arm around me and squeezes. I cry harder. "Please don't make me go," I sob. I don't feel my tears until they hit my neck or slide into my mouth. "It's not like I'm some little kid playing sick to get out of taking her math test. I *want* to finish school. I just can't go there right now." There's no way they'll make me go to school. Not when they can see how much it upsets me.

But when I look up at my father, his mouth is set in a straight line, and Mom's is, too.

"Your father and I made up our minds," she says firmly.

"*This* is what it takes to get you to agree about something!" I shout. It's almost the same joke I made earlier, about what had to happen for Chirag to take me to Bay Leaf. Again, no one laughs.

I never thought I would prefer my parents' fighting, but right now I hate their united front. I wish they would just get divorced so that I could go live with my dad. I'm pretty sure that I'd be able to convince him to homeschool me if only Mom weren't around.

"It is not my job to be your relationship's Band-Aid!"

"Maisie, I think you should stop shouting before you say something you regret."

"No," I yell, so loudly that my father stands up. Maybe all this crying and shouting is bad for my face. "You shut up. Both of you! I can't believe you would make me go to school like this. What kind of parents are you? Isn't it your *job* to protect your child? Isn't that something parents are supposed to *want*?"

My mother presses her lips together so hard that they turn white. "That's enough, young lady," she says, sounding for all the world like a normal parent trying to deal with a normal teenager who's acting up like normal teenagers do. Maybe the face transplant wasn't my chance at a normal life; maybe it was *theirs*.

"I think you owe us an apology," she says evenly.

I stand up now. "Well, I think you owe me an apology," I shout. It's never a fair fight with her. She's a lawyer. She's literally had training on how to argue.

"I think that's enough," she says finally. "We can discuss this in the morning when you've calmed down."

"I don't want to calm down!" I cry, but she's already turned her back on me; she takes my father's hand and pulls him along with her, until they're both on the other side of my door. Then, quietly, calmly, she closes it behind her. I don't even get to slam it shut.

SIXTEEN

That night, it isn't my crying that wakes the whole house. Instead, I wake to the sound of sobs coming from my parents' room. I tiptoe down the hall and stand outside their door.

"She's never yelled at us like that before." Dad's voice is thick with tears. "I used to listen to my colleagues complaining about their kids, and I'd think how lucky we were."

"We *are* lucky," Mom counters, and it surprises me to hear that it sounds like she's crying, too. "Maisie didn't mean those things. She's just hurting."

"Is this all too much for her?" he says. "Maybe she's right. Maybe we shouldn't make her go to school yet."

"I know it'll be hard," Mom answers. "Nothing about this isn't going to be hard."

Well, if you know how hard it's going to be, why are you making me go?

As if she heard my question, she continues, "But we have to do what's best for Maisie. Believe me, I know how much easier it would be on her if she could stay home, but the doctors said it would be good for her to go to school. She has to get used to the way people will look at her." She sighs, and I imagine her rubbing her temples with her middle fingers, the way she does when she's tired.

"I don't want to lose our little girl," Dad says, and I imagine his shoulders shaking as he cries harder. For a second, I'm tempted to open the door and crawl into their bed the way I did when I was very little. I want to feel my dad's arms around me and I want to tell them that I love them and they aren't going to lose me.

But then the feeling is overtaken by anger. He doesn't want to lose his little girl? *He's* not the one who's lost something here. He's not the one with this ridiculous face. He's not the one who's going to get stared at, who'll never get to wear a bathing suit, go for a run, have sex, get married, have kids.

I sink down onto the floor and close my eyes. I was never that girl who fantasized about a long white dress and wedding cake and throwing the bouquet. In fact, I didn't think I'd ever want to get married. I didn't want to end up fighting like my parents. Although they're not fighting now. Now it sounds like they're kind of lucky to have each other.

And that just makes me angrier. They're together in there, and I'm alone out here.

Six months ago, I would have texted Chirag at a moment like this.

Sorry if I'm waking you, I would have said.

No problem, he'd have answered. *I was dreaming about you.*

You were? What was I doing?

Running. Then he'd have asked, *What's wrong?*

I'm lonely.

Want me to come over?

I'd have answered *yes*, and twenty minutes later I'd sneak out of the house—quietly, quietly—so that my parents wouldn't hear. Chirag would be parked down the block, out of sight. I'd tell him everything: what my parents were saying, how they always made everything about them when it was really about me.

Maybe we'd have made out, or maybe he'd have driven around through the fog until the sun came up. Or maybe we'd have just sat there quietly, smiling at each other until morning. Just seeing him would have been enough to make me feel better. To make the world seem so much bigger than what went on in my parents' house.

I tiptoe back into my room, where I stare at my phone on my desk. Chirag would be here in an instant if I asked. But I can't ask. For all I know, he's dreaming of me right now, my old face still taking up space in his subconscious. I can't risk snapping him out of that.

I can still hear my father crying in the next room. I can't believe they're going to make me go to school on Monday. I'll be gawked at and pitied and whispered about. After a while, Chirag will have seen this new face just as much as he ever saw my old one. Maybe my new face and my old face will battle it out over which one will get to be in his dreams. If he ever dreams of me again.

Serena and I always planned to go to Berkeley together. But now I don't want to go to college with anyone who knows me, even her. I don't want to go to college less than an hour's drive from my parents' house, just a little farther from the hospital where they gave me this new face. As long as I'm around people who know what I used to look like, I'll never be seen as anything other than a victim, a puzzle, a science experiment gone awry.

At one of those special assemblies last year, they had representatives from a dozen East Coast colleges come and talk to us. They said it was to broaden our horizons, as though no one in our class had heard of the Ivy League, which was kind of ridiculous. But one of the speakers was from an all-girls college in New York City called Barnard.

What better place to be a freak than New York City?

I pull my laptop onto the bed and visit the school's website, browse through pictures of smiling students and wrought-iron gates. *That* is where I'm going to school. My grades are good enough, as long as I keep them up this year. I download the application and begin filling it out, even though it's not due for months. I won't tell anyone; let my parents and Chirag and Serena think that I still want to stay in California. This will be my secret, a decision that no one can make for me. I'll just get through this year as quickly as possible: I'll keep to the edges of the school's hallways, my hair across my face like a curtain, no longer the track star walking with her head held high, who threw her arms in the air while her classmates cheered. And when it's over, I'll move clear across the country.

Three thousand miles away from anyone who knows my old face.

SEVENTEEN

On Monday morning, in that second between sleep and waking, I'm myself again, blinking my eyes awake and looking forward to the *Step, breath, step, breath* rhythm that used to punctuate my days. But then I roll over in bed and feel the stiffness on my left side, the delicate tight skin screaming in protest when I lift my arm overhead, and I remember who I am now. I am a freak of a girl who will not be going for a run this morning, whose mother is coming into her room to wake her because she slept through her alarm.

Sometimes I wish they could anesthetize me into a coma all over again.

"You don't want to be late for your first day," Mom trills, pulling my blankets back.

In the shower, using the medicinal-smelling soap my mother special-ordered from the pharmacy because she read in one of her countless magazines that it would help my scars fade, I can feel that the muscles I built up over years of training have already atrophied from months in the hospital, where the most exercise I got was walking in circles around the nurses' station in the weeks following my surgery. My clothes don't fit the way they used to.

As I get out of the shower, I catch the tiniest glimpse of myself in the steamy bathroom mirror: The skin on my left side is pink and angry; the pink scars on my face are as dark as ever. Am I really worried my classmates will notice that I'm not as *fit* as I used to be?

"Hurry up, lazybones," Mom calls cheerfully as I pad down the stairs, like I'm a regular teenager who overslept on her first day of school. I'm wearing jeans and a long-sleeved plain white T-shirt, the same outfit I wore when Chirag and Serena visited. As commonplace an outfit as possible. Anything to help me blend in. Though clothes would need magical powers to make me look like everyone else. "Chirag will be here to pick you up any minute."

I freeze halfway down the stairs. "*Chirag* will be here?"

"Of course," Mom answers like it's obvious. This morning, she's wearing a suit; she's going back to work now that I'm going back to school. "He always drives you. Didn't he text you?" I shrug. He might have, but I've been avoiding my phone. Too scared I'd invite Chirag over. Apparently, it wouldn't have mattered if I did. Mom invited him over for me. I hate the way she talks to Chirag behind my back, like she's arranging playdates for a five-year-old.

She practically pushes me out the door and I look at the ground as I walk down the steps and toward Chirag's car, the fog enveloping me. This time of year, it usually burns off by nine or ten in the morning, but I wish it could stay today, hanging low and heavy, covering me like a quilt.

"Morning," Chirag says, and I mumble it back, letting myself into the passenger side. We haven't talked since our disastrous dinner at Bay Leaf, but Chirag doesn't point that out, nor does he remind me that we used to talk every day, a zillion times a day. Maybe he's worried that I will break if he says anything. We drive to school in silence, me sipping the coffee that he had waiting for me in the car, just the way he used to—2 percent milk, no sugar. The way I always liked it. Today, I can barely swallow it.

I'd always kind of thought my parents might get me a car for my seventeenth birthday, but I haven't driven since the accident and no one has suggested that I try. I'd imagined driving myself to school in a shiny hybrid like Chirag's, wearing new car smell like perfume. I'd hoped that everyone would look at me on our first day back as I pulled into the parking lot and expertly maneuvered my way into a spot.

Today, they're looking, but it's definitely not because of the vehicle I arrive in. I tilt my head downward. I don't want to meet anyone's eye, don't want to *see* them staring. I stare at Chirag's legs, and follow them across the parking lot.

Without stopping, Chirag pulls a folded piece of paper from his pocket. I'm careful to reach for it with my right hand. His fingers brush against mine and linger there, like he's considering whether or not we should walk into school holding hands like we used to. Quickly, I grab the page and pull my hand away from his.

"Your schedule," Chirag says, gesturing at the page. "Your mom gave it to me."

I shake my head. We usually get copies of our schedules in homeroom on the first day.

"The administration had to make some changes, so they prepared it ahead of time," Chirag explains.

I look at my classes. No physics, no track practice. No more running until my lungs ache, no more relays with my teammates, no more ribbons and medals and cheers and applause.

I have never wanted to go home so badly. Not when I was nine and my parents sent me to sleepaway camp for one miserable month. Not when I was fourteen and went to the pool only to discover that last year's bathing suit had worn so thin it was almost see-through and everyone pointed and giggled. Not even when I woke up from my coma and discovered I was in a strange hospital, in a strange bed, and I could barely move.

I take a deep breath and follow Chirag through the school's front doors. I squeeze my right hand shut tight, pretending that Chirag's fingers are laced through mine.

Even with my gaze focused on Chirag's legs in front of me, I can feel that everyone—people I've never spoken to, whose names I'm not even sure of—is looking at me. I move slowly, scared of losing my balance where everyone can see. Out of the corner of my eye, I see that mouths hang open, eyes don't blink, hands are brought to faces so that my classmates look like they're mimicking that painting *The Scream*. A few faces actually look disappointed; I guess I'm not quite the half-faced monster they'd been expecting. I wonder how many of them sat up late last night Googling "face transplants."

I can't believe I ever actually *wanted* to be the center of attention at this school. Serena used to strut down the halls and all the boys turned and stared and I actually envied all those whispers and glances.

Chirag is just a half step ahead of me. I close my eyes and breathe in the smell of him, thinking that it might calm me down, make me feel better.

The next thing I know, I've walked right into him.

"Oh my god, Maisie, are you okay?" he asks.

"Ow," I say, though it didn't really hurt; I just said *ow* as a reflex. I can perceive the pressure of his body pressing into my face, but not feel the texture of his shirt, the fibers of the fabric. He could be wearing something as rough as burlap or soft as cashmere and it wouldn't make a difference. I'm tempted to turn my head so that it's my mouth against his shirt; my lips and the cupid's bow above them would be able to feel him.

I open my eyes. We're outside my homeroom. That's why he stopped walking.

Phantom giggles come from the kids around us. I back away a couple steps.

"I'm fine," I say.

"Did I hurt you?" He looks like he thinks that my face could fall off just from colliding into his gray sweatshirt. A few months ago, I'd have made fun of him for looking so scared.

"I'm fine," I repeat, though I'm honestly not sure just how delicate this new face is. Maybe bumping into something could cause major damage. A familiar string of panic winds its way around my ribs. Chirag and I aren't in the same homeroom. He's about to leave me.

"I can come in if you want. The teachers will understand." The gentle concern in Chirag's voice makes me feel worse. "I can stay until Serena shows up, at least."

"No," I insist, shaking my head even though every bone in my body, even the new ones I don't know very well yet, want him to stay. "I'll be okay. It's just homeroom." I've sat in this classroom every morning since my freshman year.

Chirag leans down to hug me good-bye, but I duck out of reach, pretending to step closer to the classroom door. Bad enough he had to touch me when I bumped into him.

"See ya," I say, turning my back on him.

"See ya," he answers, and his voice sounds almost wistful, like maybe he was thinking about the way we used to kiss each other good-bye.

Serena breezes into class after the bell rings but before the teacher has gotten to her last name, Marcus, in roll call.

"Sorry I'm late," she says, slipping into the chair beside mine. I'm sitting off to the left, about halfway back, the same place where Serena and I have always sat in homeroom. I considered sitting in the way back, but I thought that would stand out even more than keeping my usual seat.

"You're always late," I answer. The truth is, I can't remember the last time she made it to class before the teacher had gotten to the S's. "If only I'd been blessed with a last name like yours," she used to say. With a name like *Winters*, she'd insist, she'd always make it in time.

Now, when Mrs. Martens finally reaches her name, Serena shouts, "Here!" so that the whole class erupts into giggles and cheers. Serena actually stands up and curtsies, and the boys all wolf whistle because she's wearing a short skirt that shows off her tan legs.

Finally, Mrs. Martens gets to my name. "Winters, Maisie." She says my name loudly and slowly, as though she thinks that my ears were damaged in the accident.

Didn't the administration cover that in the letter they sent home?

Mrs. Martens looks up from her list, scanning the room for me. Everyone spins around in their seats to look.

"Here," I say, my voice shaking, my head tilted down so that my hair falls across my cheeks. I don't shout like Serena, but I don't whisper it either.

"Of course you are, dear," Mrs. Martens says, and she smiles a sad kind of *I'm so sorry* smile, the same way she looked at Colby Cuthbert when her father died of a heart attack freshman year.

I think I hate Mrs. Martens.

She pauses and then moves on to the only name after mine in the alphabet—Wohl, Jason—just in time for the bell signaling first period to ring. Everyone begins to get up.

"Maisie!" Mrs. Martens's voice rises above the din.

"I'll wait for you in the hall," Serena promises as I walk to meet Mrs. Martens in the front of the room.

"There's a change in your schedule, dear." When she speaks to me, she focuses her gaze at the empty space just above my left shoulder. A lot of my teachers will do that this year, to avoid staring at my face. I wonder if they all had some kind of sensitivity training: *Don't look her in the face, it will just make her self-conscious.*

Instead, it makes me feel like one of the gorgons from Greek mythology. Like they're all scared that if they look too closely, they'll turn to stone.

I hold my schedule out in front of me questioningly. It's wrinkled from Chirag's pocket. I wonder how long he had it in there. I wonder if it smells like him.

"Yes. You were scheduled for sixth-period physical education on Monday and Wednesday afternoons," she says. *Gym,* I think but do not say. *No one calls it physical education.* "And, well, your doctors didn't think you should attend that particular class." I'd like to call my doctors and let them know that what happens in gym class hardly qualifies as rigorous exercise. Mrs. Martens continues, "So, instead of PE, I'd like to invite you to come to my studio and work on some art."

Mrs. Martens's art class is an elective popular among the slackers and the stoners. Anyone with actual artistic talent takes classes after school at the art institute in the city. She actually sounds excited, like my inability to go to gym class is good news. She probably thinks she's going to be the teacher who helps me, like a teacher in a sappy made-for-TV movie, the one who helps the troubled student. She thinks that in her studio—which is just a regular classroom—I'll work on a sculpture of my face, all the new features jammed in with the old ones, and have some kind of breakthrough, sobbing in her arms when I see the finished product.

"I'd rather not." I speak just as slowly as she does. "I mean, if it's just an invitation, it's optional, right?"

Mrs. Martens adjusts her glasses. "Of course, dear," she says. She's never called me *dear* before today. "You're welcome to spend your P.E. period in the nurse's office, resting."

From the way she says it, I can tell that that was what the administration or my doctors originally proposed.

She continues, "Certainly, that's better than sitting on the sidelines while your classmates exercise."

She smiles again, one of those heart-attack smiles, like she has any idea what it would feel like to sit on the benches while everyone else worked out. "Great, thanks," I say. I turn on my heel and walk slowly out of the room. My eyes are so distracted by the sight of the new nose, the rest of me cannot feel that before I even get to the classroom door, I start to go cross-eyed. I blink and concentrate on staring straight ahead, at Serena's silhouette waiting for me in the hall.

I follow Serena to our first class, European History. Over the summer, we were supposed to read *A Tale of Two Cities* to get ready for our unit on the French Revolution, but of course, I didn't read the book. Serena is trying to summarize it, but I can barely hear the words *fishwives* and *guillotine* over the sound of the whispers and giggles that follow us down the hall. Suddenly, spending forty minutes in Nurse Culligan's dark office sounds incredibly appealing.

I wish it were time for gym class right now.

EIGHTEEN

By lunchtime, I've received at least a dozen more heart-attack smiles, from teachers and students alike. I want to shout *Stop smiling!* each and every time, but that would probably just draw more attention, so I keep my mouth shut. If I told Chirag, he'd offer a reasonable explanation for the sympathetic smiles, the same way he did for the stares.

The fog has burned off and Serena is already sitting on one of the benches out in front of school. My friend Ellen, from the track team, and her best friend, Samantha, are sitting on the grass beneath her. We've waited three years to sit here; it's kind of an unwritten law at Highlands High that only the seniors get to sit on these benches. Our first day freshman year, Serena and I sat here cluelessly and it wasn't until the end of lunch period that a sophomore took pity on us and explained the angry stares we'd been receiving for the prior forty minutes.

I tighten my grip on my lunch bag; Mom actually packed my lunch this morning, something she hasn't done since I was in elementary school. She wanted to be the one who packed my midday dose of pills. She probably didn't think I could have done it correctly.

As though I'm not intimately aware of each pill I have to take. I'm the one who tastes them on her tongue, who feels them in her throat, who gags in between gulps of water.

Serena's face is tilted up to the sky, and she pulled the straps of her tank top down over her shoulders to avoid tan lines. Sam turns her face from the sun long enough to glance at me; I haven't seen her, or Ellen, since before my accident. They each texted me after I came home from the hospital—*Get well soon!*—but I never wrote back.

"Hey there, May-Day," Serena says, squinting up at me. "I'm starving. You?" Serena has called me May-Day for years. It used to make me think of spring, for flowers and sunshine. But now I think of the phrase's other meaning: someone crying for help. *M'aidez.*

I shake my head. "I'm really not hungry," I say carefully. "I think I'm just going to sit in the library for a while. Catch up on some reading."

"What could you possibly have to catch up on? It's the first day."

"Oh, I don't know, the last couple months of junior year?"

"Come on, Maisie, it's not like they're going to test you on something you missed."

I'd love to sit down beside Serena and face the sky. I don't even care about the risk of melanoma, but the doctors also said that my scars would be more pronounced if I got even the littlest bit of a suntan. I covered myself with SPF 100 before I left the house this morning, but that was hours ago. Now I pull my left sleeve down over my wrist, stretching the fabric until my whole hand is covered. Maybe I'll wear long sleeves no matter the weather for the rest of my life. I should move to a colder climate.

"I can't," I finally say to Serena, barely able to get the words out. A shadow of understanding falls across her sun-stained face and she gets up.

"Ellen. Sam." She turns from me to face our friends. "I've had enough sun for today. Let's go sit in the shade."

"Are you crazy?" Ellen says. "I was stuck inside a classroom all summer. I'm not missing a minute of sunshine." Ellen's parents made her take classes at a local university for the summer. They thought it would look good on her college applications. Not that she needs it; she's kind of a genius. I bet she'll end up at Harvard or Yale or something.

Ellen has yet to look at me. Suddenly, I want to check exactly how many miles are in between Harvard or Yale and Barnard.

"The sun isn't good for Maisie," Serena answers matter-of-factly and I swallow a shout of frustration. I can't believe she just flat out told them that. Couldn't she have told some lie, pretended that *she* was the one worried about skin cancer for once? I mean, it's not good for anyone to sit out in the sun. You don't have to be a freak like me to get melanoma.

"It's fine," I say, sitting down hard on the bench. "Don't worry about it." I'll bring a hat tomorrow or something.

"Don't be silly." Serena is trying to sound like her usual cheerful self, but her voice sounds borderline shrill. She stands up and walks toward the school, to the shady benches by the front entrance of the building, where the freshmen sit. Samantha shrugs and follows Serena, looking reluctant but resigned. Ellen hesitates, stretching her legs out in front of her on the grass. Clearly, she doesn't want to leave her patch of sunshine.

"Really, guys, it's okay. We can stay."

Oh my god, am I about to start crying over which bench I'm going to sit on for lunch? I glance at my watch; it's twelve-fifteen. I'm supposed to take my pills at noon. If my mother knew I was fifteen minutes late—if she knew I'd spent nearly five whole minutes in the sun—she'd drag me inside kicking and screaming, pouring water and pills down my throat as she did so.

"We're not going to jeopardize your health so that Ellen can get a suntan, Maisie." I've never heard Serena sound quite so serious before. I stand up and follow her like a dog who's been scolded.

Ellen groans as she stands up. Now she does look at me, a strained sort of scowl on her face. I'm not sure if it's because she's disgusted by what she sees or because she's just pissed about leaving the sunshine behind.

"We can still sit there," I say softly. "Maybe on cloudy days." But my words are hollow; people stake out those benches from the first day of school and keep them all year long. We're not gone five seconds before another group of seniors takes our place.

Once we're settled on our shady bench, Samantha asks, "So what was it like?"

"What was what like?"

"Being in a coma. Could you hear things? Did you see a bright light? Your dead relatives?"

Ellen pretends to be fascinated by her sandwich, but she's obviously listening, too.

"It wasn't that kind of coma," I say finally.

"How many different kinds of comas are there?"

I shrug. "I don't know."

"But don't you—"

Serena interrupts, "Jesus, Sam, can't you tell that Maisie doesn't want to talk about it?"

Defensively, Sam counters, "How am I supposed to know that she doesn't want to talk about it?"

"Would *you* want to talk about it?" Serena asks. "Besides, just because she was in a coma, she's not, like, an expert on them now."

"Fine," Sam says. She sounds disappointed. I feel like I've let her down. She and Ellen both watch as I take my pills, like I'm doing something they've never seen.

But then, I guess they never have seen anyone with a patchwork face swallow before.

NINETEEN

'm swallowing my last pill when Chirag walks up. Instinctively, my lips curl into a smile, and I have to sit on my hands to keep from holding them out for a hug hello. Old habits die hard, I guess. Actually, last year, we almost never sat together for lunch. He usually sat with his guy friends and I sat with my girl friends—but we'd always text each other to meet behind the school for a kiss before classes started again.

And last year, when he sat down beside me, he'd have put his arm around me and I'd have rested a hand on his knee. Now I just stare at the strip of bench in between us. It reminds me of seeing him in the halls before we started dating, when he was just the boy I had a crush on, the boy I wanted to touch but couldn't. Back then, even when he and I were in the same classroom, it felt like he was a million miles out of my reach.

"So . . ." he says finally, "I'll meet you out front at two-thirty." Serena, Sam, and Ellen look away, pretending not to hear.

"What?"

"I'll meet you out front at two-thirty," he repeats, and I wonder if— like Mrs. Martens, like Eric—Chirag thinks that the accident affected my hearing.

"I heard you," I say, "but why? I have class at two-thirty."

"Didn't you look at your schedule? On Mondays and Thursdays your last class is seventh period so that you can leave in time for PT. And on Fridays, too, so you can get to the hospital for your blood tests."

I shake my head. I didn't really look at my schedule. And when exactly did Chirag start referring to physical therapy as PT like he's so familiar with it? Does he know what I do with Marnie? Know that sometimes I spend the full hour doing nothing more than bending and straightening my stiff left arm, forcing the scarred skin on my left side to stretch until it feels like it's ripping wide open?

But I can't ask those questions without risking some kind of further explanation, so I say, "Why are *you* meeting me?"

"Your mom said she couldn't leave work early three days a week. So I volunteered to drive you on Mondays. The administration tweaked my schedule so I'm not missing anything."

"You have track practice on Mondays."

"Coach will understand."

I open my mouth to protest. Coach is inflexible about missing practice. She once suspended a runner after he missed practice because he had food poisoning and didn't tell her until after the fact. Even when I sprained my ankle sophomore year, I didn't miss one day of practice. I sat impatiently on the sidelines, waiting to be well enough to run again.

Before I can say anything, Chirag says, "Your mom and I worked everything out with the teachers."

My pulse quickens, and I press my left fingernails into my jeans. If I were anything like my mother, this would be the time when I raised my voice. But Chirag and I have never had an actual fight and I'm not about to start now. Not over something as small as scheduling.

Even if it doesn't feel small. I swallow and silently order my heartbeat to slow. "I guess you and my mom have been talking a lot lately." *Behind my back,* I think but do not say.

Chirag shrugs. "She called me last week to work out a schedule."

I look at my sneakers. "I didn't know that." *Why didn't you include me in these conversations?*

"I thought your mom told you."

Well, she didn't, and since when do you count on my mom *to tell me anything that has to do with you and me?*

How can Chirag act like this isn't a big deal? He knows how I feel about my mother treating me like a little kid, something she did plenty even before the accident. Maybe he thinks I don't mind that kind of thing anymore. *Or,* I want to say, *maybe you agree with my mom—maybe you think that now I need to be treated like a little kid?*

But instead I nod and say, "Okay. I'll meet you out front at two-thirty."

"Great." Chirag smiles as he stands. He hovers above me for a second, like he's trying to decide what to do. Before, I'd have tilted my face up for a good-bye kiss. Now I keep my gaze fixed firmly on the ground in front of me. Finally, Chirag leans down and kisses the top of my head.

"You smell different." He has such a deep voice that everything he says sounds solemn. I nod. That stupid soap my mother made me use. Plus, I threw away my old perfume last night. I hate the way it smells now.

"You still smell good," Chirag says, but it sounds forced, like that's the kind of thing he thinks he ought to say.

"Thanks," I mumble. Chirag loved the way my old perfume smelled. I should have kept it, for him, whether I liked it or not. He would have done that for me.

"I gotta go," I say, packing up my now-empty pillbox and shoving it into my bag. "I'm going to be late."

"What for?"

The bell rings; it's sixth period. "Late for staring at the ceiling in Mrs. Culligan's office."

As I walk away, I hear Ellen saying, "I'm gonna catch five minutes of sunshine before gym."

The nurse's office is quiet and cool. I guess there aren't any other sick kids on the first day of classes. I lie down on one of the beds in the dark, the paper Nurse Culligan puts over the pillowcase crinkling beneath the weight of my head. Serena, Samantha, and Ellen are getting ready for gym right now. They're probably complaining as they change in the locker room; we all hated gym class, even me. They probably think I'm lucky not to have to go.

Being here now is just another in the long list of today's humiliations. I never knew you could be humiliated alone before. I roll over to face the wall even though I'm not supposed to lie on my side. Wow, how pathetic. Other kids rebel by staying out late, breaking curfew, drinking, doing drugs. My rebellion is to roll over.

I don't want to fall asleep; don't want Nurse Culligan to shake me awake in time for seventh period. Worse, she might let me sleep right through it. Then Chirag would have to come searching for me because I wouldn't be out front to meet him at two-thirty like he and Mom planned. And he would call my mother to say that I wasn't strong enough to make it through my first day.

Tattletale.

I shake my head, hearing the paper wrinkle beneath my cheek. Chirag is just trying to do the right thing. And it's not like there's some playbook for how to act after your girlfriend has a procedure so rare that most people in the world don't even know it exists.

If I'd chosen not to do the transplant, I wouldn't be here right now. Maybe I'd still be in the hospital, or maybe I'd be at home, taking long laboring breaths through my mouth beneath a skin graft. They said the grafts would never be more than a mask over what was left of me, but this face I cannot feel, this nose, these cheeks, this chin: What are they if not a mask? And with skin grafts, I wouldn't be wearing someone else's skin and bones, literally wearing *death* on my face. They'd have taken skin from the undamaged parts of my own body, my inner thighs maybe. Or my lower back.

If I'd chosen differently, Ellen and Sam could have had their lunch in the sunshine. Serena wouldn't have to explain me to them. And Chirag wouldn't have to look at the remains of the girl he used to hug and kiss and hold.

I don't feel the tears that drip across my nose and my cheeks. Dr. Boden said there's no guarantee I'll ever regain full sensation. For now, we just have to wait and see.

The mattress squeaks beneath me. At least *this* is only temporary. Next year I'll go to Barnard and my mother will be too far away to coddle me, and Chirag won't feel obligated to take care of me, and no one in New York will know that this isn't the face I was born with.

No one will know that I used to be an athlete, that there used to be freckles on my nose, that I used to have a dimple in my left cheek. They might wonder how I got these scars, but they'll be too polite to ask, and I won't ever tell.

TWENTY

'm dreaming, but not about my donor for once. In this dream, people are laughing. Even though I can't see them, I can tell that they're laughing at *me*. I want to ask them what I've done, but my mouth can't make the words.

I wake up only when my chin slips from the heel of my hand and my nose hits the desk in front of me.

"Careful," someone calls. "You don't want to have to replace it a second time."

"Gregory Baker!" The teacher—Mr. Wolf, my English teacher—shouts. "Apologize this instant."

I blink. Oh my god, I was asleep in class. I slept through a discussion of *One Hundred Years of Solitude*. The laughter continues now that I'm awake—the giggles from my dream belonged to my real-life classmates. But more humiliating than the laughter, more humiliating than what Greg said, more humiliating than the fact that our teacher is forcing an apology out of him, is the fact that Mr. Wolf didn't try to wake me.

Greg mumbles an apology, and Mr. Wolf asks if I need to go to the nurse's office. If anyone else had been dozing in class, Mr. Wolf would have woken them and sent them home with an extra paper to write. But me—the sick girl, the broken girl, the damaged girl—no teacher would begrudge *me* some extra shut-eye. Mr. Wolf doesn't scold me. He doesn't even ask for an explanation.

I'd love to tell him that I'm tired. More tired than he could possibly imagine or understand. It's a tiredness that comes from inside of me, that makes me aware of every heartbeat, every breath, every movement. My hands feel like they're stuck in cement and I have to concentrate on gripping my pencil or holding my eyelids open.

They added some new drugs to my regime a few weeks ago. (My *regime*; war words again.) At any moment, my immune system could revolt and try to expel our new territories, i.e., my face. Now, in addition to taking the orange-and-turquoise CellCept capsules twice a day, I'm also taking the creamy-colored Prografs twice, too. And it's not like I was full of energy before they adjusted my meds.

Screw you, Greg. And you, too, Mr. Wolf. You don't have any idea what it feels like to be drugged into oblivion.

I gather up my books and shuffle down the hall to the nurse's office. I spend more time there than any other student, more than the slackers who fake illnesses to get out of class, more than the football team with their injuries so constant that the parents are talking about eliminating the football team altogether. After the first week of school, the administration decided that I'd have to take my medication in the nurse's office each day, instead of on my own where everyone could see me. At first, I thought they were doing it for my benefit, like they thought it would be less embarrassing for me to have to slip off to the nurse's office than pop a pill in front of everyone. But when I tried to argue that going to the nurse's office was even worse, the real reason became apparent. They were concerned that if my classmates saw me taking drugs, they'd want to buy them from me. As if anyone would pay to feel like *this*.

It's October. The days are getting shorter, the nights longer, and everyone is talking about their costumes for the school's annual Halloween party. I haven't decided what I'm going as, but I know one thing for sure: My outfit will include a mask.

School has never been so hard for me. Dr. Woo wasn't kidding when she warned me about the side effects of antirejection drugs. In addition to fatigue, there's migraines, weakness, and nausea, to name just a few. My GPA is slipping, slipping, sliding down out of the acceptable range for Barnard. I should ask Dr. Boden to write some sort of note to go along with my application: *Please excuse Maisie's grades; she used to be really smart, she just can't stay awake in class because of the myriad drugs her team and I insist she take.*

But even if Dr. Boden does write me a note, even if all my doctors and nurses sign it like some kind of petition, it won't be enough. What will I do once I get to New York? I'll never be able to pull an all-nighter to finish a paper. I won't ever stay up late bonding with my roommate.

Oh god, my poor hypothetical roommate. She'll have to live with a girl who goes to bed early, then wakes up screaming in the middle of the night.

Maybe I can get Dr. Boden to put something in that note about how I'll need a single room.

But then what? What about graduate school and my first job, and the rest of my life? I will never *not* have to take these pills. They will never *not* be fraught with side effects.

How will I make it through the rest of my life if I'm always this tired?

I can't remember what it feels like to have energy. How did I ever get straight As, and run track, and shop with Serena, and kiss my boyfriend, all in the course of a single day?

It would have been easier if I hadn't been a miracle, if the rest of me had died along with my face. I'm not saying I wish that was what happened, but it certainly would have been a lot simpler that way.

TWENTY-ONE

We're about halfway through dinner when the phone rings. Serena jumps up to get it. She has dinner with us at least once a week, mostly to help me with our calculus homework since I have so much trouble paying attention in class.

"Winters residence," she recites politely. After a moment, she hands the phone to my mother. "It's Nurse Culligan," she whispers, sinking into her chair beside me as Mom disappears into the kitchen. My father isn't home from work yet. He's been working late ever since I went back to school; I guess he has a lot to make up for after taking off so much time over the summer.

Or maybe you just don't want to come home to the daughter you can no longer recognize.

"Nurse Culligan?" I echo. "Why would she be calling here?"

"She said she heard about Mr. Wolf's class this afternoon. What happened?"

I sigh. I'd been hoping to keep it to myself. "I fell asleep."

"You fell asleep?"

"Yeah."

"How?"

"What do you mean *how*? I closed my eyes and I guess I just forgot to open them back up again until Greg Baker made a crack about my nose job."

"You didn't get a nose job."

"I know I didn't get a nose job." I shove my plate away. I wasn't all that hungry to begin with (nausea from the pills, of course), and now I'm not hungry at all.

"What book are you analyzing this month?"

"What difference does that make?"

"When I had Mr. Wolf for sophomore English, I could've fallen asleep in every single class he spent talking about *Moby Dick*. If I had to hear him rhapsodizing about the whiteness of the whale one more time—"

When Serena talks to me, she looks me directly in the eyes. My eyes, at least, are the same.

"It's the drugs, Serena," I say irritably. "Not the book." In fact, I hate having missed a second of Mr. Wolf's talk on *One Hundred Years of Solitude*. It's the most beautiful book we've ever read in class. And anyway, Serena knows full well that before, I never would have fallen asleep in class, no matter the subject.

"Okay, but seriously, they should record his lectures on *Moby Dick* and give them out instead of sleeping pills." Serena, like everyone else, can't understand this kind of tiredness. I didn't know it was possible to be this tired before.

"I'll tell my doctors you said so."

Serena laughs. "Hey," she says suddenly, "do you just want to copy my calculus answers?"

"What?"

"I had some time between classes this afternoon, so I went ahead and did the homework. Why don't you just copy it?"

"Cheat?"

Serena rolls her eyes. "I forgot what a goody two-shoes you could be. It's just that with midterms coming up . . ." She sighs, trailing off. Spending hours helping me with my homework is digging into her study time. Serena actually looks stressed. I squeeze the knife in my left hand, even though it hurts. I'm not the only one trying to get into college.

I've never cheated on anything before, but it's tempting: It would be so much quicker to copy Serena's answers. I never understand anything anyway, no matter how much time she spends explaining. Feeling like this, it's impossible to understand that one plus one equals two, let alone what x stands for.

"Yes," I decide. "I'll copy your answers after dinner."

"Seriously?"

I shrug. "Maybe I'm not such a goody two-shoes anymore." Serena grins as my mother comes back into the room. Mom would freak if she knew what Serena was smiling about.

"The school nurse would like our permission to call a special assembly," Mom says matter-of-factly as she sits back down.

"Why?"

"To educate the student body about your injuries—"

"They don't need an education about my injuries. My injuries are right here for all to see." I point at my face and without meaning to, I stick my finger into my nose. One of the more delightful side effects of not being able to feel my new appendages is that my depth perception is off-kilter, along with the rest of me.

"Well, it sounds to me like they need a little education after what happened today."

"Nothing happened! I fell asleep. That has to do with the immunosuppressives, not the other kids' lack of education."

My mother looks at me evenly. She takes in my whole face. She probably read that the best way to get used to how I look now was to stare at me every chance she got. "You didn't just fall asleep. The other students—"

"It doesn't matter."

"It doesn't matter? It doesn't matter that they were laughing at you? That they made jokes about your surgery as you walked out of the classroom and to the nurse's office, crying?"

"Wait a minute," Serena interrupts. "I thought it was just that idiot Greg Baker?"

I close my eyes. So maybe it wasn't just Greg Baker. Maybe a chorus of yawns and applause accompanied me out of the room. Maybe even after he apologized, Greg Baker pulled his own cheeks out perversely, so that he looked nothing at all like himself. And maybe I did cry, just a little bit. It doesn't matter; it's not like I could feel the tears.

"According to Mr. Wolf, it was practically the entire classroom. Nurse Culligan thinks, and I agree, that a school-wide assembly would give you the chance to explain—"

"Wait a second, they want me to *talk* at this assembly?"

My mother nods. "You, and Dr. Boden, if his schedule allows it, and Nurse Culligan, and perhaps the guidance counselor—"

"Okay, stop."

But my mother keeps going. "This is an *opportunity*, Maisie. You can do some real good here. Let this be a teachable moment for your classmates. People go their whole lives without being touched by someone like you—you could make a real difference. I'm sure if they knew what you'd gone through—"

She says *teachable moment* proudly, like a little kid who's just learned a new vocabulary word.

I shake my head. She wants me to be one of those special people who make it through the other side of a horrific injury as a shining example of the human spirit. Someone who says she's *glad* this happened to her, it made her a *better* person, made her life *richer*. Like those people they talk about in the last five minutes of the news, the human interest stories that are supposed to make you feel better about all the crappy stuff they spent the previous hour talking about. Tonight, it was a story about a surfer who lost her arm in a shark attack. She's still surfing, and she just got married.

Well, she wasn't in high school.

"Believe me, Mom, none of those kids give a—"

"Maisie!" Mom shouts before I can finish. I roll my eyes. I don't see the point in mincing words right now. Sometimes it feels like my mother is the only person in the world I'll say anything to. Like I don't care what she thinks of me.

Serena looks at her lap; she's sitting between my mother and me, so it's impossible for her to avoid the cross fire. It's not like she's never been around when my mother was yelling before. After more than a decade of playdates and sleepovers, it was impossible to hide Mom's temper.

"I am *not* a teachable moment, Mom," I say. "I'm not an after-school special." Arguing is so much harder when I'm this tired, but I refuse to give in. Finally I say, "I'm just trying to make it through the year, okay?"

Mom shakes her head. "A special assembly is an excellent idea. We don't want this happening again."

"It *won't* happen again," I say with certainty. The truth is, I'd rather it happened a thousand times than have to get up in front of the whole school. But Mom doesn't see it that way. One more time and Mom will bring up the assembly again. Next time, she won't take no for an answer.

So it's up to me to make sure that there is no next time. I just have to figure out how.

Later, Chirag texts me: *Heard what happened in Mr. Wolf's class. You okay?*

I don't answer right away. Before, he'd have written *Why didn't you tell me?* Before, Chirag would have written *Want me to come over?* or maybe just *I'm coming over.* Now he waits politely, carefully, gently for an invitation I'll never give.

I'm fine, I write finally.

You sure?

Yeah, I answer. *I feel pretty good tonight,* I add. I think it's the first time I've ever lied to him.

I'm glad.

Good. One of us should get to be glad about something.

TWENTY-TWO

Serena is turning into a vampire. Her skin is three shades paler than usual, her lips a dozen shades redder. She's wearing tight black shorts with shiny black tights and leather boots with three-inch heels and somehow she still looks like giggly, warm, sweet Serena. She could layer on pounds of makeup and still look like herself. My stomach aches jealously as she leans over the magnified mirror she stole from one of my mom's makeup drawers and propped up on my desk, shoving aside my pill bottles to do so.

Serena and I have gotten ready for Halloween together every year since the first grade. When we were twelve, we decided that we were too old for trick-or-treating, but we dressed up anyway, counting the days until we'd be old enough to go to the annual Highlands High Halloween Spooktacular. I can't remember a time when we didn't know about this party. Everyone in town knows about it. Some of the more daring kids even try to sneak in while they're still in middle school, but Serena and I waited patiently for our freshman year.

"I can't believe this is our last Halloween party." Serena studies her profile, checking for any spots she might have missed, making sure that her honey-colored skin doesn't show through anywhere.

"They'll have Halloween parties in college." I'm careful not to say *at Berkeley*. As long as I don't say it, I'm not officially lying to her about my real plans.

"Yeah, but it won't be the same."

Nothing is the same anymore, I think but do not say. My own costume is much simpler than Serena's: brown pants, brown sweatshirt, werewolf mask. Last year I went as a witch, but it was really just Serena's way of forcing me into a skimpy outfit. I wore a black miniskirt and a sequined black tube top and a pointy hat. I didn't wear tights and I was freezing all night, goose pimples dancing up my arms and down my legs and into my shoes. My parents would never have let me leave the house like that if it hadn't been Halloween, or maybe they were just so busy fighting that they didn't notice my outfit at all. Chirag and I weren't a couple yet, and I pretended not to notice the way the boys looked at me when Serena and I made our way to the center of the dance floor. I can't remember how it felt, to be looked at like that. Now when they look at me, it is without even the shadow of desire. Maybe they think: *Man, what a shame. She used to be hot.*

"Are you sure you can wear that?" Serena asks, gesturing to my mask.

"Are you kidding?"

"I mean, what if it presses on your nose or your chin or something? Could it—I don't know—hurt you?"

I shake my head. "It doesn't actually hurt at all."

Serena's face softens; even under her makeup, I can tell she's blushing. "It doesn't?"

"I can't feel a thing."

"It *looks* like it hurts." She must mean the jagged pink scars on my cheeks. It's been a long time since I looked in the mirror closely enough to consider whether they've faded like the doctors promised. Now Serena's face tells me that they haven't, at least not much.

If I were one of those special people—the kind of person my mother wants me to be—I'd have picked a costume that showed them off.

Instead, I yank the mask over my head. "There," I say, my voice echoing inside of it. *Now you don't have to look at it.*

As though she can read my mind, Serena mumbles, "I'm not the one who's trying not to look at it."

With my face underneath the mask, Serena can't see my surprise.

Serena bounds out to Chirag's car like a puppy. We're late because we had to wait until after eight p.m. to leave so that I could take my pills before we left. The fog hangs heavy and wet in the air, making everything feel damp, so that Serena's voluminous hair sticks to her cheeks and her face.

Chirag is wearing a bloodstained tracksuit; he's supposed to be our victim. I consider pointing out that, mythically speaking, vampires and werewolves don't really work together, but then Serena might insist that I be a vampire, too. What would it be like if I let Serena paint my face to match hers? If she pressed white powder onto my cheeks, across the bridge of my nose, and over my chin? I shake my head, tugging my mask down lower, even though I can barely see out of the eyeholes. I wonder if my donor dressed up for Halloween last year.

At the party, hoping for some kind of transcendent caffeine high, I chug Diet Coke like it's every bit as delicious as the Halloween candy Serena and I collected when we were little. I have to lift my mask for every sip, resting it across my forehead like a sort of rubber headband. Before, I never clung to Chirag at parties because I was cool, independent, fun. Now I keep my distance because I have to go to the girls' room about a dozen times over the course of the night.

"I like your costume," I say to Ellen on one of my myriad bathroom trips. She's dressed as a zombie prom queen, wearing a hot-pink strapless dress made of taffeta that's been ripped and shredded. She's painted pale blue makeup across her arms, face, and chest.

"Is that you under there, Maisie?" Ellen asks, giggling. Even though I can't feel the mask on my face, I can smell it: a dirty, rubbery swell that's now tinged by my own sweat because it's hot under here.

I don't answer, but she takes my silence as a *yes* and says, "Well, thanks. It would have looked better if I'd lost a couple pounds like I'd planned on and if this stupid zit—ugh, you know how sometimes, you forget you have a pimple for a while and then you catch a glimpse of yourself in the mirror and you're like oh my god, I can't believe I've been walking around with *that* on my face all day."

Wow, that must be really tough. The voice in my head is dripping with sarcasm.

Ellen giggles. "Sorry," she says hollowly. "I know I'm not supposed to say stuff like that to you," she adds. I wonder if Serena took the girls aside on the first day of school and told them that they shouldn't complain about things like pimples and diets around me.

"It's okay. Even my mother is back to complaining about her wrinkles these days."

"I guess there's only so much a person can take," Ellen answers before trotting back out to the party. I'm not sure if she meant me, my mother, or my friends, and I'm not about to ask.

I don't exactly intend to sneak out after her, but I find myself following her out of the bathroom, the gym, and into the hall, careful to keep far enough behind that she won't notice me.

Part of what makes this party such a big deal is that every year, the senior class finds the most unlikely spot to hang out, someplace where the chaperones can't keep an eye on us. Every year the school administration threatens to cancel the party, and every year the students promise to behave, but we never do—we just get better at hiding our indiscretions. Last year, the seniors took turns disappearing to the boys' locker room.

Tonight, I have no idea where my classmates are sneaking off to. After all, there's no reason why anyone would tell me: You can't exactly party hard when you're on an antirejection regimen. Or maybe the cool kids just kept the location to themselves because they wanted a place to hang out where they wouldn't have to lay eyes on the class freak.

It's eerie, walking through the nearly empty halls of our school on a Saturday night. Strange to be here without the din of lockers slamming shut, the clatter of high heels against the linoleum floors, the squeak of sneakers. I follow Ellen past the science labs (where the senior class set up camp two years ago), and past the hallway that leads to the gym (where the seniors hung out three years ago), and up the stairs to the teachers' lounge.

Wow, I think, impressed. *I can't believe you guys chose the teachers' lounge.*

I don't follow Ellen all the way inside. Instead, I hover by the door. The lounge is carpeted, and from here, I can see kids strewn across the couches inside. Eric and Erica are making out, and Ellen plops down right on top of them.

"Sorry to interrupt," she giggles, but Eric and Erica don't even seem to mind. After all, they have all the time in the world to make out. If I'd known that my time to kiss Chirag was limited, I don't think anyone could have torn me away from him.

Just to the left of the door, so no one inside can see me, I slide down the wall and sit on the floor, lifting the mask a little bit so that I can rest my chin on my legs. I breathe through my mouth; it's quieter that way. I allow myself to close my eyes. If anyone saw me sitting here like this, they'd say *Poor Maisie. Someone better take the sick girl home.*

I hear Eric's voice: "Come on, Chi-Dog, loosen up."

"Nah, I'm driving tonight."

Erica's voice now. "Eric, you know that nurses can't actually have fun while they're on duty."

Eric. "But nurses at least get a night off once in a while."

Chirag. "Come on, guys, cut it out."

I should leave. I should get out of here before they discover me, before they know that I've heard them. Sweat plasters my hair to the back of my neck. Even the hair on the mask itself feels damp, wilted.

"Dog," Eric says, "this is your senior year and you're missing it. You're *wasting* it." He sounds so sincere, like he's truly concerned about Chirag.

"Did you see the way Alexis Smith was looking at you tonight?" Erica adds.

Alexis Smith is a junior. She has blond hair and blue eyes. She dressed as a French maid tonight, waving her feather duster around the gym like it's a magic wand. She's on the track team, too. She has freckles, though not as many as I used to have. Just a tiny little sprinkling across her nose. Maybe Chirag thinks they're sexy like he used to think mine were.

Erica continues, "You could be in here with her. You know that, right?"

All at once, an image of Chirag kissing Alexis flashes behind my eyes. Chirag kisses her smooth cheeks, her soft neck, the tip of her nose. Alexis would be able to *feel* all that. Alexis would be able to kiss him back without worrying that pursing her lips might be bad for her scars. I squeeze my eyes shut, but I can't stop seeing Chirag kissing the smooth crook of Alexis's elbow, holding her left hand in the car while he drives. All those things he can't do with his current girlfriend, who is quite literally damaged goods.

I can't take a deep breath with this stupid mask over my face. The rubbery odor starts to smell like something else; it reeks like something is burning.

For the first time, I remember how it smelled the day of my accident. I remember the scent of my flesh on fire.

I rip the mask off and throw it on the ground beside me, trying to fill my nose with the scent of anything else. I try to inhale the scents drifting into the hallway from the teachers' lounge: Erica's perfume, Eric's sweat, Ellen's berry-flavored lipstick. I'm so hot that I wave my hands in front of my face like a fan before I remember that my face can't actually feel the breeze.

Finally, Chirag says, "I can't do that. You know I can't do that. Maisie—"

It's Ellen's voice that cuts Chirag off. "Look, Maisie was always great. No one is arguing that. She was one of my best friends. But she's different now."

"I know," Chirag admits. "I see the old Maisie sometimes, just for a second." He says the words *old Maisie* like he's talking about a girl he used to know. Which I guess he is.

I lift my werewolf mask from the floor and hold it in my lap like it's a stuffed animal.

"Come on, man," Eric scoffs. "You don't *see* the old Maisie. That girl is *gone*." When he says *old Maisie*, the words sound like a joke. Maybe it is. Maybe I am. Ellen snorts, and Erica starts laughing, hard and loud, like she wants to make sure that everyone in the room knows how funny her boyfriend is.

"Dude," Chirag says, his deep voice a warning. "She's not some kind of punch line." My heart floods with gratitude. It's exactly what you'd hope your boyfriend would say when you weren't around to hear him.

"Fair enough," Eric answers. "But she's not some kind of girlfriend, either."

What perfect response will Chirag have now? I close my eyes and imagine what I'd most want to hear: That he cares about me so much. That he's taking care of me because he believes that the old Maisie might come back someday. That he doesn't care what I look like, he loves me no matter what.

My heart beats fast and my stomach twists as I feel the familiar rush of adrenaline. I've never actually heard him say that he loves me out loud.

But instead of anything even resembling *I love her,* Chirag sighs heavily and says, "I know. I *know*. It's not just that she doesn't look like the old Maisie, doesn't move like the old Maisie. She's just . . . different. It's like having a perfect stranger in the car next to me."

"With a stranger's face sewn onto her skull," Eric adds, and I wince.

You have no right to refer to my donor that way! She's not a punch line, either.

My heart starts to pound. What if one of them decides to get up, sees me here, realizes what I've heard? As quietly as I can, I take a deep breath and silently order my heart to slow.

"Shut up," Chirag says, his deep voice more solemn that I've ever heard it. "Seriously, dude, just shut up. I know it's over. I can't even touch her anymore."

Can't, or don't want to? I shake my head. Both answers are probably true: No one would want to touch a patchwork face that wouldn't be able to feel his caresses, just as no one would know how.

Ellen's voice: "So why don't you end it? Say you just want to be friends. I mean, that's all you are anymore, anyway."

"And then you can start touching Alexis Smith," Eric adds. I can practically hear his grin.

I imagine Chirag nodding slowly, his head bobbing up and down as though it weighs a million pounds, just like mine after the transplant. "I can't," he counters. "I'm going to be a doctor someday. I can't just abandon someone who's not well."

"Dude, you haven't taken your hypocritical oath yet, Dr. Srinivasan."

"Hippocratic," Chirag corrects. "And it doesn't matter. I can't be that guy."

"What guy?"

"The guy who breaks up with a girl that unhappy. I have to wait until she's better."

TWENTY-THREE

Carefully, I slide my way back up the wall and slip my mask over my head. I'll sneak away before any of them know I'm here, before any of them can guess that I've been listening, before Chirag knows that I heard his rational, levelheaded explanation for why he's still with me.

That's what drew me to him in the first place, right? I wanted to be with that guy who didn't raise his voice when he disagreed with me, nothing like my overly emotional, high-volume parents. And yet . . . I kind of wish that Chirag had been a little less logical just this once. Isn't he at least a tiny bit sad about the way things turned out? Doesn't he miss me, the way I used to be—the old Maisie, as he put it?

I'm literally on my tiptoes when I nearly walk head on into Serena. Who is holding hands with Greg Baker.

Jesus. How bad is this night going to get?

The white makeup Serena applied so carefully is smeared. Maybe she was sweating while she danced, or maybe Greg rubbed his fingers all over her while they made out. I don't think Serena has made it through a school dance without kissing someone, not since ninth grade.

Beneath my mask, I close my eyes and try to imagine Chirag kissing me. I should go back to practicing kisses on the pillow like a fifth grader.

"Hey!" Serena says, dropping Greg's hand to take mine—my left hand. "I was wondering where you were."

"Don't let me spoil your fun," I say, trying to twist my hand away. No one but Marnie, my doctors and nurses, and my dad, once, has touched my left hand since the accident. "I have to go," I add blandly. Serena won't release her grip. Her skin is smooth over mine. "I was just looking for a quiet place to call my mom."

There is nothing lamer than calling your mom to pick you up early from a party, but I don't care. It's not like I have some cool-girl reputation to protect anymore. I just want to go home. I want to be alone in my room where I can't hear what people are saying about me. Where I can hide under the covers and close my eyes and imagine that Chirag's arms are around me. Around the old me.

"Say it ain't so, Maisie!" Greg moans, his voice thick. "This party is just getting started." He leans in and nuzzles Serena's neck.

"Quit it, Greg," Serena says, shoving him away. "Maisie, are you okay?"

I don't answer, but somehow Serena still knows.

"Greg can drive us home," she says. "Come on."

I shake my head. "I don't want to spoil your fun," I say again. Bad enough that I'm spoiling Chirag's.

Serena laughs. She leans in and whispers, "Do you really think I'd rather hang out with Greg Baker than with you? He's my designated driver. Come on."

Serena leads the way down the hall and out of the school. She holds my hand the entire time, and it doesn't feel nearly as bad as I thought it would. *Why can't it be like this with Chirag?* I drop her hand only once, to take off my matted, smelly mask and deposit it into a trash can.

Serena is lying on my bed beside me in borrowed pajamas. Greg seemed really disappointed when Serena got out of the car with me. He'd probably hoped that driving me home was Serena's excuse for leaving the party to be alone with him.

My phone vibrates with a text from Chirag: *Where are you?*

I don't want to write back, but I'm scared he'll call my mom at best or send out a search party at worst, so I write: *I went home. Got tired and didn't want to ruin your night.*

"Do you think Greg went back to the party?" I ask, staring at the ceiling in the darkness. I feel Serena shrug.

"Probably. Otherwise, he'd have to wait until Monday to start telling everyone what a frigid tease I am."

"God, Greg is such a jerk."

"I know," Serena agrees, laughing. "Good thing I'm such a tease."

"Serena!"

"What, you don't think I was going to hook up with Greg Baker after what he said about you in Mr. Wolf's class, do you?"

I release fists I didn't even know I'd been clenching. Marnie would be so pleased; my left hand hurt so little that I didn't even notice it until after the fact. "I figured you forgot about that." *Or you just didn't care enough to let it stop you from kissing Greg.*

"Of *course* I remembered." Serena shifts, rolling onto her side so that she's facing me. Unlike everyone else, we never really outgrew sleepovers. Even last year, whenever we had some big test to study for or a paper to finish, Serena would just set up camp in my room for days at a time. My mother never complained because she knew we really were studying.

But Serena doesn't know that I've barely slept through the night since I got home from the hospital. She doesn't know that in a few hours, I'll probably wake up crying after one of my donor nightmares. Maybe I should warn her. A dry run for whoever might end up my freshman roommate next year.

Instead, I say, "Greg might be telling everyone that you're a frigid tease right at this very moment."

"I don't care."

"Come on, you care. Everyone cares."

"Greg was going to talk about me no matter what I did tonight." In the darkness, Serena can't see more than my silhouette. Is she imagining that I still look the way I used to, that this is just another sleepover? Is she ignoring the fact that we wouldn't be here at all— we'd still be at the school, or headed to an after-party at someone's house—if I still looked the same?

"So why not avoid him altogether?"

Serena shrugs. "I guess I just don't care that much about what jerks like Greg are saying about me."

I used to think that Serena and I would never grow apart after high school the way so many girls do. We've been best friends since kindergarten; we made it through being put in different classes in fourth grade and middle-school cliques; we didn't skip a beat even when I turned out to be an athlete and Serena someone who only pays attention to competitive sports when forced.

But now, I wonder if I'll make a new best friend when I get to college—to Barnard. Someone who wouldn't recognize my old face if she walked right into it. Someone who doesn't know that I used to run track and mock yoga.

Whoever my new best friend is—this nameless girl who doesn't know my old face—she won't have Serena's charisma, because no one does. She won't be so confident that she doesn't care what people say about her. And I won't know that she can only fall asleep lying on her right side, her left arm above the covers. I won't know that she wakes up with a smile on her face every morning, as though she's just had the most amazing dream. I won't have been there the day of her first kiss, and she won't have sensed the instant I started falling for my first real boyfriend.

Whoever she is, and however close we become, my history will never be all twisted up with hers.

Serena asks, "Are you going to tell me what really happened tonight to make you leave the party?"

"I was tired. You know these meds make me tired."

"If you were so tired, you'd be asleep by now instead of lying here staring at the ceiling like you're waiting for some kind of message to appear."

She's right. I can't sleep. I can't sleep because I keep hearing the words Chirag said over and over in my head, an endless repeat, a record skipping over a scratch.

"Chirag wants to break up with me," I admit finally.

I feel Serena nodding. "I know," she says.

"You *know*? Did he say something to you?"

"Of course not. He knows I would kick his butt if he even talked about hurting you."

"Then what do you mean *you know*?"

"Listen, Maisie, don't take this the wrong way, but *of course* Chirag wants to break up with you. He's been more of a caretaker than a boyfriend to you since school started, and that's not—"

"It's not what?"

She shrugs. "It's not fair," she says finally.

"Well, I don't think it's fair that I have to walk around deformed for the rest of my life."

"No," Serena agrees. She doesn't try to argue that I'm not deformed. "That's not fair either. But two unfairs don't make a—I don't know, don't make a right, I guess."

"We never even got to tell each other *I love you*. Not officially, anyway."

"There's still time."

"I can't say I love you to a boy I just heard tell a roomful of people he wants to dump me."

"Sure you can."

"Maybe *you* could." Serena is brave like that.

Serena shakes her head. "I've never been in love, Maisie."

"You have a new boyfriend every semester."

"What, and you think that means I fall in love every few months? No one's ever told me he loved me and I've never said it, either. Your relationship with Chirag was never perfect, but you two loved each other. We could all see that."

I shake my head. That's not how I remember it. Imperfect, I mean.

Serena continues, "You don't know how lucky you are."

"Not another person telling me I'm lucky," I groan. Slowly, I add, "He won't, though."

"Who won't what?"

"Chirag won't break up with me. He's too worried about me. What does he think, if he dumps me I'll jump out the window or something?"

"No," Serena says. "He knows you're stronger than that." I smile. "I think he just doesn't want to add to the things that are hurting you."

I close my eyes. "I just wish it could be the way it was between the two of us. *Before*." When I was the old Maisie. The girl who was fun at parties. The girl who didn't have to worry that she might overhear someone saying that the boy who was supposed to be her date was really just her nurse. Now I decide that I am officially never going to a school party again. Maybe not even once I get to Barnard. *If* I get to Barnard.

"I know," Serena agrees gently. She puts an arm around me in the darkness. "But I don't think it can be."

I lean against my friend. I should nod. I should say *you're right*. Chirag would say so. Chirag *did* say so. Why can't I?

Instead of saying anything, I cry quietly until I fall asleep.

TWENTY-FOUR

The next day, when Serena is in the shower, I sit at my desk with my laptop and look up that surfer who lost her arm, the one who was on the news the other night. She was eighteen when the shark attacked her, one of the most promising female surfers in years. Now she's a motivational speaker. She travels the world telling people that even when life is at its darkest, there's still hope. Her website is scattered with pictures of her recent wedding; her new husband stands beside her, handsome and tan, a surfer like her, except he has all of his limbs.

I read her bio twice, but it doesn't say whether she was dating her husband before the accident. It doesn't say whether he fell in love with her before she became a broken-down freak, or whether she was a virgin when that shark took her arm, or whether she's planning on having kids even though she might not be able to hold them by herself. And it doesn't say how long after the attack she was able to sleep through the night.

I'm still searching for more information when my mother comes into my room to watch me take my pills. I slam the computer shut so hard that the pill bottles on my desk rattle.

My god, I hate these stupid pills. I don't care if they're keeping me alive. Without these pills, I wouldn't have fallen asleep in class and Greg Baker wouldn't have laughed at me and Nurse Culligan wouldn't have called and my mother wouldn't be looking at me like this, still so disappointed that I don't want to be an example for my classmates to admire. Without these pills, my grades wouldn't be slipping and I wouldn't have to copy Serena's homework. Midterms are coming up and I can't even muster the energy to stay awake when I study. These pills are going to keep me from getting into Barnard. From getting out of here and away from these people.

These pills have made me different. Like Chirag said, I don't just *look* different. I'm a perfect stranger sitting in the car next to him.

The solution is so obvious that I can't believe I haven't thought of it before: I have to stop taking them.

My face won't, like, fall *off*, right? It's not like I'd be going off of them for the fun of it, like to stay up late at some other school party. I've already decided that I'm never going to a Highlands party again. But plenty of kids take Ritalin and Adderall to stay up and cram for tests. I wouldn't even be doing anything that bad. It's actually the complete opposite.

So I do something I've seen countless patients do in the movies. I pretend to swallow my pills, then hide them under my tongue. I hold my breath waiting for Mom to leave the room. Part of me doesn't believe she'll actually walk away without discovering what I've done. There are so many pills in my mouth that I can't speak. My heart is pounding by the time she turns on her heel for the door, and I wait, listening to the sound of her footsteps as she walks down the hall and into her own room. Serena is still in the shower, but I run into the bathroom and spit the pills into the toilet, gagging. Butterflies dance in my stomach as I hold down the lever to flush, the same way they did before the SATs, before a big track meet, before my first kiss with Chirag.

This is the answer. *This* is how I make sure that what happened with Greg Baker never happens again, so that Mom and Nurse Culligan don't get to force me to stand up in front of the entire school and tell my story. *This* is how I concentrate in class and get good grades again. *This* is how I stay awake to study. *This* is how I get into Barnard.

And maybe, just maybe, this is how I go back to being the girl that Chirag loved.

TWENTY-FIVE

At school on Monday—day two off the pills—it's even easier with Nurse Culligan. Instead of hiding my midday dose beneath my tongue, I take a handful of vitamins I swiped from Mom's bathroom. I even swallow a white Tic Tac for good measure.

Today, I stay awake in class. I raise my hand and participate in history, throwing in my two cents about Henry VIII and the Protestant Reformation. My history teacher looks so pleased I can practically hear her thinking that the girl I used to be—star pupil, teacher's pet—is back.

Later, during sixth period, instead of lying down in the nurse's office when everyone else is in gym class, I do my calculus homework. I slip a copy of it into Serena's locker. We'll cheat with *my* answers this time.

After school, Chirag drives me to PT. I greet Marnie with a smile. It's not just that I have more energy without the drugs in my system. I also just really like having a secret. It makes me feel powerful.

Today, the ball Marnie brings out is not a rubber one for squeezing but a tennis ball.

"We're playing catch," she informs me, tossing the ball in my direction. I catch it with my right hand and Marnie shakes her head.

"Left-handed catch," she says. "Don't act like you didn't know that."

"I'm a righty," I protest.

"Right-handed baseball players catch with their left hands," she answers.

"I wasn't planning on pitching for the Yankees," I counter, tossing the ball back to her. "No rigorous exercise, remember?"

"Oh, Maisie," Marnie sighs, throwing the ball so far to my left that my only choice is to try to catch it with my left hand or just let it sail by. "If only all my patients were as funny as you are."

An hour later, my left hand feels like it's on fire all over again, but I'm still in a good mood. I'm smiling as I walk out to the waiting room to discover Chirag standing there, not my mother. Even on the days when Chirag drops me off, it's always Mom who picks me up and takes me home.

"What are you doing here?"

"Your mom called. Said she has to work late tonight."

Late. Like after eight o'clock. I won't even have to pretend to take my pills later.

Chirag continues, "I thought we could grab some dinner or something. But don't worry," he adds quickly. "I'll get you home before eight."

I shake my head. "Don't worry about that," I say, the lie slipping out easily. "I'm actually on a different regimen now. In fact, let's drive to Sausalito for dinner. How about that seafood place?"

Chirag took me there for Valentine's Day last year. It was a surprise: He literally blindfolded me before letting me get in his car.

"No peeking," he said as we stood in my driveway. "Promise?"

"I promise," I said, bouncing up and down to keep warm. I'd bought a new dress for the occasion and I wanted Chirag to see it so much that I hadn't bothered putting my coat on when I walked out the front door.

"How many fingers am I holding up?"

"If I didn't want you to know I could see I would just lie, silly."

"Good point," he agreed. "This is an honor thing."

I banged my head as I lowered myself into his car. "Maybe you should have waited to blindfold me until I was inside the car," I suggested.

"Small price to pay for romance," he said.

Now if I banged my head he'd probably insist on rushing me to the hospital just to make sure I was okay.

But that night, I rolled down my window and felt the fog on my face and smelled the salty air off the bay. I guessed we were going to Sausalito about ten minutes before we pulled into the restaurant parking lot.

"Can't get much past you, huh, May?"

I grinned, but I didn't take the blindfold off. When we got to the restaurant, Chirag leaned over; I thought he was going to take off the blindfold but instead he kissed me. I gasped in surprise and then pressed my face against his, returning the kiss. His cheekbones and jawline were more defined than my own. Sometimes, when he hugged me tight, the bones of his face pressed into mine sharply, as though they had pointed edges. Next, he slipped the blindfold over my head slowly, his fingers lingering above my eyebrows. I kept my eyes closed as he smoothed back my hair and then kissed me again.

I'd never been to such a romantic, grown-up sort of restaurant. There were candles everywhere, and our table was right by the window, the lights of the Golden Gate Bridge just barely visible through the fog. Chirag made me try oysters for the first time. He said I wasn't anything like other girls, who squirmed and squealed at the thought of pouring raw shellfish down their throats.

"How many other girls have you taken here?" I joked, but Chirag shook his head.

"No other girls," he answered seriously. "Just you." He gave me an old edition of one of my favorite books, and I gave him an old edition of one of his.

"Great minds think alike," I said, reaching my hand across the table and placing it on top of his. His palm was warm and he leaned down to kiss the freckle on my left knuckle that isn't there anymore.

Tonight, Chirag looks surprised at my suggestion. "You're not too tired?" he asks, and I shake my head. I know that technically, I'm *off* drugs right now, but it feels like I may as well be *on* them. A different kind of drugs, I mean. The kind that make you feel good.

Now, as Chirag opens the passenger side door for me, I say, "Remember what I said last time we ate there? That oysters were my new favorite food?"

Chirag nods. He looks positively nostalgic, and I don't blame him. We had so much fun that night. After dinner, Chirag gave me his jacket and we sat outside looking at the bay and kissing until our lips were sore. I bring my fingers to my lips now, remembering, fingering the scar just to the left of my cupid's bow, the result of one of the milder burns around my mouth.

Maybe tonight, off my medication, I won't shy away if Chirag gets close.

Maybe, after the waiter takes our order, I'll even be able to look Chirag in the eye, so that when he leans in to hold me, he won't end up pressing his lips to the top of my head.

Maybe by the time they serve dessert, the old Maisie will emerge like magic, and Chirag will see the girl he used to know. Then he'll fall in love with me all over again, and tomorrow morning we'll walk into school hand in hand just like we used to.

TWENTY-SIX

On Wednesday morning—day four off the pills—I sneak out of the house at dawn, tiptoeing just as carefully as I did when I'd sneak out to meet Chirag while my parents slept. A taxi waits for me on the corner, right by the old tree stump. I ask the driver to take me to Highlands High.

Dinner with Chirag did not go the way I planned. I ordered a half dozen oysters, but I didn't like the way they tasted, not anymore. Still, I forced myself to eat them because I didn't want Chirag to notice another thing that was different about me. He'd have asked, with his scientific curiosity, for an inventory of which tastes and smells have changed for me. So I kept quiet and ate my oysters, telling myself that without the medicine making me tired and achy and scared of sunshine, I could at least *act* the way I did before.

I was forcing the last oyster into my mouth when my knees accidentally brushed against Chirag's under the table. Reflexively, he pulled away from my touch, the way you do when you're out with a total stranger. With someone you don't want to touch.

Maybe I expected too much. After all, I'd only been off the pills for two days and I was already trying to re-create one of the most romantic nights we'd ever spent together. Maybe there are more steps I have to take before I can go back to being the girl I was before.

Step one: Stop taking the pills.

Step two: Stay awake in class and go back to being the teacher's pet.

Step three: Start running again.

This morning, the fog is so thick that I can't even see the track behind the school, but of course I know it's there. That track is the reason I got up so early this morning, the reason I'm dressed in my old running clothes. I left my parents a note telling them I'd gone to school early.

It's not like I expect I'll be as fast as I used to be. I'm out of practice. My muscles are weaker. I just want to make it around the track a few times. If I do well enough, I might be able to run with Chirag after school one day this week, just like we used to. I won't be strong enough to race him, not yet, but still—it'd be a little bit of the old Maisie, the girl he used to know. The girl he fell for. The girl he wanted to touch.

The girl who wanted to touch him.

I pay the driver and walk across the parking lot and toward the track. This is where I used to win medals and receive cheers. Where Chirag used to wait at the finish line, shouting for me to run home.

I bend down and tighten the laces on my sneakers. These are my old running shoes, the backup pair that sat mostly forgotten in the bottom of my closet. I was wearing a newer pair the day of my accident and I haven't seen them since. I imagine they've long since been thrown away in the hospital Dumpster, along with the clothes I wore that morning, the clothes they had to cut off of me.

Or maybe by the time the ambulance came, my clothes were almost gone, burning away into smoke and ash. Maybe the rubber on the bottom of my sneakers melted; maybe the laces caught fire.

I stretch carefully, hearing Marnie's voice ringing in my ears: *No rigorous exercise.* Out loud—there's no one here to listen at this hour—I say, "I won't be rigorous, Marnie, I promise. Just a few laps around the track. I feel great. I can do it. I know I have it in me."

I imagine Marnie's answer: *It doesn't matter if you have it in you or not, Maisie. It's dangerous.*

I step onto the track, savoring its texture beneath my feet. I start out slow, barely more than walking. Out loud, I say, "The last time I went running, I nearly died. I think I've set the bar pretty high on what qualifies as dangerous."

In answer, it's not Marnie's voice I hear, but my mother's: *Stop running, Maisie. The doctors said—*

"Screw the doctors, Mom. They also said I had to take those pills. I haven't taken them for days and I feel better than I have in months."

I shake my head. Just a few gentle steps in and I'm panting. Hard. The cool foggy air feels thin in my mouth and going down my throat, barely filling my lungs, like it doesn't have as much oxygen as air is supposed to have. Between labored breaths, I manage to say, "Screw the doctors. Screw the pills."

I repeat it with each step: "Screw the doctors. Screw the pills. Screw the doctors. Screw the pills."

It's a good thing no one else is here at this hour to hear my labored words. Every muscle in my body aches in protest: The skin on my left side feels tighter than ever, like it's stretched to the limit, barely able to hold my body together. I imagine that if I were to look down my shirt, I'd be able to see the bones of my rib cage beneath a layer of skin that's been stretched to translucence: thin as tracing paper, dry as desert grass. Even my feet hurt; the calluses I'd built up after years of running have disappeared, leaving my toes soft and vulnerable, like a child's.

Pain is a warning that something's wrong, Maisie.

"Screw the doctors. Screw the pills. Screw the doctors. Screw the pills." The words are nothing like the old *Step, breath* that used to punctuate my runs. I try to pick up the pace—I used to believe I could outrun the pain, back when it was just the normal pain of running—but now it only hurts more. Each time my toes bounce against the pavement, I wonder what kind of damage I could be doing to my face. I remember the weight of it immediately following the surgery, the way my neck ached from holding my head up. I imagine that with each bounce, the sutures and staples that hold these features to my skull are coming loose. I imagine my nose, cheeks, and chin sliding right off of me, like melted cheese down a slice of pizza.

I haven't even run a quarter of a lap when I stop.

I let out a shout, still panting. I kick off my sneakers and throw them across the track. Then I double over, my heart pounding, my breath ragged. It hurts. I mean, something *always* hurts: My neck from holding my head up, the nerves not yet fully integrated. My hand, the skin still too tight where it burned. My left side, protesting every time I twist my torso. But right now, it all just hurts so much *more*. I groan miserably.

Through the fog, I hear a voice. And not one of the voices in my head this time.

"Maisie?" Someone is jogging across the track toward me. "Are you okay?"

"Ellen?" I ask as my friend—former friend, I guess—comes into view. She's wearing tight black leggings and I can see her muscles working beneath them. My legs used to look like that. "What are you doing here?"

"Running," she answers, like it's obvious, which it is. She's been on the track team since freshman year, just like me—it's how we became friends in the first place—but unlike me, she was never the type to get up at the crack of dawn for a practice run. I guess I'm not the only one who's changed. "Coach says I actually have a chance at finals. Maybe even a scholarship now."

Now. As in, *Now that Maisie is off the team.*

"Oh my god, Ellen, please just go away."

"What?"

I blink. Did I just say that out loud? I really didn't mean to say it out loud. I open my mouth to apologize. "I'm sorry."

"It's okay—" Ellen begins, but I cut her off.

"I'm sorry I'm not as much fun as I used to be, but I'm not a lot of the things that I used to be. I don't even have the same nose that I used to have!"

Ellen looks as though she's been slapped. I don't think I've ever spoken to anyone like this, not even my mother. I take a deep breath, but when my ribs expand, the skin on my left side just aches all the more.

"I guess Chirag told you what I said on Halloween," Ellen says finally.

"*That's* all you can say? You're only interested in *how* I found out that you don't like me anymore?"

"I never said I didn't like you anymore—"

"No, you just said that I used to be great and now I suck." I can't believe I'm saying these things out loud. I blame the run, the aches in my side and my feet and the back of my neck. The pain must be distracting me so that I can't remember which are the things I shouldn't say. I lean over and rest my hands on my knees. "Well, I'm sorry I'm not fun anymore. *This*"—I gesture weakly to my face—"isn't fun."

"Maisie—"

"Chirag didn't tell me anything," I interrupt.

"But then how—"

I straighten up. "I heard you, Ellen! The accident didn't affect my hearing, you know."

Understanding washes over Ellen's face. She's picturing me crouched in the corner, eavesdropping like a little kid. Hiding from my supposed friends.

And she's realizing that if I heard what she said, I also heard what Chirag said.

"Don't say anything to Chirag," I add quickly. "He doesn't know I was there."

"But, Maisie—"

"I mean it." I turn away from her, walk a few steps. Without my sneakers, there's only my socks between my feet and the track, moist with fog and dew. I shiver. My hair sticks to my damp forehead and I brush it away; I didn't pull it into a ponytail before I started running. I haven't worn it up since my accident. "Just don't tell anyone, okay?"

"I really don't think it'd be right for me to—"

"Listen, Ellen, the broken-down deformed girl who used to be one of your best friends is asking you for a favor. It's the least you can do. Please."

Much to my surprise, Ellen actually looks ashamed. "Okay," she says finally. "I promise. But, Maisie—"

"Yeah?"

"Just because I won't say anything doesn't mean that you shouldn't."

The fog is starting, just slightly, to lift. In the distance, cars are rumbling into the school parking lot, teachers and administrators arriving ahead of students. In a few minutes, I'll text Chirag to let him know that I don't need a ride this morning.

Will he wonder why I came to school so early? Will he suspect, even just for a second, the real reason: that I heard him on Halloween, and I'm trying to prove him wrong, prove Eric wrong, prove Ellen wrong? Would he ever guess that I tried to run to prove that the old Maisie is still in here somewhere?

Would he know that I failed, just like I failed at dinner the other night?

Pills or no pills, right now, standing here—struggling to catch my breath, the taste of words I never thought I'd say out loud still sour in my mouth—it feels like being able to call Chirag my boy-friend is all that remains of the girl I was before.

I look at Ellen and nod. "You're right," I agree softly. "I'm just not ready yet."

TWENTY-SEVEN

I have dinner at Serena's house after school. We're doing our calculus homework when my phone starts buzzing: text after text from my mother.

Maisie, it's a quarter to eight. You have to be home to take your pills in fifteen minutes.

Maisie, it's eight o'clock, where are you?

Maisie, it's eight-fifteen. Do you have an extra set of pills with you?

Maisie.

Maisie.

Maisie.

I don't come home until almost nine. When I open the door, Mom is sitting on the couch in the living room, her back to me. The TV is on, but she's not watching.

"You're late," Mom says, instead of hello.

I shrug, heading for the stairs. "Less than an hour," I answer. My parents never actually gave me a curfew; they didn't have to worry that I might not be home in time to get a good night's sleep before school the next day. That's how studious I was. I'd insist Chirag have me home by eleven (even if I sometimes snuck out to meet him after midnight). I'd only sleep over at Serena's if she promised we'd study. I was the kind of kid who gave *herself* a curfew.

No wonder Serena called me a goody two-shoes.

Mom stands up and turns to face me, her lips pressed into a thin white line, an expression I've gotten used to. "Didn't you get my messages?"

"Come on, Mom." I roll my eyes, starting up the stairs. "I don't think an hour is going to kill me. I'll take them now."

"Do you have any idea how worried I was? When you didn't write back, I thought—"

"What did you think?" I ask, stopping halfway up the steps and turning to look down at her. "You really don't have to worry, Mom. I'm pretty sure the worst thing that's ever going to happen to me has already happened."

I turn back around and head for my room. Silently, I beg my mother not to follow. If she comes upstairs after me, she'll watch me take them. Or *not* take them.

But the sound of her footsteps trails behind me like a shadow, up the stairs and down the hall. Before I can reach for the pill bottles, she is there, setting out my evening dose on my desk.

"What's this?" she asks slowly, fingering the pills.

"What's what?" I echo, playing dumb.

"Why are there multivitamins in here?"

I step toward the desk, trying to push her aside. "What are you talking about?" I grab a CellCept out of her hand and head to the bathroom with it in my mouth, lean over the sink to drink directly from the faucet. Maybe if she sees me take one—just one—she'll back down and leave me to take the rest on my own.

But instead, when I come back to my room, the contents of all my pill bottles have been poured onto the desk and my mother is counting out loud. She looks like a mad scientist, frantically sorting. I can tell she's struggling not to shout when she says, "Maisie, what have you done?"

"Nothing," I answer, but inside, I'm kicking myself. I should have flushed the doses I was skipping with Nurse Culligan instead of leaving them in the bottles.

"How many doses have you missed?"

I swallow, considering whether to tell her the truth. I can feel the CellCept making its way down my throat and into my belly.

"How many doses, Maisie?"

"What do you care?" I spit out finally. "You didn't even want me to get the surgery. You said they didn't have enough time to evaluate me."

"What are you talking about?"

"I heard you and Dad at the hospital. He wanted me to get the transplant and you didn't. He thought it was my chance to live a normal life, but you—" I pause. A lump is making its way up my throat, more enormous and rock solid than any pill. "You understood that I'd be a freak either way."

Mom shakes her head, her hands curled into fists. Maybe if my face wasn't so delicate, she'd reach out and slap me.

"How many doses, Maisie?" she repeats, ignoring everything I've said.

For the first time in my life, I want to be a lawyer, just like her. I want professional training to make my case. Then I could explain to her how well I'm doing without the pills. Maybe then she'd agree that I shouldn't take them for a while.

"Since Sunday," I say finally.

Mom shakes her head. "I've watched you take your pills since then."

"I didn't swallow them."

Mom's voice is louder as she echoes, "You didn't swallow them?"

"I haven't taken a single pill in days, and you know what? I feel fine. I feel *better* than fine. For the first time in months, I don't have a headache. I can stay awake in class." Mom looks horrified, but I continue, "Those pills made me *sick*. Being off them makes me feel *better*. Maybe Dr. Boden and his team were wrong."

I guess the rest of my team would be angry at me right now, like I'm the one who dropped the baton in our latest relay race.

"Maisie, your face—"

"My face feels fine," I say, though it's not technically true. I still can't feel it at all. "Stop acting like you're such an expert anyway. You're a lawyer, not a doctor."

Mom surprises me by leaving the room. I hear her feet stomping down the hall and her bedroom door slamming shut. I sink down onto my bed, relieved that's over. She'll probably insist that I see Dr. Boden tomorrow or next week or something, but I don't care. What's one more trip to the hospital?

Besides, I want Dr. Boden to see how much better I am without the pills. He'll take one look at me and realize that I'm the exception to the rule. Clearly, I don't need the pills the way other patients do. Maybe my body has accepted my face already and we don't need to worry that it'll reject the foreign tissue. I mean, my case is already so unusual, what's one more miracle, right?

I hear Mom moving around in her room, opening drawers and slamming them shut. She'll send my father in to talk to me when he gets home from work. He's working late tonight. He works late most nights these days.

I sit on my bed, looking anywhere but at the pile of pills on the desk.

The sound of Mom marching her way back down the hall makes me stand up, like I need to be ready to fight. She storms into the room with a file of papers in her hand, holding it out on front of her like a shield.

She picks out a picture of what looks like gray, muddied mush. It actually kind of looks like one of the oysters I ate on Monday night. I swallow a gag.

"Do you know what this is?" she asks. "This is a kidney in the early stages of tissue necrosis. And *this*," she says, bringing out another photo, this time of what looks like a black, bloody rock, "is a kidney in the advanced stages of tissue necrosis. Do you want your face to look like this, Maisie?"

I don't say anything. I don't even shake my head. I ball my hands into fists to steady myself, even though my left hand aches when I do. *Necrosis* is what happens when tissue dies. I must have heard Dr. Boden and Dr. Woo use the word a dozen times. But no one ever showed me what it looked like.

"If you don't take your pills, your immune system will attack your new tissue. It will turn black. It will bleed. It will die. It will disintegrate. Your *face* will disintegrate."

Weakly, I insist, "I've been off the pills for four days—"

"And it hasn't happened yet? That's because the life cycle of immune cells is about a week or two. It would take five to ten days for the immunosuppressives to get out of your system. Five to ten days for your immune cells to start attacking the transplant."

"Mom—"

"What?" she asks, so angry that she's shaking. "I'm not a doctor? I don't know what I'm talking about? You think I didn't research every single aspect of your transplant?" She waves the papers at me. "You think I don't know everything that could happen to you if your body rejects your new nose, your cheeks, your chin? You think I was going to let them touch one hair on your head if I didn't understand every aspect of what they were doing to you?"

When she stops shouting, she's panting as though she's just been sprinting.

"So I can be off the pills for five to ten days, then, right? Before anything bad happens?"

That means my window is almost halfway closed. Is that enough time—to stay awake in class, to ace my midterms? To actually be the one who helps Serena with her homework instead of the other way around? To show Chirag—

Mom's shout interrupts my train of thought. "*That's* what you got from what I just said?"

"Mom, you don't understand—" I hate the way my voice sounds. High-pitched. Childish. *Desperate*.

"No!" Mom counters. "Clearly *you* don't understand. Don't you care about all the doctors who fought to save your life after the accident? The doctors who stood in that OR for hours to perform the transplant—you're going to throw all that hard work away?"

"It's their hard work, not mine."

"And what about your donor? The woman who *died* for you to have this face—how can you treat her sacrifice so cavalierly?"

"She died either way, whether I had the transplant or not." Mom takes a shaky step backward, away from me, like she can't believe I said that. Well, I can't quite believe it either. I press my fingers into the corners of my eyes and take a breath, trying to regain control of this conversation. "You have no idea what this has been like for me—"

"Your body will adjust—"

"I don't have *time* to wait for my body to adjust!" My voice rises with each syllable. So much for controlling myself. "Midterms are *next week*. If my grades keep slipping, I'll never get into—"

I stop myself a heartbeat before I say the word *Barnard*. "Into college," I finish finally. My grades have never been more important than they are right now. Before, Coach used to say that my skills on the track would get me in wherever I wanted to go. But no one wants someone for the things she *used* to be able to do. Doesn't Mom understand that?

"I'm going to turn eighteen this summer, Mom. An adult. You're going to have to start treating me like one."

I brace myself for another onslaught of shouts. But instead, Mom releases her file and the pages flutter down to the floor slowly. She stops panting, and her voice is almost normal when she says, "Why don't you read about what happened to the *adults* who made the decision you just made?" She spits the word *adults* like it's a curse.

"Mom—"

She holds up her hand. "It's not a choice between pills and no pills. Between migraines and staying up late to cram for your exams." She closes her eyes like she can't bear to look at me when she says, "Maisie, it's a choice between life and death. But you're right. You're almost eighteen." She opens her eyes. "So you choose. *You* choose. Life or death."

She leaves the room before I can come up with a response. She walks normally now, so that I can barely hear her footsteps as she makes her way down the hall and into her own room. This time, she doesn't slam her door shut.

Alone, I slide my sweater over my head and slip out of my jeans, leaving the day's clothes in a pile on the floor, right on top of my mother's articles and photographs. I don't touch the scars on my side when I put on my pajamas. I avoid the mirror while I brush my teeth.

It's after ten. I ought to have taken my pills more than two hours ago.

TWENTY-EIGHT

I n bed later, when I lean over to turn off the light, one of the pictures my mother left behind stares back at me. Not a kidney or a heart, not something that goes inside of the body like the images she held up earlier. This is a hand. It's black. Not, like, African-American black, but black-black. Green-black. *Dying* black. The fingertips are darkest. They don't even look like fingertips but like burnt charcoal about to crumble into ash. In the center of the palm is an ugly red spot, as though the skin above it just disappeared to reveal the blood, tendons, and bone underneath.

Instead of turning off the light, I reach for the paper. The photo is part of an article she ripped out of a magazine about the world's first hand transplant. The patient was from New Zealand, and claimed to have lost his hand in an industrial accident. His donor died in a motorcycle accident. The patient was happy with his new hand, or at least he said so in the beginning. Soon, he regained sensation in his fingertips; he could hold a phone, eat with a fork and knife.

But before long—like me—he came to hate his immuno-suppressive regimen. The pills made him feel weak, he said, like he always had the flu.

When he stopped taking his medication, his doctors came to the conclusion that he was mentally disturbed. Only a crazy person would go off his meds, they said. They discovered that he'd lied about his injury. He hadn't lost his hand in an industrial accident, but while he'd been in prison, serving time for fraud.

Soon, the hand became swollen and red and immobile. Eventually, it had to be amputated. The article doesn't say what happened to him after that. The doctors concluded that he was just a bad candidate. A good candidate would have taken his pills no matter what the side effects. A good candidate wouldn't have given up.

I was supposed to be a good candidate. The girl who never gave up, who finished every race she started, even those she didn't have the slightest chance of winning.

I pick another article up off the floor and read that the long-term risks of immunosuppressive therapies are vast because you're literally choosing to debilitate the very system that protects you from disease and infection. You're trying to keep your immune system weak enough to accept the new parts—otherwise your body would treat the foreign tissue as a disease or infection that must be destroyed—while still hoping that your system will remain strong enough that you won't get diabetes or cancer or the slew of other diseases you're now highly susceptible to.

But without the regimen, death after a transplant is almost a certainty: The article states that a face transplant recipient in China died when he began using alternative medicine instead of taking his immunosuppressives.

I close my eyes. My stomach muscles are sore from running just a few yards this morning. At dinner with Chirag on Monday, our conversation was as stilted as my parents' at the dinner table after a fight, even more awkward than it was when he took me to Bay Leaf back before school started. We discussed our classes and our teachers the same way my parents talked about work and their colleagues: carefully and clumsily, with long pauses and silences in between almost every sentence.

Before, sitting across from my parents, I'd sometimes want to shout *You two made a baby together, took a honeymoon, built a home! Whatever happened to all that intimacy?* I didn't understand how it could just vanish into thin air, into nothing at all.

I drop the article to the floor and get out of bed. *You choose,* Mom said. *Life or death.* I walk toward my desk, toward the mess of pills Mom left behind. I organize them, dropping the correct pills back into their correct containers. All but one of each. One of each I place on my tongue, and this time I swallow.

Because I do want to live. For whatever that's worth.

PART III

WINTER

TWENTY-NINE

t's raining. Unless it's one of the drought years, winter is the rainy season in Northern California, when it's easy to forget that we spend the summer months completely parched. Some days the rain never becomes anything more than a drizzle, and some days it just feels like the fog is a little bit thicker, slower to burn off. But some days, rain pounds down like a waterfall, ripping the remaining leaves from the trees, soaking the ground so that the earthworms crawl to the surface, so that tires are coated in slicks of red mud, so that clothes and hair and skin never feel dry. Every morning when Chirag picks me up before school, I run to his car feeling like the Wicked Witch of the West, scared she might melt in the rain.

Tonight, Mom knocks on my door. She doesn't wait for a response before opening it.

"Mom!" I shout. "What if I had been changing or something?"

"I've seen you naked before."

No, I think. *You haven't.* Not since I've been home from the hospital. Not since the scars on my left arm faded into little white stripes, like I'm a zebra or something.

"It's time to go," she says.

"It's going to rain."

"So?"

It was raining the day of my accident, I think but do not say.

"Maisie," she says. "You're not getting out of this. Nurse Culligan thinks it's a good idea."

"Since when is Nurse Culligan such an expert?"

Mom rolls her eyes. "We put a lot of work into this, Maisie," she says. "You're going."

This started a few weeks ago, when Nurse Culligan called during dinner yet again and told my mother she thought I might benefit from some kind of support group for people who are recovering from what the nurse delicately referred to as "life-altering injuries."

Mom says, "Even Dr. Boden thought it was a good idea. They recommend therapy for transplant patients and you haven't been in therapy since you came home."

Since you came home. It sounds like I might have been anywhere. On vacation. At summer camp. "Sure I have. I go to physical therapy twice a week." The fingers in my left hand gripped a tennis ball for five whole minutes last Thursday.

"That's not the same thing."

I shrug. "Neither is a support group."

"Would you prefer to go to a psychologist?" Mom asks. "Plenty of patients struggle emotionally after a surgery like yours."

There aren't exactly *plenty* of people who have had a surgery like mine. We're a small, select group. In fact, it was almost impossible to find a support group for me in the first place. It turns out that most kids my age who need support need it for more normal sorts of problems: cancer, parents with addiction, eating disorders and peer pressure, that kind of thing. Eventually, Mom and Nurse Culligan had to ask Marnie for help. Marnie tried to find a group for teenagers, but apparently, most people make it further into adulthood before they're horribly disfigured. Or maybe it's just that injuries like mine are so rare that it's hard enough to find twelve people within driving distance to sit around and talk about it, let alone twelve people the same age.

"It might make you feel better, knowing you're not alone in your Depression," Mom adds, emphasizing the final word like it begins with a capital D. She shoots a meaningful glance at my pill bottles as if to remind me of the harm I almost did. Doesn't she understand that I didn't stop taking the pills because I was, like, *suicidal* or something? I wasn't trying to kill myself. I was trying to get my life *back*.

I didn't want to die. I *don't* want to die. And she should understand that by now because I haven't missed a single dose since that Wednesday night. Although she doesn't watch me take them anymore. She stayed true to her word: It's *my* choice. But I suspect she sneaks in here and counts them when I'm not around.

Mom sighs at my silence and says, "It will be good for you, Maisie."

"You don't know that," I mutter. The group Marnie finally suggested is for adults. I'll be the youngest one there. Maybe they'll take pity on me and let me keep quiet.

"I know that you're still not sleeping through the night."

I glance at the wall that separates my parents' bedroom from my own. I thought I'd gotten a lot quieter. Quiet enough not to wake her.

"We'll be there with you the whole time. Come on, Maisie, you spend half your free time reading about injuries. It's time you gave the real thing a try."

"What's that supposed to mean?"

"It means I know you're up here every night Googling face transplants and hand transplants, survivors of shark attacks and earthquakes. You're not exactly subtle about it," she adds, pointing to the books on my desk: one about carnival freak shows and another about the Elephant Man. I'm tempted to tell her that it's partly her fault. She's the one who left me alone with all those articles last month.

But instead, I say, "I get to see the real thing every time I look in a mirror, Mom."

"And how often do you do that?"

In the car on the way to the support group, which is held in the basement of a local church, my parents argue. At first, I'd kind of hoped that my father was insisting that I didn't have to go to this meeting if I didn't want to. But much to my dismay, they still have a united front when it comes to me. Instead, they're arguing about nonsense, just like they used to. My father didn't make the bed this morning. I don't think he's made the bed once in their twenty-year marriage, but today, it seems, my mother has finally noticed.

By the time we get to the church, I've decided that I don't want them to come inside with me after all.

"You can pick me up in an hour," I say, opening the door and hurrying across the parking lot. Even rain is preferable to spending one more second inside that car with them. I don't look back to see whether my parents are startled by my sudden enthusiasm.

My bag rattles like a maraca as I rush across the parking lot. I started carrying an extra dose of pills with me outside of school, just in case I get stuck in traffic, or the car runs out of gas, or, I suppose, I'm in some kind of terrible *accident* between points A and B.

The church is still decorated for Thanksgiving even though the holiday was more than two weeks ago. An overflowing plastic cornucopia is perched on a table just outside the entrance. There is a garland of lights in the shape of turkeys above the door, dripping with rain. The bulbs in at least half of the turkeys aren't working.

Inside, it smells like mildew and pine needles—a result, I guess, of the towering redwoods that ring the parking lot. I haven't actually been inside a church since I was five years old, when my parents sent me to Sunday school for nearly a full year before they decided that we weren't religious after all.

I'm early. In the basement, a circle of plastic chairs is waiting to be filled with freaks like me. There's a bulletin board covered in fliers. Apparently, this isn't the only support group that meets down here. Looks like Monday nights are AA and Tuesdays are Al-Anon, and every other Sunday, there's a group for cancer survivors. I look around, wondering just how much misery this room has soaked into its walls over the years. Fluorescent lights flicker on the ceiling, washing the chairs in wet yellow light.

I sit down and take *One Hundred Years of Solitude* out of my bag. Mr. Wolf's class has long since moved on—we're discussing *Beloved* now—but I keep reading the book over and over again, looking for anything I might have missed that day that I fell asleep.

I don't look up from my book when the room begins to fill with footsteps and murmurs and the sound of chairs squeaking against the ground. The pattern on the tan linoleum floor reminds me of the hospital, though here I can see dust bunnies in the corners of the room. I guess a church basement doesn't have to be cleaned as often as a hospital. I pretend to be so absorbed in my book that I don't hear the tapping of crutches as someone limps across the room, the squeak of a wheelchair that needs oil, or even when someone asks if I'd like a cup of coffee. No one asks why I'm here; my reasons are written plainly across my face.

I still haven't put my book down when a man sitting a few chairs down from me says, "Who'd like to start tonight?"

I close my book and look up. It's a circle of despair. Directly across from me is an elderly woman with a glass eye who can't stop blinking. Beside her is a man only a few years older than I am who's missing both his legs so that he has to be strapped into his wheelchair, and beside him is a girl with a jagged scar running up her right arm and no left hand at all, not even a prosthetic.

"Car accident," the person sitting to my left whispers.

"What?" I ask, turning.

And then I see a face that might be even worse than mine. Half of it—the right half—is perfectly normal. There's stubble running across his cheek; his eye is big and round and bright hazel and it narrows when he smiles at me. But the other half is mangled, as though someone chewed it up and spat it out. His left eyelid is barely open, the left half of his mouth is turned downward into a perpetual frown, and his skin—it doesn't even look like skin anymore.

I break my gaze, trying not to shudder. Just because I'm deformed myself doesn't mean I'm not still shocked by deformities.

"Cassie was in a car accident," he says, nodding in the direction of the girl across from us. He leans close, speaking softly. I'm tempted to back away but stop myself. He holds out his hand. "I'm Adam. You're Maisie, right?"

"How do you know that?"

"Marnie told me to look out for you." His strange, crooked face lights up somehow when he says Marnie's name. He has a crush on her, I realize, almost smiling. A big crush. An obviously hopeless crush.

"She your physical therapist, too?" I ask as I shake his hand. He nods. Like mine, his right hand is unmarred. His left hand is nearly as mangled as the left side of his face.

"Hey, Clyde!" he calls out suddenly, startling me so that I drop his hand like it's hot. The man who asked us who'd like to start tonight looks our way. He has a prosthetic right arm. I wonder if his name is on a list somewhere, a potential recipient for an arm transplant. I lace the fingers of my hands through each other, like I'm scared someone might take them away. "We got a new kid. Maisie."

"Hi, Maisie," everyone choruses, just like they do at AA meetings in the movies. No one stares at me the way they do at school, taking in my face like I'm an animal at the zoo. No one flashes me a heart-attack smile, either, or tries to avoid looking at me altogether. They don't observe me with laser focus like my mother, or study my features like my doctors.

"Way to put the poor girl on the spot, Adam," Clyde answers, but he's smiling. How anyone can smile in a room filled with this much loss is beyond me. He crosses the circle and uses his left hand to shake my right.

"Tell us about yourself, honey," Clyde says kindly. He sits back down in his chair.

"I was really just going to—" I pause. I can't tell the truth: *I was planning to sit quietly and read my book while you all told your sob stories.* Finally, I mumble, "I thought maybe for my first day I could just observe or something." With my right fingertips, I trace the bumps of the scars on my left hand.

"Scaredy-cat," Adam says, poking me in the side—my left side, right on top of my stripey scars. I shift in my seat, hoping he couldn't feel them through my sweater. Turning to the group, he adds, "Okay, then, I'll start today, since Maisie isn't ready yet. I'm Adam."

"Hi, Adam," everyone but me says.

"Well," Adam continues, "as most of you know, I served in the Middle East last year."

"Such a long way to go for a brand-new tattoo," the man with no legs interrupts mock-seriously, pointing at Adam's face. I wait for Adam to stand up and shout; I expect Clyde to scold him for making a joke in what's supposed to be a safe space. But instead, Clyde is laughing, and Adam is laughing, and then the whole room is laughing. I remember the night Chirag took me to Bay Leaf, his stony face when I attempted to make a joke about what had happened to me.

"Yeah, Michael," Adam agrees, chuckling. Later, I'll learn that Michael is a veteran, too. "I wanted something to remember the experience by." But then his voice turns serious and soft as he talks about the RPG that flew overhead, the explosion that followed. I can tell he's shared all of this before, though it doesn't sound like the kind of story you ever get used to telling.

Adam's burns were less severe than mine. He doesn't say so, but I can guess that some of them were second degree; the scarring on his face and down his left arm almost matches the marks on my left side. But he also has skin grafts where the burns must have been third degree. His face was mutilated, not destroyed like mine.

I guess his fire just didn't burn as hot.

THIRTY

After Adam, Cassie speaks. And then the woman with the glass eye, whose name is Maureen. I know I should be listening, but I can't help thinking about a game that Serena and I used to play called Would You Rather. It's supposed to be kind of dirty and sexy—and it was when Serena was the one asking the questions—but when it was my turn, it always turned kind of depressing. Would you rather lose your hearing or your sight? (I said hearing, Serena said sight.) Would you rather have no hair or no teeth? (Hair, we both agreed, but only after a long discussion about hats and wigs and headscarves.) Would you rather lose your mind or your parents?

This room is a veritable treasure trove of Would You Rather scenarios: Would you rather have no legs or no eye? Would you rather have no arm or no face?

Someone is saying my name, pulling me out of my thoughts. I look up and see Clyde standing over me. "I know you're not ready to share with us, Maisie," he says, "and that's okay. But maybe you could just tell us how you were injured?"

Marnie wasn't wrong: I'm definitely the youngest one here. Even though Clyde looks nothing like a teacher, it feels like this is a classroom and I've just been asked a question I don't quite know the answer to. "Lightning struck a tree near my house. The tree tore down some wires and there was a fire."

"An electrical fire," Adam breaks in. "Totally destroyed part of her face." I guess Marnie isn't bound by patient confidentiality rules the way doctors are.

To my surprise, *I* want to be the one telling my story. I don't want some stranger sharing the details for me. "I had second-degree burns all down my left arm and side, but my nose, cheeks, and chin burned off." I pause, waiting for someone in the room to gasp, or cringe, or at the very least look away, but no one does. "So a few months after my accident, they performed a partial face transplant."

The faces in the circle nod and smile, taking it in like it's nothing they haven't heard before.

When the group breaks up, Adam leans over me. "Want to grab a cup of coffee?" he asks. He's tall, taller than I noticed before. Probably six foot one, at least. It should make him look even more like a monster—this enormous man with the disfigured face—but somehow, it has the opposite effect. Despite his height, he moves gracefully, the tiniest bit of a strut in his walk, a relic of the confidence he must have had before he was ruined. You can tell—looking at the right side of his face—that he was handsome, before.

I shake my head. "My parents are waiting for me. I need to be home by eight, to take my pills." My bag rattles as I lift it off the floor, reminding me of the extra dose inside. It never occurred to me to use it for something frivolous, like grabbing a cup of coffee with someone I barely know.

I yawn, my eyelids growing heavy.

"Am I that boring?" Adam asks.

"Sorry," I say. "It's not you. It's the—" I hold up my bag in front of me, like he has any idea what's inside of it.

"Antirejection drugs, huh? They're brutal. Marnie told me."

I never realized what a big mouth Marnie has.

"I know," Adam laughs. "Marnie can be a real talker sometimes."

"What?" I didn't say that out loud, right? That Marnie had a big mouth? That was just that one time with Ellen, right?

"No point in being polite here," Adam explains. "Call Marnie a big-mouth, a pain, a jerk, whatever you need to. This is where we get it all out."

"I don't think I would ever call Marnie a jerk."

"Seriously? Because sometimes, when she's working my left side so hard that I can't even see straight, that's probably the kindest of the choice words I have for her."

"You have a point there," I say drily.

"Anyway, you're not the only one in here on immunosuppressives." Adam nods across the room at the woman with the glass eye, Maureen. "Kidney transplant."

"I thought she was here because of her eye."

"That, too." Adam shrugs, like it's no big deal, like people have multiple life-changing events all the time, like human beings are equipped to handle that much tragedy. "Anyway, maybe next time for the coffee." He smiles as he slips on his raincoat. *Next time.*

The old Maisie would have hated coming here, would have hated being around all this sickness, all this hurt. She'd have run away as fast as her legs could carry her. But this Maisie's legs can't carry her all that fast anymore.

Coach used to have nicknames for everyone on the team. She called me Fish because she said I was a fish out of water, the most competitive member of the team—not exactly the picture of a laid-back California girl. All my teachers noticed my competitiveness, actually. In the comments section of every report card, there was always some note: *Maisie is bright and talented, but her competitive nature limits her ability to excel on group projects*, or *Maisie is a wonderful student, but class debates bring out her competitive side*. I think back to Chirag's and my first interaction, debating over Hemingway. Was I trying to beat him at literary analysis?

Well, that was the old Maisie. Eric was right when he said she was gone. I glance around the room, at all these tragic figures pulling on their coats, shaking out their umbrellas.

No one here knew the old Maisie. Here, among all these strangers, I can give being someone else a try. A new Maisie. Maisie 2.0.

My parents are still fighting about their bed in the car on the way home. It's almost impressive that they've managed to talk about pillows and sheets for so long, in the time that three people in the support group shared their stories, plus me. By the time we put up our Christmas tree, Dad is sleeping in the den again. I guess if you don't share a room, you don't have to fight over whose turn it is to make the bed. Not that they don't find plenty of other things to argue about.

In the backseat, I finger my bag, listening to my pills clicking and clacking inside. I chose to take them. I chose *life*. So why does it feel like I gave up, gave in, accepted defeat, *failed*?

I close my eyes and make a mental list. Old Maisie: Competitive. Straight A student. Runner. Morning person. Cool girlfriend. Goody two-shoes (according to Serena). Parents on the verge of a divorce. And—even though I'd never have admitted it then—pretty.

New Maisie: Tired all the time. Bad girlfriend. (Not a girlfriend at all, really.) Grades slipping. Shy. Loser. Jokes mostly fall flat. Parents still fighting. Afraid to drive. Ugly.

How come pretty girls aren't supposed to admit that they're pretty but I don't feel any guilt acknowledging that I'm ugly now? There must be some kind of feminist argument to be made there, but thanks to my immunosuppressives, I'm far too tired to try to figure out what it is.

I sigh. Maisie 2.0 sucks. The original Maisie would have kicked her butt. I may have chosen life, but I have no idea how to live it like *this*.

THIRTY-ONE

Group—that's what everyone calls it, just Group—meets every Wednesday at six, and when my parents are both working late one evening, Chirag drives me. I watch him out of the corner of my eye, his long graceful fingers wrapped around the steering wheel at ten o'clock and two o'clock, his coffee-colored eyes focused on the wet road in front of us. I look away before he can see me staring.

Back in September, Mom could have asked Serena to drive me to school, could have recruited my best friend to carpool me to PT instead of my boyfriend. But Serena is always late and much as she loves me, Serena would never be able to sacrifice her senior year to play nurse.

My mother knew that Chirag was the one we could count on. Knew he was a *good guy*, just like Eric said.

The windshield wipers wave back and forth with a steady hum. The church is covered in brightly colored lights now. There's even an inflatable Santa Claus beside an illuminated nativity scene. Christmas is just a few days away.

Chirag puts the car in park and takes off his seat belt, like he's planning on getting out of the car with me.

Quickly, I say, "You don't have to walk me inside or anything."

In Group, Maisie 2.0 is starting out slow. For the past couple of weeks, she's just listened to everyone else's stories, like maybe she thinks she can soak up their well-adjustedness through osmosis or something.

The old Maisie wouldn't have been scared to speak, but then she'd never have had to ask the questions that run on constant repeat in Maisie 2.0's head: *Does anyone else avoid mirrors? Does anyone else hate the drugs that are keeping them alive? Do any of you really believe that you're still lovable* (ugh, just the word makes me cringe) *even now, looking the way you do? The way we do.*

"I thought I might——" Chirag looks shy. "I was wondering if I could sit in. Maybe see what you talk about in there."

I don't talk about anything at all, and I certainly wouldn't talk in front of you.

I shake my head. "It's not that kind of group. Everyone in there is injured." *No one in there is like you.* In that room, *Chirag* would be the freak, the one the rest of us wouldn't be able to stop staring at.

"I know everyone's injured," Chirag says softly.

"Well, then why did you think you should come inside?" I snap.

Chirag looks so hurt that I almost apologize. But if I say I'm sorry, he might think he can come in after all, and that's the last thing I want. It's bad enough that he has to see *me* all the time. He shouldn't have to endure a whole room full of ruined people.

"Pick me up in an hour," I say finally, like he's nothing more than a cabdriver. I get out of the car without saying good-bye.

I walk into the church slowly, breathing in its already familiar musty odor as I take the steps down to the basement. Tonight, when Clyde asks if anyone wants to start, I raise my hand. Everyone's gaze swings in my direction, though no one looks surprised. Maybe they all know I have this perfect boy waiting for me in the parking lot. Maybe they all know that I need them to tell me how to let him go.

I know that some members of the group are married. Maureen was still married when she lost her eye, and she and her husband stayed married afterward, until the day he passed away. Clyde wears a wedding ring.

And Michael—the man who lost his legs—has a girlfriend who picks him up most nights. "Can I ask you something?" I begin, shifting in my seat to face him.

Michael rarely talks about his girlfriend. Most nights, he talks about skiing. He's a Paralympian; he speeds down snow-covered mountains sitting in one of those chairs balanced on a single ski with poles in each hand. He's flying off for some competition in Tignes, France, next week; tonight will actually be his last meeting for a while. He drums his fingers against what remains of his left leg— cut off halfway up his thigh, unlike his right, which is completely gone—like he has all this pent-up energy he's just waiting to release.

I take a deep breath and ask, "Did you start dating your girl-friend before you lost your legs, or after?"

"Both," he answers. He fidgets with the fingerless leather gloves he wears to make pushing his wheelchair easier on his hands.

"What do you mean?"

"She was my girlfriend before I got injured, and when I came home it was a disaster. I couldn't handle it when she tried to touch me. I got angry when she had the nerve to so much as look at my injuries."

I nod. "So she broke up with you? Because you were being such a jerk to her?"

He shakes his head. "I think I could have gone on being a jerk to her forever and she'd have taken it."

I sigh, leaning back against my chair. "Because no one wants to be the person who breaks up with someone like us, right?"

Michael shakes his head. "No," he says firmly. "Because she loved me."

I bite my lip. I don't know what to say in response to that.

"I actually tried to break up with her before I was deployed. I thought I was so strong—you know, *I'd rather you hate me now than have to mourn me later.*"

"What happened?"

He shrugs. "She said whatever happened, we'd cross that bridge when the time came." Michael continues, "But then when the time came, neither of us could quite cross that bridge, you know? So finally, my mom broke up with her for me."

"Your mom?" I echo. I can't think of anything more mortifying. Michael laughs.

"Yeah. She saw how I was treating Julie and she hated every minute of it. We were running on fumes, you know?"

I nod, thinking of dinner with Chirag in Sausalito, when I tried and failed to duplicate what Chirag and I had been before. But then, fumes aren't the worst thing in the world. I inhale, imagining Chirag's smell.

Michael continues, "So one night, Mom told Julie to get out and not to come back, not to call, not to text. She said that I needed some time on my own to recover—and so did Julie."

"Wow. Your mom sounds tough."

"Yeah," Michael agrees. "Tough enough to say the things I couldn't. The things I should have, from day one."

"But you got back together?"

"A couple years later."

"A couple of *years*?" Even though the whole group is watching us, it feels like a private conversation. "Didn't you miss her?"

"Of course. But the thing is, I missed her even before we broke up. I was so much not myself that we weren't *our*selves, either. Our relationship didn't even resemble what it had been before."

I nod. Sometimes I think that the only time I don't miss Chirag is when I'm in bed alone at night, imagining he's there with me, picturing us dancing at prom. Daydreaming of the way things used to be.

"And now?" I prompt.

Michael shrugs. "It's still different. We had to get to know each other on these new terms. Lucky for us, we each fell in love with the people we'd become."

Michael smiles, his love for Julie written plainly across his face. I look away, wincing. The look on my face never communicates anything but *damaged* anymore, like I'm wearing an enormous OUT OF ORDER sign.

"Why didn't you break up with her on day one, like you knew you should have?"

"I was scared," Michael answers. "Who was going to want me? Who would want what I was now? Wasn't I better off hanging on to the person who'd wanted me before, who still remembered what I'd been like before—who still loved who I'd been before?"

Across the room, someone whistles in agreement: Clyde. Michael continues, "I knew I was never going to be that guy again. But I just couldn't let her go like I should—I don't know. It felt—"

"It felt like losing that guy all over again," I supply. "Severing your last tie to the person you'd been before."

Michael nods. I rub my neck with my good hand.

After a few seconds of silence, Clyde says, "Okay, who wants to go next?"

After Group, Adam walks me out. I Googled him the other day, the same way I Googled the surfer who lost her arm, the snowboarder with the traumatic brain injury, the Elephant Man. There were plenty of articles about Adam Robert Rosoff, hometown hero—star of his high school's soccer team, honors student, homecoming king—back from the war. Now he gives motivational speeches to troubled youth. He's exactly the kind of person Nurse Culligan was hoping for when she suggested that special assembly. The kind of patient my mother wanted me to be. That special person who becomes even stronger after having been maimed, who talks about it bravely instead of wishing that everyone would just ignore it.

As always, Adam asks me for coffee.

"I can't," I answer, as always.

"Right, your parents are waiting."

Clutching my umbrella, I shake my head. "Not my parents tonight."

"Who, then? Your boyfriend?"

I nod. Saying the word *yes* out loud feels like it would be a lie. Adam pulls his hood up over his face in the rain, casting his scars into shadow. "So that's why you were interrogating Michael tonight, huh?"

"I wasn't interrogating him," I insist defensively.

"When are you gonna do it?"

"Do what?"

"You know what," Adam says. "Give him the old heave-ho."

"The old heave-ho?" I echo. "What are you, eighty years old?"

"Wise beyond my years, darlin'," Adam answers. When he smiles, the left side of his mouth doesn't curl up nearly as much as the right, and the result is a crooked almost-smirk. "Anyway, I had to break up with my girl, too, back in the day."

Before I can stop him, Adam is jogging across the lot toward Chirag's hybrid car, which is still parked exactly where it was when he dropped me off. He looks back at me and winks. "I gotta meet this guy before you give him the slip."

I let myself in the passenger side, ignoring the sound of Adam's voice telling Chirag how special and brave I am. Chirag has rolled his window down and the two of them talk with the familiarity of old friends. I always loved that about Chirag, how he could step into any situation with ease. If I'd let him come inside tonight, they probably would have loved him.

But if he'd come inside tonight, I'd never have asked Michael the questions I asked.

"I've got to get home," I interrupt.

Chirag turns from the window to face me. "Adam invited us out for a cup of coffee."

I shake my head. I should do it *tonight*, with Michael's story still fresh in my ears. Give Chirag the old heave-ho. The slip. Adam made it sound so easy.

"I have to take my pills."

"You have a dose with you, don't you?"

"It's for emergencies," I protest. "Anyway, how do you know that?"

He shrugs. "I guess your mom mentioned it."

I didn't know she knew I carried extra pills around with me. Did she check my bag when I wasn't looking or something?

"I guess you talk to my mom all the time now, ever since she enlisted you to be my nursemaid." The old Maisie never would have said that. She and her boyfriend never fought. Now, when Chirag tries to smooth things over with a *Maisie, don't be ridiculous* look, I shake my head.

Smoothing things over won't get this done any faster. But being angry might. *Fighting* might.

I certainly know how to pick a fight. I'm an expert, in fact, after years of watching my parents.

"I know driving me around town is the last thing you want to do."

"I only wanted to help—"

"Help what? Help my parents take care of the freak who used to be their daughter?"

They use words like *freak* and *creepy* and *ugly* in Group all the time. Out here, in the damp December air, the word sounds harsh and out of place. I shiver.

I wonder if Chirag sat in his car in this parking lot for the past hour. Maybe he didn't drive away, didn't get a drink or a bite to eat, didn't pull out a book to pass the time. Maybe he just sat here, waiting for his girlfriend to walk back across the parking lot. I exhale heavily, so that my stomach curls in like the letter C.

"Chirag," I say finally, "we have to go." He nods a good-bye to Adam and rolls up his window. I wave as we pull away. I think Adam mouths the words *Good luck* back at me.

I'm going to need it. Because I know what to give Chirag for Christmas. And I'm giving it to him tonight.

THIRTY-TWO

As we drive, Chirag opens his mouth at least a dozen times, like there is something he wants to say but doesn't think he should.

"Say it already," I demand as we pull onto my street, past the place where the tree used to be, past the stump that used to be our finish line, past the redwoods whose bark looks spongy in the rain.

"Say what?"

"Clearly there's something you want to say to me."

"Maisie, there are about a million things I want to say to you."

Quietly, I whisper, "Then say them."

Chirag pulls into my driveway and parks. He shakes his head. "I can't."

"Okay, then," I nod. "I'll say them for you." I unclick my seat belt and take a deep breath, trying to ignore the angry butterflies in my stomach, the rush of nervous adrenaline shooting through my body.

Finally, I manage, "You want to break up with me."

"What?"

I swallow hard and set my shoulders the way I used to before crouching into position at the start of a race. "You can admit it. You want to break up with me. You want to go out with Alexis Smith."

"What does Alexis Smith have to do with anything?" He sounds defensive. Or maybe just surprised. I can't tell.

"Oh, come on, Chirag. Alexis is totally your type." She's what I used to be. Pale and freckly, a runner. Never had so much as a paper cut.

"Maisie, you know I think you're—"

I press my hand over his mouth before he can say anything like *You know I think you're beautiful/pretty/attractive/special no matter what*. It's the first time I've touched him in months and for an instant, I can feel the warmth of his breath and the press of his lips. It takes me a second to realize that I'm covering his mouth with my left hand. He can probably feel the scars on my palm against his lips.

"Don't, Chirag. Please."

He shakes his head, my hand still on his face. His beautiful, smooth face. I used to touch him every day: slipped my hand carelessly into his, pressed my cheek against his, rubbed his nose with mine. Gestures that seem impossible now. How did I ever touch him so easily? I can't remember how it felt anymore.

I drop my hand and tuck it beneath my legs. "It's okay," I say. "I'm not the girl you fell in love with." It's the first time I've said the word *love* out loud to him, unless you count saying things like *I love Indian food* or *that shirt* or *beating you when we race*, which I certainly don't.

"Maisie, you're still—"

"I'm still what? Still beautiful on the inside?" I laugh again, but it comes out sounding like a cackle, struggling to get around the lump in my throat. "Come on, Chirag, you don't actually think I'm going to fall for that, do you?"

My palms begin to sweat. I've never yelled at him, not once, not ever. But Maisie 2.0 can't be scared to shout.

"Why have you been taking care of me all this time? Driving me around, missing track practice? What, did you think those acts of charity would look good on your college applications?" I'm mean, meaner than I knew I could be. "You want a girlfriend you can kiss and hold and look at without gagging." I shake my head: Which of us am I trying to be mean to—him, or me?

"Maisie, I never—"

"Come on. I look like something out of one of your sci-fi movies. Like Frankenstein's monster, made up of someone else's spare parts." Immediately, I regret referring to my donor that way. She didn't deserve that.

"Maisie, stop," Chirag says, and even now, he isn't yelling. His voice is as calm and even and solemn as ever. "I'm trying to be a good guy here, but you're making it really hard."

Can't he see that for once, finally, I'm trying to be the good guy, too? "You *are* a good guy, Chirag. Nobody says you're not a good guy. And nobody will think that you're not a good guy if we break up. You've more than paid your dues. Everyone thinks so."

"Do you really believe that I want to be good to you because I'm worried about what other people will think of me? You know me better than that."

Why is he making this so hard? Why is he fighting back? He *wanted* this. He should be *relieved*.

He takes a deep breath and continues, "Look, your new face has taken some getting used to. Maybe you're not as pretty as you used to be—"

My hand flies up from beneath my legs, across the car, toward his face. A string of panic tightens around my rib cage, but it's differ-ent from the one I felt the day I woke up from my coma. This one is higher, somehow, closer to my heart. I was freezing before, but now I'm hot. I feel so hot that if I don't get out of this car soon, I think I'm going to suffocate.

Oh my god. I can't believe I slapped him.

And I can't help thinking *Wow, I did it with my left hand, Marnie would be so proud.* Although, when I bring my hand back to my lap, it's shaking uncontrollably. For a second, I wonder if I might have damaged it beyond repair. But the shaking slows, and finally stops.

Chirag takes a deep breath and—softly, calmly—says, "Maybe we should just hit rewind and pretend we never said any of this."

I don't answer right away. Because it's tempting: go back in time, not that far, just back to the church parking lot. Say *yes* to Adam's offer for coffee and spend a pleasant evening in a diner somewhere. Adam would be able to tell Marnie he was taking good care of me like she'd asked, earning one of her triple-megawatt smiles. And Chirag and I could go on like we have been, him chauffeuring me from place to place, waiting for me to be better so that he could break up with me.

But what would be *better* enough? When my scars fade just a few shades lighter? When I can stay up past ten and sleep through the night?

I've made up my mind. I'm setting him free tonight.

I open the door and step outside, leaving my umbrella beneath the passenger seat. The rain soaks my hair, drips down my neck beneath my shirt. I let the damp air fill my lungs, lower my tempera-ture. Even from the driveway, I can hear my parents yelling, though I can't make out what they're fighting about this time. Something ridiculous, I'm sure, like cleaning the grout from between the bathroom tiles or sorting the laundry. Nothing so serious as Chirag and me.

I bend down so that Chirag can see me. "I never loved you anyway," I say, and I hope he can't hear the way my voice wavers beneath the weight of the lie. "Don't come back here."

"Maisie—" Chirag begins, but I slam the door shut before I can hear what he says next.

I walk up the steps to my front door, but I don't go inside. Instead, I turn around and watch Chirag restart his car, slide the gearshift into reverse, and drive away.

I wait until he's out of sight to collapse onto my front steps. I can't believe I told him I didn't love him before I ever got to tell him that I did.

I don't care about the rain soaking every part of me. I'm crying so hard that I can't breathe, crying so hard that my throat aches and my teeth chatter and my eyes sting. I'm crying so hard that it takes me a while to notice that something has happened that hasn't happened in a long time.

I can feel the tears dripping down my nose and falling onto my chin.

THIRTY-THREE

I call a cab to drive me to school the next day, and the day after that. Luckily the day after that, finals are over and Christmas break begins. But by the first day of school after the new year, I've run out of cash left over from babysitting gigs and birthdays to use for cab fare, so I ask my mother to drive me to school. She looks surprised by the request. I should have gotten up earlier and asked my dad. Lately, he leaves for work before I've even woken up.

"Chirag's not taking you?"

I haven't actually told my parents that Chirag and I broke up, even though it happened almost three weeks ago. I kind of just assumed they'd figure it out. I didn't even tell Serena at first. It wasn't hard; like everyone else, she was distracted by end-of-semester finals, and then she left town with her parents for Christmas. But on New Year's Eve I finally told her. It was the first time I said it out loud and I hated the way the words sounded coming out of my mouth.

Afterward, we sat in my living room waiting for the clock to strike midnight, Serena gently shaking me awake each time I nodded off. We both knew there were at least a dozen parties Serena could have danced her way through instead of sitting quietly on my living room couch. Before my accident, I'd been looking forward to going to one of those parties with Chirag, to kissing someone at midnight for the first time in my life. Instead, Serena and I hugged and then fell asleep in my bed. In the middle of the night, she rolled onto her side, and the tickle of her hair falling on my nose woke me.

Now I say to my mother, "No. Chirag's not taking me."

I step from the doorway into her bedroom. She's sitting at her desk—she calls it a desk but it's really a vanity, with a mirror propped up behind it and drawers for makeup and lotions and curling irons and rollers. When I was little I used to sit there playing for hours, staring at my reflection, imagining that when I grew up, I'd have a desk just like my mother's, with a mirror that I could gaze into every morning. Sometimes I'd play at being the wicked queen from *Snow White*, chanting *Mirror, mirror, on the wall*. I believed that if there was such a thing as a magic mirror, it looked like this one.

I wonder what my six-year-old self would have made of the handheld mirror Dad gave me that night in the hospital, the first time I saw that my face was gone. Surely she'd have thought that such a big moment deserved a special, beautiful mirror like this one instead.

"I wish you'd told me that sooner, Maisie." Mom sighs heavily without taking her eyes off her reflection as she brushes blush onto her cheeks. "I'm going to be late for work now."

"I'm sorry it's so inconvenient for you," I mutter sarcastically.

"Don't you think it's a little early in the day for that tone?" She sighs again putting her makeup down. "You used to be such a morning person. My goodness, when you were little, you'd wake up with a smile on your face."

She looks so wistful that I want to pick up the alarm clock from her nightstand and hurl it at the mirror, smashing the glass into a thousand pieces.

"I guess smiles don't fit on my new face so easily."

She spins around to face me. "They'd fit just fine if you'd *try* smiling once in a while," she counters.

"Maybe I just don't think I have all that much to smile about."

"Are you serious? Do you have any idea—"

"I know, I know. I'm so very *lucky*," I say, and my voice sounds so ugly I barely recognize it. "I'm the luckiest girl on the planet. Lucky to have been such a morning person that I was out running the day of a thunderstorm. Lucky to have survived the fire that should have killed me. Lucky to have been waiting in a hospital bed the day a car killed a total stranger so that I could have her face plastered to what was left of my skull." I am so sick and tired of the word *lucky* that I nearly gag every time I say it. "Lucky that I had a boyfriend who was such a good person that he'd chauffeur me all over town even though I didn't look a thing like the girl he fell in love with, even though I barely talked to him and never let him touch me, up until the day that we broke up."

I stop then, my heart pounding.

"You and Chirag broke up?" Mom asks. She doesn't look angry at me, despite my outburst. She looks kind of sad.

"Yes," I answer, and I start to cry.

"Oh, sweetheart." Mom stands up and puts her arms around me. I can't remember the last time I let her this close; not since I've been home from the hospital, at least. And not for a long time before my accident. I used to think maybe she'd gotten so used to being angry at my father that sometimes she forgot she wasn't angry at me, too.

Her sweater is fuzzy against my cheeks. "I'm so sorry," Mom coos. "I know exactly how you feel."

My muscles stiffen. I wipe my eyes and pull away. "Are you kidding? You don't have any idea how I feel."

"I know it seems that way now. But believe me, I've had my heart broken, too—"

"Not like this." Does she really think that whatever heartbreak she had can compare to mine? I mean, seriously, she never had to break up with someone because she *literally* wasn't the same person she'd been in the beginning of a relationship.

She continues, "I just never thought that Chirag would do that. He seemed so devoted to your recovery."

My hands curl into fists at my sides. I savor the tightness of the skin over my left hand. *Of course* she assumes that Chirag broke up with me. Everyone at school will think so, too. Eric and Erica have probably been high-fiving him in the hallways behind my back, proud that he finally did what they thought he ought to have done months ago. Maybe some people will think that Chirag was a bad guy for having broken the deformed girl's heart, but once they hear what really happened, they'll change their tune. The whole school will agree that I was the jerk. All poor Chirag wanted was to help me. They'll shove him into Alexis Smith's waiting arms.

Now I tell my mother, "I broke up with him."

"You did?" I don't think I've ever seen my mother look so confused. "Why?"

I shrug. She'll never understand that deciding to break up with Chirag took so much more time and felt so much harder than deciding to go through with the transplant.

"But—" she begins, then stops herself. I know what she's not saying, because I'm thinking the same thing: I was a fool to end it. I'll never have another boyfriend, not the way I look now.

"You can just say it." I shrug.

"I thought you loved him," she says finally, surprising me.

It's because I love him that I broke up with him, I think but do not say. *It was my turn to be the good guy.* Out loud, I say, "I'll be waiting in the car." The old Maisie would have wanted to wash her face, make sure she didn't look too splotchy, after all that crying. The new Maisie just stomps out to the car, tearstained.

Walking into school without Chirag at my side is disorienting, like I've forgotten my chemistry textbook at home or didn't do my French homework last night. I keep my head down on my way to homeroom. Without Chirag, the whispers are a little bit louder, the stares a little bit longer.

Had they actually been holding back when Chirag was here? Are the floodgates open even wider now?

Eric stops me in the hallway. "Yo, Daisy-May," he says, a name that no one has ever called me before.

"Hey, Eric," I answer as I enter in the combination for my locker.

"You seen Chi-Dog this morning?"

What is it with this guy and the nicknames?

"Why would I have seen him?"

"Oh, I don't know, just because you two have been attached at the hip for the past year?"

I shake my head. Doesn't Eric know we broke up? I thought the whole school would know now that finals are over, the new year stretching out ahead of us. I study his face, looking for a sign of mockery.

"Anyway, when you see your boy, tell him Coach changed the practice schedule around this semester. Again. What a pain. A whole new roster to memorize—"

When I see *my* boy? He really doesn't know?

"I'll tell him, Eric," I say, interrupting his latest rant about the freshmen on the track team who just can't keep up. He laughs at his own pun. "Later," I call out as I turn around and head down the hall and around the corner to my homeroom.

Chirag is waiting for me outside the classroom. His lips curl up into the beginning of a smile when he sees me, a habit left over from before my accident, when we couldn't see each other without grinning.

"Didn't you tell anyone that we broke up?"

Chirag looks startled. Maybe he thought I would open with *Happy New Year*, or at least *Hello*.

"No," he says slowly. "I didn't."

"Why?"

He shrugs. "I just didn't think it was anyone's business."

I exhale.

"How was your break?" Chirag asks.

"Fine."

"Get any good presents?"

"Not really. Did you want to talk to me about something?"

"What?"

"I mean, what are you doing here? I made my way to homeroom just fine by myself after we broke up."

"I know," Chirag answers quietly, and the string around my rib cage, the one up near my heart, tightens again. Was he watching me—keeping an eye out for me, even after the breakup?

"I just wanted to ask if you needed a ride to PT this afternoon. I thought maybe now that some time had gone by and you'd calmed down, you might—"

"I might want to get back together?" Oh my god, my voice sounds hopeful. I'll have to add Chirag to the list of things I cannot have: running, alcohol, staying up late.

"Of course not," Chirag answers quickly. "I just meant, maybe we could—maybe I could—still help."

Ouch. This hurts more than when he said out loud that I wasn't pretty, more than everything I heard him say on Halloween. Because we could go back to the way things were before the breakup and still be completely broken up. There was nothing romantic about what we were doing, and Chirag knows it; he said as much on Halloween. He could chauffeur me around town all while dating Alexis Smith. I bet she wouldn't even mind. A girl who looks like me couldn't possibly be a threat. To her, I'd just be Chirag's good deed, part of what makes him such a great catch.

But doesn't *Chirag* care? Isn't it just a little bit hard for him, to imagine me sitting in his car every day, all the while *not* being his girlfriend? But then, I guess he's had more time to get used to it than I have. Breaking up was, after all, the rational thing to do, and Chirag understood that months ago. He waited for my sake.

For my emotional, irrational, foolish sake.

I shake my head. "My mom said she'd drive me," I say.

"And you're okay for Thursday, too?"

I shake my head. Sometime over the holidays, our insurance company decided that they were only willing to pay for my outpatient PT once a week. So I'll only see Marnie on Mondays now.

"No more Thursdays," I say to Chirag finally.

"Okay, then." He reaches into his bag and pulls out a blue umbrella. "Here," he adds, holding it out to me. "You left this in my car." I take the umbrella without saying thank you, squeezing it so hard that its metal bones dig into my hand. I turn and walk into homeroom. By the end of the day, the whole school knows we broke up. But Chirag isn't the one who said anything.

Chirag would never do that.

THIRTY-FOUR

At Group on Wednesday, I wait until two people have shared and then I raise my hand. When Clyde nods in my direction, I smile, my cheeks warming slightly.

I can blush now.

"I regained sensation a while back," I say. "My parents practically stood up and cheered when I told them. I mean, literally, they hadn't been that excited about my SAT scores."

A murmur of laughter floats through the room. "They called my doctors to arrange a spontaneous meeting with my team. The mood in the meeting was *triumphant*. You'd think everyone in the room— about thirty doctors and nurses, plus my physical therapist and my parents—had regained sensation, instead of just me." I pause, almost sighing. "I know it's a big deal. There was no guarantee that I'd ever regain sensation, and the doctors didn't know just how long it would take if I did. When they attached my new face to what remained of my old one, they just kind of crossed their fingers and hoped for the best. I mean, okay, they probably did a lot more than cross their fingers. But we just had to wait and see if the nerves from my old body would grow into my new flesh."

I bite my lip. Maybe I've said too much. Across the circle, Adam nods encouragingly, his sandy blond hair falling across his scars. So I start again. "Dr. Boden—he's my plastic surgeon—said this was a big deal, not just physically, but psychologically. He said patients who regained sensation had the best chance of really acclimating to their new features. Soon, he promised, this nose, these cheeks, this chin, would feel more my own than they had before."

I swallow. "And everyone looked at me, like they were expecting me to—I don't know. To be excited about that. To be thrilled that this nose and these cheeks and this chin were going to feel *more my own than they had before*. But I couldn't. I'm not exactly thrilled. I mean"—I play with my hair, untucking any strands that are hooked around my ears—"I know it's a good thing. And the truth is, I've kind of already started thinking about them sometimes as *my* nose, *my* cheeks, *my* chin. The semantics are just too confusing otherwise." Another murmur of laughter, which feels good. "But I'm not sure I *want* to get used to these features. Not completely. Not entirely. Because if I start thinking of them as my own . . ." I shake my head. "I don't know."

Clyde speaks. "*I* know," he says. "I wanted to hate this prosthetic arm. I didn't want to wear it. It wasn't *mine*, it wasn't real, it couldn't replace what I lost. I didn't want to get *used* to it. Because getting used to it meant I'd accepted what happened to me."

He doesn't continue; doesn't say that I should just suck it up and accept it, doesn't regale me with stories of how much better he felt once he did. He just shrugs, silently pointing out the obvious truth: *There is no going back.*

Maureen raises her hand. "Is it okay if I ask a question?" she says, looking with her good eye not at Clyde, but at me. I nod. "I don't understand—what exactly do you mean about regaining sensation?"

"Oh, right." I guess I forgot that not everyone here is familiar with all the details the doctors have drilled into my parents and me, time and time again. "When they transplanted the new features onto my face, they attach the blood vessels immediately—that way the transplanted tissue survives. But it was just sort of sitting on my tissue bed, not yet integrated in my nervous system. So it felt kind of like just a flab hanging off my face, for lack of a better term." Oh, if Dr. Boden could hear me now. "But as my nerves grew into the tissue, the weight lessened, until it disappeared. A literal weight being lifted off my shoulders," I add, and everyone laughs again.

I continue, "But I wasn't going to be able to move or feel the new tissue until the nerves grew to reach the new muscle. And nerves have a growth rate all their own—they grow a certain amount every day, but depending on the distance between my nerves and the new muscle, it could take months to a year for them to reach the new tissue, if ever. And actually, the ability to move is a totally different set of nerves from the nerves that control sensation. Though for me the movement nerves weren't as big a deal because you don't really have to move your nose and cheeks and chin the same way you have to move, say, your mouth if they'd had to replace my jaw. So I was able to smile from day one, eat from day one. Just very very carefully."

I stop. That's the closest I'd ever come to really calling myself *lucky*. Lucky that I hadn't had to worry as much about the nerves that control movement, because I got to keep my own jaw.

Maureen shakes her head. "Wow," she says. Adam lets out a low kind of whistle.

"I know," I say apologetically, running my fingers through my hair. "It's super gross. I shouldn't have gone into that much detail." I probably should have edited myself more. The truth is, I sort of just got used to how disgusting it is.

But when I glance around the circle—much to my surprise—everyone looks *impressed* by me. For the first time in a long time, despite my slipping grades, I actually feel smart about something. Dr. Boden used to say that this was such *exciting* medicine, so *thrilling*. Chirag said it was *cool*. Finally, I kind of understand what they were getting at.

Who knew that *not* editing yourself could be so rewarding?

Later, when Adam asks me to get coffee with him, I say yes.

"What about your pills?" he asks, the tiniest bit of a teasing smile playing on the edges of his lips.

"Shut up," I answer, but I'm laughing.

THIRTY-FIVE

text my mother that I'm getting a ride home and turn off my phone so I can't see the slew of questions she's sure to send in response, then follow Adam to his car. I don't ask him where we're going and I don't watch the clock. Instead, I look out the window and gaze through the darkness at the fog.

When I was little, my father told me that walking through the fog was the same thing as walking through clouds and I didn't believe him. Clouds were fluffier than fog, I argued. They'd be warm as cotton blankets, not cool and damp. And anyway, I insisted, surely you couldn't just walk through clouds. They're too thick. My father laughed out loud at that, at his precocious little girl and the adorable things that came out of her mouth. I wonder if he would have laughed so hard if I'd had scars then.

I know this is a terrible thing to say, but I used to wonder whether all parents thought their children were beautiful. Like, were the parents of truly ugly children so blinded by their love that they simply couldn't see what the rest of the world saw? Now I know the answer. I mean, I don't think my parents would have loved me any less had I been a less attractive child, but I know they liked it that I was pretty.

When I was little, my father used to rock me to sleep repeating my name in a little singsong: *Maisie Rose Winters, a pretty name for a pretty girl. Maisie Rose Winters, a pretty name for a pretty girl.* I'd protest that I wasn't pretty, but my father insisted.

"You'll see it for yourself, someday," he promised.

Now Adam pulls into the parking lot of a coffee shop. He holds the diner's swinging front door open for me and walks inside without waiting to be seated. On one side of the restaurant is a row of booths beneath the windows; on the other side is a counter and behind that, the kitchen. The place is full of cooking sounds—hamburgers being flipped, the sizzle of butter melting and the rhythm of onions being chopped. Adam slides into one of the booths; he's such a regular here that when the waitress stops by our table he doesn't even have to place his order. The waitress just says, "Your usual, honey?" and Adam nods. Quickly, I glance at the plastic menu and order a sandwich and coffee.

"Milk?" the waitress asks me, and I answer, "Black." Ever since the surgery, I like stronger tastes: I take my coffee black, I sprinkle Tabasco sauce onto my hamburger, I ask for extra wasabi when I eat sushi. It must be connected to the changes in my sense of smell. Still, my favorite scent hasn't changed: Ivory soap and clean sheets with a hint of curry. Chirag.

I sigh heavily. Adam doesn't ask why.

When my coffee comes, I take out my pillbox and begin swallowing one after the other. It takes me a second to realize that no one here is staring at *me*. The waitstaff here may be used to Adam's damaged face, but the other customers certainly aren't. My face looks almost normal next to his.

"How can you stand it?" I whisper, nodding in the direction of the people at the next table. A mother and her little boy, who hasn't taken his eyes off Adam since we walked in.

"I don't blame them," he answers with a tiny shrug.

Adam was the kind of person who was always going to be stared at. Before his accident, they would have all turned to look at the tall, handsome man taking up almost his entire side of the booth with his long arms and legs. Before, he'd have been the kind of handsome that would make Serena swoon and make me shy. Now he leans back against the vinyl, stretching his arms overhead. I can see his muscles beneath his T-shirt as he arches his back.

I guess no one ever told him *no rigorous exercise.*

"But it's so rude," I say, though I keep my voice down. I don't want people to know we're talking about them, even though they're the ones who are staring.

"Most of them don't even realize they're doing it. And little kids—" He stops and turns to face the little boy sitting in the booth behind us. His mother is trying to distract him by offering him a french fry. Adam smiles at the boy. "He's cute," he says to the mom, smiling his crooked smile. The damaged parts of his lips are more purple than pink, like a bruise that just won't heal.

"Thanks," she answers, blushing. I think she wants to apologize, but can't figure out how to do it without acknowledging—out loud— that Adam is a freak. She winces, like it's painful for her to look at Adam's face. As though, looking at him, she can't help imagining just how much it hurt to be burned like that.

To the boy, Adam says, "My face got burned in an explosion."

"An explosion?" the boy echoes, his eyes going wide. Adam nods.

"Does it hurt?"

"Not anymore."

The kid smiles. "That's good."

Adam grins back. "I think so, too."

The boy goes back to his french fries; his mom looks visibly relieved. Adam turns back to me and says, "Little kids are better than grown-ups. They'll actually ask the questions everyone else is thinking. And they don't avert their eyes when you notice them staring."

I shake my head. "I don't care whether it's a kid or a grown-up. I'm not some kind of sideshow for their entertainment."

"They're not staring because they're entertained," Adam counters. "They just want to know my story. They don't understand how this could happen to someone. It's human nature."

"Chirag said that once." After our disastrous meal at Bay Leaf.

"Smart guy," Adam says and I nod. "The worst are the cheerful people who pretend n   to notice at all."

"Oh my god, yes!" I agree, adding in a singsong voice, *"Oh, half your face burned off? It's hardly noticeable!"*

Adam laughs.

"But you're wrong." I shake my head. "Those people aren't the worst. The worst are the people who know what you used to look like." I shudder, thinking about the kids at school, the stares that still haven't stopped, even though it's been months now, even though each and every one of them knows my story. They can't stop comparing my new face to my old one. "How am I supposed to forget what happened to me when the people who knew me before the accident stare at me like I'm Humpty Dumpty and they're trying to figure out how to put me back together?" I can't wait until I move to New York next year, where no one within a thousand miles knows my old face.

Adam shakes his head. "The point isn't to forget what happened to us."

"I didn't mean forget, like, I wouldn't actually *remember* what had happened. I just don't want to be constantly reminded of what I look like now."

"Like Clyde said, eventually you have to accept it."

I shake my head. "That's not what Clyde said."

"Yeah, but you know as well as I do that that's what he was getting at."

"Well, now you've deprived me of the chance to figure it out myself. I'm going to tell Clyde on you."

"Tattletale," Adam says, grinning. "Seriously, though, Maisie—acceptance is the key. Acceptance is everything."

"Don't use your motivational speech stuff on me."

"How do you know I give motivational speeches?"

"I Googled you."

"You Googled me?"

"Right after we met." I don't add that I haven't looked up any other injuries since I Googled his.

"Guess I made quite an impression, huh?"

Wait a second. Is Adam *flirting* with me? He knows Chirag and I broke up—does he think that's the reason I finally said yes when he invited me out for coffee? All that time, it never even occurred to me that he wanted to hang out because he *liked* me. I thought he was just doing it because Marnie asked him to keep an eye on me. Marnie, on whom he has such a hopeless crush. Marnie, beautiful and unmarred, the kind of girl he'd surely have been dating before he became damaged goods.

"Nah," I answer "I was just impressed you found a way to parlay your injury into a lucrative career." Am I flirting back? Do I even still know how?

"Ouch!" Adam says, but he's laughing. I blush, savoring the warmth in my cheeks, on my neck.

"Can I ask you something?" Adam says, his face turning serious. I nod. "When was the last time you looked at yourself in the mirror?"

"I look in mirrors every day," I lie. "Getting dressed, brushing my teeth—"

"No," Adam interrupts. "I mean *really* looked."

It would be easy to clam up and ask him to take me home, easy to slam his car door shut in my driveway, the same way I did with Chirag weeks ago. But instead, I say, "Not since I got home from the hospital."

"When was that?"

"September."

Anyone else would tell me that I should look. Would tell me that my reflection won't be as bad as I expect. Would promise that my scars have faded. But Adam says, "I went six months without really looking."

"Six months?" I echo incredulously.

"Hey," Adam says, pretending to be defensive. "You've gone four months, way to horn in on a guy's record."

"Watch out, Adam, I'm coming for you," I say mock threateningly.

Adam shakes his head. "They were the worst six months of my life."

"Why?"

"Because I was pretending that I was still the old me. Like you said, I wanted to forget what had happened to me. But then, whenever I did catch a glimpse of myself—it was impossible to avoid it entirely—it was like losing my face all over again."

I nod. "It's strange the tricks your mind can play on you," I agree. I accidentally saw myself when I was brushing my hair this morning. I was so surprised that I actually dropped my brush. It fell with a clatter onto the tiles in my bathroom and my mother came running in, worried that I'd fallen.

Adam says, "I was like an addict in denial or something."

"I'm not in denial," I say firmly. I gave in and took my pills, even though they make me feel useless. I tried to run and practically passed out. I broke up with Chirag even though I never got to tell him *I love you.* I walk through school each day and everyone stares. I'm perfectly aware that I'm not the girl I used to be. "I'm not in denial," I repeat, more softly this time.

"Sure you are," Adam counters. "You don't even know what you look like."

"You want me to believe that looking in the mirror has magical powers?"

"Of course not. At first, it was torture, staring at this new noggin. But until I looked, I wasn't mourning what I lost."

The word *mourning* sounds out of place, at odds with all the *lucky* talk I'm used to.

"I didn't die," I say softly.

Adam nods. "For a long time, I didn't think I had the right to mourn, no right to feel sorry for myself when I had plenty of friends over there who didn't make it home."

I swallow. "I keep thinking about my donor's family. They lost a daughter, a sister, a friend—I don't even know, since I don't know anything about her. And I'm not allowed to ask, because then the doctors will start worrying about the psychological impact the transplant has had on me and suddenly I'll go from a success story to a failure." A *loser*, I think wryly, remembering the story of the hand-transplant recipient in New Zealand who gave up. "And everyone keeps saying how lucky I am—"

"That's the worst!" Adam interjects, laughing. In a high-pitched voice, he says, *"You're so lucky the doctors got to you in time. So lucky that the fire missed your eyes. So lucky that you still have your hair, your lips, your jaw."*

"Wow, how do you know the exact words my mother says to me?"

"You think I don't have a mother, too?"

We're laughing so loudly that the other patrons' stares aren't about the way we look anymore.

"But there is something that our parents and our doctors and our friends don't understand."

"Just one thing?"

Adam winks and shakes his head. "Part of us *did* die. Literally—that tissue on your face, the part they removed. It *died*. And you can't recover from *any* kind of death without mourning it."

Adam reaches across the table and takes my left hand in his. I try to pull away, but he holds fast. The scars on his hand press into the scars on mine, all ridges and lines, pink and white. He squeezes tightly, and after a moment, I squeeze back.

Before Adam drops me off at home, he gives me his number.

"Does this make you my sponsor?"

"What?"

"Like in AA, in the movies. You get a sponsor to show you the ropes. To call before you fall off the wagon."

Adam grins. "Sure, I'll be your sponsor. Call if you need anything."

It feels like we've been flirting all night, almost like this was a date. But Adam doesn't lean in to try to kiss me, or even hug me good-bye. Maybe he thinks I'm not interested. Because he knows he looks even worse than I do.

I smile. "I need a lift to Group next week."

"You got it."

THIRTY-SIX

n my room, I undress slowly. There's a full-length mirror on the back of my closet door. My father hung it there when I was twelve. Before that, the only way I could see myself from head to toe was to stand on a chair in the bathroom facing the mirror above the sink. But then I fell off it once and Mom burst into the room yelling. She was scared that next time, I'd break my arm, my leg, my nose.

Now I turn off the lights before I approach the mirror. Maybe some other night I'll keep the lights on, but not today. Not yet.

I sit in front of my closet in my underwear. First, I look at my arms, my legs, my stomach. The shadows of my old muscles are still there. I used to make Serena punch me in the stomach, just to show her how strong my abdominals were, how much better running was than yoga. Now I flex my bicep until it bulges, though not nearly like it used to.

It's not quite dark in my room. Moonlight shines in from the window, and a sliver of light comes in from the hallway outside my bedroom door. I take a deep breath and shift my gaze. I can just make out the angles of my face. I tuck my hair behind my ears and over my shoulders. My cheeks don't look quite as round as they did when I left the hospital; I guess the doctors weren't lying when they said the swelling would go down. I press my hands into them and I can feel my own touch, the ridges on my fingertips, the tops of my nails. I press harder, so that I can feel how the skin on my left fingertips doesn't match the skin on my right: My left pointer finger has a rough scar right on its tip, but the skin on the ring finger is actually perfectly soft: brand-new, like a baby's. When I was in kindergarten, my whole class got fingerprinted. Serena said it had something to do with finding us, in case we were kidnapped someday. But my fingerprints have changed.

This nose is so much sleeker than my old one; it's even slimmer than it was the first time I saw it. It must have still been swollen then. I stick up my chin, leaning back until I'm almost facing the ceiling. I try to angle my face so that I can see my own profile, feeling like an infant who's just discovered she has hands and feet and can't quite wrap her mind around all these new parts.

Even stranger than my new features are the shadows of my old ones underneath them. Even though so many of my old bones are gone, even though they sewed on these new ones, something about my old face remains. I thought that having a dead girl's face sewn onto my skull was walking around with death on my face. But it's the old parts of me that seem like ghosts, like they're haunting this new face. No wonder the people who know what I'm supposed to look like can't stop staring.

I shake my head, my hair swinging back and forth, tickling my shoulders. Not what I'm *supposed* to look like. What I *used* to look like.

I try to imagine someone else here with me. Someone watching me undress. Someone undressing alongside me. After all the flirting we did tonight, maybe one day it will be Adam and me in the dark together. Maybe he'll reveal his scars, too. Maybe it would be better that way than with someone like Chirag, someone with no scars of his own. Maybe that's the whole reason Adam asked me out. It's been a few years since his accident; I wonder if he's been alone all that time, scared to let anyone see him.

Until I came along, someone just as damaged as he is. Someone he wouldn't have to be embarrassed in front of.

Someone *I* wouldn't have to be embarrassed in front of.

I press my hands to my belly. Just thinking about Chirag used to fill my stomach with butterflies. I go over the past few hours in my head, trying to remember everything Adam said to me, every wink and every smile. But my belly remains butterfly-free.

Maybe people who look like Adam and me don't get to have that kind of butterflies. Maybe our butterflies are reserved for doctors' appointments and test results. Maybe romance butterflies are another part of my old life that I have to say good-bye to. That I need to *mourn*, just like Adam said.

There are steps to mourning, right—stages? I grab my phone and look them up: *denial, anger, bargaining, depression, acceptance.* I've definitely got anger covered, between fighting with my mom and breaking up with Chirag. And maybe giving up the pills was a kind of bargaining: I will take this new face *if* I don't have to take the pills—and the side effects—that come along with it. And depression—that seems too big to be a single stage. That's more like the undercurrent beneath everything else.

If you ask me, the two stages that really count—the big ones— are denial first and acceptance last.

I thought I would throw up or cry or scream if I looked this closely. Now I set my jaw and square my shoulders.

I will look in this mirror every night. I won't stop until I can look with the lights on. I won't stop even then. Every race I ran, I used to keep going for yards past the finish line. I didn't like to give up, even after I'd won.

I stand and hold my left arm out in front of me. Just above my elbow is a long white scar. I trace it with my right hand, imagining the flames that burned me there. In between the scars my skin is soft as silk.

I turn to look at myself from the side. Where my shoulder and neck meet, the skin is almost completely normal. Somehow, the flames didn't touch me there. Maybe I was curled up into myself, my shoulders hunched up around my cheeks. For the first time, I realize what a miracle it is that I still have my hair. My ponytail caught fire, but someone must have doused those flames before they traveled up to my scalp, so that only the tips of my hair were singed off. Someone in the hospital trimmed it for me before I left, so that the ends were even. I haven't cut it since.

It's strange, when you think of it, that fire can travel. I imagine a flame packing up a bag, getting ready for a journey.

I'll wear black tomorrow. No one at school will think anything of it. People wear black all the time. It'll be my secret that the color is symbolic, a sign that I'm mourning the part of myself that died, mourning all the things in my old life that are different now.

No one will know that I'm waiting to get to the fifth stage, the one where I can accept what's left of me.

THIRTY-SEVEN

decide to start driving myself. Adam says he doesn't mind ferrying me back and forth to Group on Wednesdays, and Serena tries to be on time when my mother can't take me to school or a doctor's appointment, but I'm getting sick and tired of counting on other people for everything. If I'm going to make it on my own in Manhattan next fall—even though there, ironically enough, I don't think I'll actually need a car—I need to start making it on my own here first.

On Wednesday, I text Adam that I don't need a ride. I tell my parents that I'm taking my mother's car, and they don't argue. In fact, I think they're relieved. Mom even says I can drive it to school in the morning. She'll get a ride into the city with Dad, even though that will be the most time they've spent alone together since Christmas.

Before I pull out of the garage, I take my time adjusting the rearview mirror. I'm getting good at looking in the mirror—last night, I even turned on the little light by my bed when I looked at myself, studying the shadows it cast across my face.

As I drive, I stop to study my reflection in the windows and mirrors. Sometimes, I am truly startled to discover that there aren't any freckles sprinkled across my nose. Sometimes, it feels like I'm looking at a stranger I'm desperate to get to know, but sometimes I understand that I'm looking at myself.

When I pull the car into the parking lot of the church, I feel almost the way I used to after a race. My heart is pounding and I can't stop smiling.

Maureen smiles as I sit down in the circle. "You look like you're in a good mood, honey." I barely notice her glass eye anymore. "And it looks like those are fading," she adds, pointing to my cheeks.

"Really?" I ask. Lately, I've been thinking that the scars on my cheeks look less like war paint and more like poorly applied blush. "I kind of thought so, too. But I wasn't sure."

She nods. "They are. Absolutely." Anywhere else, even if my scars had vanished entirely, no one would have said a word. It's not polite conversation. But here, I can take what Maureen said as the compliment she'd intended it to be.

When Clyde asks who'd like to start, I raise my hand.

"I drove myself here tonight," I begin proudly. Adam sticks his fingers in his mouth and whistles. It's a pretty weak whistle since his mouth is lopsided, but it starts everybody cheering and clapping nonetheless.

The old Maisie wasn't all that proud when she passed her driver's test. It just felt like something I was *supposed* to do on my sixteenth birthday, something to check off of my life's to-do list. Tonight actually feels *better* than that did. "My donor was killed in a car accident. I don't know the details—I don't know if she was the one driving or not. Maybe she wasn't in the car at all; maybe she was a pedestrian on the sidewalk, just running errands, walking her dog." I pause. "Maybe she was out for a run, like I was."

Maybe she was covered in sweat and panting, forcing herself up the next hill and the next and the next. Or maybe she was nearing that moment when you start to feel invincible, when you think you can go on running forever, through the rain and the fog and the wind and the sun.

"I miss running," I continue. "I ran almost every day before my accident. I loved it. I miss being on the track team. Coach thought I might be able to get a scholarship someday. My boyfriend—ex-boyfriend—is still on the team. We used to run together." I pause, and add, "I fell in love with him on a run."

In fact, I remember the precise moment I realized I loved Chirag. It was over a month before my accident. Long before he held up his sign saying that he loved me. It was after school. We'd started out on the track, running in circles, but Chirag said he felt like a gerbil and veered off into the street. I followed him. His legs were about six inches longer than mine and I loved watching his easy, loping stride. When he ran, he always landed on his toes instead of his heels; he'd read somewhere that it was better for your knees that way. Soon, I was running like that, too.

It was the middle of March—almost exactly a year ago—that time of year when you think it should be spring already but winter hasn't given up its hold yet. It wasn't raining, but it was misty; the fog had never quite burned off that day. We were about a mile from school, on a path in the park, when Chirag reached down and took off his shoes, tossing them into the trees beside us.

"What are you doing?" I shouted in between breaths. *Step, breath. Step, breath.* He was a few yards ahead of me. I took advantage of his pause to pass him; I wasn't about to let him beat me.

"There's a tribe of Indians in Mexico who are the best runners in the world," he shouted. "They run barefoot for miles and miles and never break a sweat."

"You're not that kind of Indian," I shouted back, and Chirag laughed, his golden skin shimmering beneath his sweat.

"You should try it, too!"

"No way!" I replied without turning around to face him. "The ground is filthy. There could be glass or splinters or something."

"Aw, come on, Maisie," he cooed, coming up on my left side and getting a few steps ahead of me once more. "I dare you."

I never could resist a dare, and Chirag knew it. So I took off my sneakers and tossed them into the brush just like Chirag had. Then I put my head down and sprinted to catch up with him. I tackled him, but he was too strong, and instead of falling to the ground, he lifted me up over his shoulder.

"I win," he said, throwing his arms over his head.

"You do not. I was just about to pass you," I protested, panting. The bones of his shoulders pressed into my belly but I didn't care.

He turned his head and kissed my arm. "I have you," he said simply. "I win." He turned around and carried me back down the path. We spent the next half hour searching for his left sneaker. By the time he found it, I knew I loved him.

Now Clyde seems to understand that I don't have anything else to say. He glances around the circle and says, "Who'd like to share next?"

I drive to school the next day. I go early, and when I pull into the parking lot, the fog is still heavy. There are only a few cars in here at this hour: teachers who came in early to grade papers maybe, the janitor who's inside somewhere, taking out the trash and wiping down the blackboards.

I recognize Ellen's car immediately. Cherry red, two doors; her parents gave it to her as an early graduation present. Or maybe it was a Christmas present. Either way, she's been proudly driving it to school all semester long.

I open the car door and slam it shut behind me, the *thwack* echoing across the lot. I don't think students are even allowed inside the school building this early. Not that there's ever much need for enforcing that rule.

I push Mom's keys into the pocket of my black jeans and pull my dark gray sweater more tightly around myself in the morning drizzle. I painted black nail polish onto my fingers a few days ago. It's already chipped.

I take a deep breath and walk around to the back of the building. I hear Ellen before I see her, the slam of her feet against the track. *Step, breath. Step, breath.* I can tell, from the sound alone, that she's landing hard on her heels, exactly the way Chirag taught me not to. It's the sound of someone running harder than her body wants; the sound of someone who will never run as fast as she hopes to.

Ellen's head is bent down low, her chin nearly on her chest, so she doesn't see me coming. I could walk away, go back to the car and pick up *One Hundred Years of Solitude* yet again, read it until the bell rings for homeroom. Ellen would never have to know I was here. Instead, I stand at the edge of the track and watch Ellen run. Watch the strands of her ponytail falling out of its elastic, the sweat dripping from her chin to her chest, the way the muscles in her legs vibrate each time her feet hit the ground.

No rigorous exercise. Maisie 2.0 is a girl who cannot run. And not just races. Maybe I'll never even be able to run to catch a train or to get inside when it suddenly starts to rain or just for the sheer joy of it, just a short way—running into someone's arms for a hug.

Suddenly, I hear myself saying, "Try landing on the balls of your feet."

Ellen doesn't hear, so I repeat it, louder this time. When she still doesn't stop, I walk toward the middle of the track and wait until she's about to run headlong into me. Then I grab her arm, expecting her to stop the instant she feels my touch. But I underestimated the momentum she'd built up and our legs get twisted and we both fall onto the track.

"What the—?" Ellen begins angrily. Then she sees that it's me on the ground beside her. "Oh my god, Maisie, are you okay?"

I'm on my hands and knees. My right wrist is aching—I threw out my hands to keep my face from hitting the ground. I'm panting as though I was the one who'd been running. Because what if my face had hit the ground? What if I'd broken this nose, this chin? What then?

My stomach lurches with a familiar rush of adrenaline.

"I'm fine," I say finally, nodding.

"But your—" Ellen hesitates, biting her sweaty upper lip.

"My face? It's fine." I shake my head, trying to look calmer than I feel.

"What were you thinking?"

I sit back on my heels and shake my wrist out. It's muddy from the damp track.

"I guess I thought I could help."

"What?"

Ellen is drenched with rain and sweat and fog, her bangs sticking up from her forehead in all directions. Her fair skin is covered in red patches from the effort of her run. It doesn't look bad: It's a mark of the work she's put in. I swear my freckles used to change color from brown to magenta when I ran. She's wearing shorts and a tank top and her arms and legs are so white that they practically glow in the fog. No wonder she hated me for cutting off her tanning time back in September.

"I thought I could help," I repeat, pushing myself up to stand. I offer her my hand—my left hand; my right hurts too much—and help her stand. Her fingertips brush against my scars. She drops my hand like it's hot. But she doesn't seem disgusted, just embarrassed.

"I don't need any help."

"Yes, you do."

Ellen presses the heel of her hand against her forehead. She's still panting. "I guess I deserve that."

"Deserve what?"

"You being nasty to me. After how I acted last semester."

"I'm not—I wasn't trying to be mean."

"Then what are you doing here?"

I shrug. "I'm early," I say finally. "And your car was in the parking lot. I was just watching you run."

"Why?"

"Because I love running." The words I don't say hang in the air: *And I can't run anymore.*

"Oh." Ellen rubs her nose with the back of her hand, brushing away some lingering sweat.

"I was just trying to tell you that you should try landing on the balls of your feet."

"What?"

"You were coming down hard on your ankles. The impact is bad for your knees, and it slows you down—it forces your body to come to a sort-of stop in between each step." My explanation isn't nearly as scientific as Chirag's was, when he explained it to me. "If you land on the balls of your feet, you can build up more momentum. It's kind of like ice skating—you just flow from one step into the next."

"Okay," Ellen says. "Well . . . I wanted to get in another mile before homeroom." Ellen was never like me when it came to running. I always thought that she'd only joined the team because it would look good on her college applications, alongside her perfect grades and AP classes. But now—with me gone—she's the best runner on the team. I'm sure Coach is piling the pressure on.

Guess I'm not the only one my accident changed. I mean, I know it changed things for my parents, for Chirag, for my doctors. But this is a kind of change I never could have predicted, a change in someone I'm not even friends with anymore.

Maybe Ellen is trying to find out how it feels to be someone who really cares about running. Ellen 2.0, just like me.

"You should try it," I say. "Running on the balls of your feet. For your last mile."

Ellen looks surprised. She probably thought I was going to walk away and leave her alone. Instead, I climb onto the bleachers and watch. It takes her a couple of laps to get it right: Her body is so used to landing on her heels that it tries to keep doing it even when her brain wants to land on the balls of her feet. I can see her struggle. I probably look the same way in PT, when my body is screaming out *not* to do the very thing that Marnie orders me to do.

But after two laps, Ellen catches her stride. Her footfalls are softer now, and she leaps from one step to the next buoyantly. I'm not sure if she's actually going faster than she was before, but her head is held up higher now.

When she's finished, she walks over to me. "Thanks," she says.

"No problem."

"Can I ask you something?"

I nod, bracing myself for a question about Chirag or my face. But instead she says, "Why'd you help me?"

"What do you mean?"

"I thought you hated me now."

I shake my head. "I don't hate you. And I helped you . . . I don't know. Because I *could*, I guess. Because I know how to run." I think of Michael; he doesn't have legs, but surely he remembers how to walk. Of Maureen, who can't see out of one eye, but certainly remembers what the world looked like when she could.

"I never told Chirag, you know. About Halloween. I didn't even tell Samantha, and I tell her everything."

"I know. Thank you."

"I just wanted you to know that."

Our conversation is awkward, as though our friendship is another skill that I remember but can't use anymore. Like we both can recall what it was like to be friends, but neither of us can actually *feel* it now.

"I bet if you asked, Coach would let you come back to the team, as, like, a student coach or something. I'd tell her how much you helped me. And she wouldn't say no to you, you know, because . . ."

"Because no one wants to say no to the class freak?"

Ellen looks away.

"It was a joke, Ellen. It's okay."

"It wasn't funny."

They would have laughed in Group. "Guess it was kind of an inside joke."

Ellen shakes her head, confused.

"That's a really nice idea, though, student coaching." I pause, looking down at my dark clothes. The old Maisie received ribbons and medals; crowds cheered for her, other teams booed her. But now, Maisie 2.0 receives applause from Marnie just for catching a ball with her left hand. For driving to Group all by herself. "I'm not sure I'd want to be on the team like that, you know? A part of it but also outside of it. Feels like it would be a kind of . . . denying that things have changed."

Ellen nods. "I get that. It sucks, though."

"Yeah," I agree. "It does. There are a lot of things I don't get to have anymore." It comes out sounding sadder than I mean it to. Ellen looks so devastated that I want to reach out and comfort her. "I just meant—I have to find new things to look forward to."

PART IV

SPRING

THIRTY-EIGHT

got into Berkeley!" Serena practically tackles me with the news. Before I can respond, she says, "Wait, shouldn't we go sit in the shade?"

It's lunchtime and I'm sitting on the bench where we sat for just a few minutes on the first day of school, my face tilted toward the sky. It's not raining today—the rainy season is almost over—and right now, I can actually *feel* the heat from the sun on my skin. I'm like a vampire who's just discovered she can walk in the sunlight after all. I don't even care that people are staring at me, don't care that the group who usually sits on this bench is tossing me dirty looks.

I don't have a migraine. For six months, I woke up nearly every morning with a throbbing at the base of my neck that radiated up until it reached my temples. But for now, the ache has vanished. And yesterday, I made it through the whole day without taking a nap. Today, only my socks and sneakers are black. Still, nothing like Serena's peach-flowered top.

"Congratulations!"

"Thanks!" Serena twists her long dark hair around her fingers. "Have you gotten yours yet?"

I don't answer, and Serena says, "They're probably just doing them alphabetically. Marcus comes way before Winters, you know?"

I nod, but the truth is I got my acceptance letter from Berkeley two days ago. But if I have to lie to Serena about something, I'd rather it be whether I got my acceptance letter than pretending to be excited that we're going to go to school together in the fall. Besides, it's not totally a lie: I am still waiting for an acceptance letter. Just from Barnard, not Cal.

"Seriously, though, shouldn't you get out of the sun?"

Serena looks so solemn that I laugh.

"You sure latched on to that particular side effect."

Serena folds her arms across her chest defensively. "It's the only one your mother told me about."

"Yeah, but it's not like you haven't gotten to see the other side effects up close and personal." Serena blushes. "Anyway," I add, "I don't think ten minutes of sunshine will kill me."

"Yeah, but the seniors who usually sit here might." She nods in the direction of the group that's scowling at us.

"Come on, can't they give a poor disabled girl like me a break?"

Serena laughs. She's this beautiful, almost dainty kind of girl, but when she really gets going, she has the most absurd, nasal, honking laugh I've ever heard.

"Hey, can I ask you a random question?"

"Sure."

"You know that when I got out of the hospital, Chirag took me to Bay Leaf?"

"He hates that restaurant," Serena says, wrinkling her pretty nose. I can't wrinkle my nose yet. I tried, looking in the mirror last night.

"I know!" I agree. "Which is why, when he took me there after I got out of the hospital, I said, *What do I get if I lose a limb next time?*"

Serena plops onto the bench beside me. "That's funny."

"Chirag didn't think so."

She shrugs. "He never really laughed at your jokes."

"He didn't?" I ask, genuinely surprised.

"It drove you crazy how serious he was!" Serena almost shouts, standing up and taking my arm—my right arm—to pull me into the shade. The sunny bench we left behind is quickly taken over by its usual inhabitants.

"Oh my god, speaking of Bay Leaf," she continues, "remember that night last year when a huge group of us were there and Chirag complained about it the entire time?"

I nod. "Yeah."

Serena tries to make her voice as deep as Chirag's: *"My mother's food is so much better than this . . . real sag paneer isn't this creamy. Traditional naan does not look like this."*

"That's the worst impression I've ever heard."

"Who else have you ever heard do a Chirag impression?"

"No, I mean, it's the worst impression I've ever heard anyone try to do of anyone."

Serena scowls, but she's trying not to laugh. "And remember halfway through dinner he practically sat on your lap and ate all the food off your plate? I thought you were going to break up with him then and there."

"Seriously?"

"Dude, you were fuming! 'Course, you never said anything to him about it. You'd have rather gone hungry than have an actual fight with the guy."

"What are you talking about? Chirag and I never fought."

"Exactly!" Serena nods, her hair falling across her face. She exhales, blowing strands away from her eyes. "You'd just come to me and moan about the things he did that pissed you off. How he was scientific about *everything*, all those movies he made you watch—"

"I liked some of those movies!"

"Yeah, but he always refused to watch any of the movies you loved. I was the one who had to come over to watch *When Harry Met Sally* . . . and *Two for the Road* and *The Philadelphia Story*."

I shake my head. "I guess I forgot about that." I forgot that there was anything about Chirag I disliked before my accident.

"Well, I remember," Serena says, pulling an almond butter sandwich out of her bag and sitting cross-legged on our usual shady bench. "I think you were just scared to fight with him. Scared of being anything like your parents."

"Guess I got over that fear. You should have heard the way we fought the night I broke up with him."

In between bites, Serena says, "Breaking up with him doesn't mean you're like your parents. I mean, it kind of means you're the opposite, right? Because their relationship stopped working a long time ago and they still haven't broken up. It'd be way more like them to *stay* in a bad relationship."

I smile. "When did you get so wise?"

"I've always been wise," Serena answers with a flip of her hair. "I just don't like to show off."

I lean over and kiss her cheek. It's the first time I've put my face this close to anyone else's, and Serena doesn't flinch when my nose rubs against her cheekbone.

When I pull away, she says softly, "Listen . . . did you hear about him?"

"About Chirag? What?" I ask quickly. *Does he have a new girlfriend? Is he okay? Should I feel bad because I thought about the girlfriend question before I thought about the is-he-okay question?*

"He got into Stanford."

"Oh." I nod. "Good for him." He always wanted to go there. Before my accident, we used to talk about how easy it would be—me at Berkeley, him at Stanford. We thought we wouldn't have to break up the way other high school couples do when they go to different colleges. Berkeley and Stanford are less than ninety minutes away from each other.

"We'd be rivals," I said once. I tried to imagine what it would be like to show up at a track meet and root against Chirag. I didn't think I'd have been able to do it.

"Like the Capulets and the Montagues. Or the Sharks and the Jets," Chirag answered.

"Didn't end well for those folks," I said. A joke that Chirag didn't, I remember now, laugh at. Instead he leaned in and kissed me for a long time until my knees literally felt weak.

What did I think would happen when I went to Barnard? Did I know—even back in September, when I decided to apply there—that I'd break up with him?

Serena says, "Maybe you should congratulate him."

I shake my head. "I'm not sure. We haven't exactly been talking since our breakup." The last conversation we had was when he asked if I needed a lift to PT. Since then, we kind of just nodded in each other's direction when we passed each other in the halls. Lately, I've just avoided making eye contact with him entirely. When I see him coming, I pretend I'm totally engrossed in a conversation, or a book, or a text message. Once, last week, I just turned around and walked the other way.

"But you know how much getting into Stanford means to him."

"Getting into college means a lot to everyone." I press my feet into the ground, still muddy from a season of rain.

"Don't pretend you don't care, May-Day."

"I'm not," I insist. "But we didn't exactly have the most friendly breakup in the history of Highlands High. I said terrible things."

"I'm sure you didn't really say anything that bad."

"I did," I say firmly.

"But you could still try to be friends—"

"I didn't want to be his friend." I interrupt. "I didn't want to be with him if I couldn't, you know, *be* with him."

"I get that," Serena says. "I do. But maybe you won't always feel that way. Maybe you'll want to be friends someday. And you could, I don't know, keep that option open by doing the right thing now. Go. Congratulate him. Throw in an apology while you're at it."

"For what?" I say, and I'm not being sarcastic. I have so much to apologize to him for that I wouldn't know where to start.

"I don't know. For everything."

"I'm not sure a blanket apology will be enough in this case."

Serena shrugs. "It's a place to start."

I glance at my watch. It's time for my midday dose. "I gotta go." I get up and head for the nurse's office.

I'm on my third pill when I realize that Serena's right. I know how much this meant to Chirag. The truth is, I want to congratulate him.

I take my remaining pills two at a time, eager to get to Chirag before the bell rings for sixth period. Before I lose my nerve.

I have to find him first. I still know his schedule by heart, so I know where to look. But he's not on the benches out front. And he's not near his locker. He's not sitting in a classroom, early for his sixth-period class. I'm about to give up when I think of the one place I haven't looked. Out on the bleachers by the track, where we sat together on our second date. I turn on my heel and head in that direction.

There are plenty of people spending lunch period out here. It's nothing like that January day last year when we sat out here alone.

As I climb up the stairs in the center of the bleachers, only about half of my classmates are staring, averting their eyes, or whispering to the person sitting beside them. I'm not sure if they're used to me or if they're all just too engrossed in their own lives to pay attention to the freak walking amongst them, the one whose pulse is pounding because she's looking for the boy who broke her heart, whether he meant to or not.

I hear his voice, deep and solemn, before I see him. Just the sound of it tightens that string around my rib cage, the one up by my heart.

I spin around, looking for him. He's just a few feet in front of me, a couple of steps higher than where I'm standing. Smiling and handsome in the sunshine, pushing his hair back from his forehead.

He's sitting next to Alexis Smith, her right leg slung across his left. Her short, pale fingers are laced through his long dark ones. She looks away, then rests her cheek on his shoulder. Chirag kisses the top of her head like it's nothing: No big deal, he's kissed it a thousand times before and could kiss it a thousand times more.

The top of my head is the only place he kissed me after my accident.

How long has this been going on? Has Serena been keeping it from me? Or have I just refused to see it all on my own, every time I looked the other way, every time I avoided the places I knew Chirag would be?

The string hanging from my chest tightens again, making my breath come fast and hard. This is what I wanted. I ended it so that he could go on with his life and have the senior year he deserved. He deserves a normal girl like Alexis. A girl he can take to senior prom and who can dance the night away without sneaking off to take her pills. A girl whose hand he can hold without feeling her scars. A girl he can kiss with his eyes open, a girl who gets stared at because she's so pretty, not because she's a monster. I bet that when he tells Alexis he loves her, she'll just say *I love you, too*, instead of shooing him away so that he can't hear her parents' fighting.

I told Ellen that I needed to find new things to look forward to. I need to give up Chirag, just like I gave up the track team. I mean, I know we broke up months ago, but it wasn't until right now, this moment, that I really understood what it meant. Chirag isn't in love with me anymore, not even with the old me. A rational person like Chirag would never be in love with someone who doesn't exist. And the Chirag I fell in love with has disappeared, too. I'm not the only one who's different now.

The string pulls itself so taut that it finally snaps.

THIRTY-NINE

T wo coffees, please," Adam says, smiling his crooked smile at our waitress. "One with milk and sugar, one black."

We're sitting in the diner after Group. He doesn't look away when I take my pills, one right after the other. Tonight, as I gulp them down, he actually sings an old song about how one pill makes you larger and one makes you small until I'm giggling so hard that I can barely swallow the last one.

"Better be careful," I say. "If my mom finds out you're making it harder for me to take my pills, she'll ix-nay this whole relationship."

My tongue trips over the word *relationship*. I mean, I guess that word applies to pretty much every kind of human interaction, but people usually only use it for romantic ones, right? Or not-quite romantic ones, in our case. Maybe tonight will be the night Adam makes his move.

"I don't really get the feeling that you're in the habit of listening to your mother when it comes to who you hang out with."

"Whom," I correct teasingly. Adam rolls his eyes. "Anyway, not listening to her has never made her shut up before." In a singsong voice that sounds nothing like my mother's, I recite: "*Take your pills.*

Have you done your stretches today? Well, I didn't see you do them so do them again. Go to school, to see Dr. Boden, to PT. Chirag will drive you." I shake my head. "I'm so sick and tired of her pushing, pushing, pushing me."

Adam shrugs. "That's what parents do."

"She was always like that. Even before the accident. It really pissed me off. I mean, I was a good kid. I got good grades and ran track and I stayed out of her way when she was fighting with my dad."

"The perfect daughter," he says, but it's clear from his tone that he knows I'm far from it.

"I know," I groan. "I *know*. I could be a brat, and it's been a lot worse since the accident. But she has no idea what this is like. *This*," I say, pointing to my face. "She's so determined for me to handle it the way she wants me to handle it—the way she thinks *she* would handle it. But she has no idea what it's like to be stared at, to look in the mirror at a reflection you still don't always recognize."

"Most people can't understand. That's what Group is for."

I nod. "I know. And I'm grateful. I just can't remember the last time I had a conversation with my mother when she wasn't asking whether I'd done everything she thought I was supposed to do." I close my eyes. I can see it now, the way she scrunches up her nose as she goes through her mental list; her nose has freckles on it, just like mine used to. "Thank god I don't have her nose anymore."

I clap my hand over my mouth. "Oh my god, I can't believe I just said that."

Adam takes a bite of his sandwich. "Said what?" he asks, his lopsided mouth full of turkey club.

"About my nose. Her nose." I point to my face, tracing a finger down the slope of my nose. "*This* nose."

"It's a nice nose."

"Yeah, but it's not *my* nose. I mean, not my *real* nose. My real nose was my mother's nose. This is my donor's nose."

I press my finger to the tip of it: hard and pointy, so different from the nose I had before the accident.

"Let me ask you something," Adam says. "Did you like your nose? The one you had before the accident?"

Slowly, I shake my head. In fact, I'd hated it. I used to whine to Serena about how round and bulbous it was, used to wonder whether Chirag thought it got in the way when he kissed me. "I used to joke that someday, I'd get a nose job or something. You know, upgrade. But I never would ha . I was scared of the surgery." That sounds ridiculous now.

Adam says, "Well, at least now you don't have to."

"Don't have to what?"

"Don't have to get a nose job. Think of your new nose as a bonus."

I shake my head. "*This* isn't the nose I would have chosen. Someone else's nose."

"But you said you got your old nose from your mother." Adam takes another bite, chews and swallows. "Either way, you're walking around with someone else's nose on your face."

Adam is one of the few people in my life who has never even seen a picture of the old Maisie. He doesn't know the way that I used to look, the freckles on my round nose and the dimple in my cheek.

Adam has scars, too. He's broken, just like I am.

Maybe he hasn't tried to kiss me or even just take my hand because he thinks I'm not ready yet. Maybe he thinks I'm fragile.

Maybe *I* have to be the one to make the first move. Maybe it will be the beginning of a lifetime of first moves, because boys will always be worried that I'm too delicate.

Not that there's exactly a line of people waiting to make a first move with me. There's only Adam.

"Hey," I say suddenly, as though I've only just sat down and noticed him sitting across from me, "do you want to go to prom with me?"

"What?"

I press my hands flat on the sticky table, looking at them instead of at him. "I know, it's not traditional for the girl to ask the guy, but it's not like you even go to my school—"

"Or any school. Maisie, I graduated from high school a long time ago."

I look up. "I know, but—"

The look on Adam's face shuts me up. He's mortified.

Oh god, what was I thinking? That just because Adam is damaged, he'd want to go out with me? That just because he has scars, Adam wouldn't be disgusted at the idea of seeing my face up close while we slow-danced, of *feeling* my scars through the layers of my dress? Not that there is a prom dress in the world that could cover them up. I'd need to wear long sleeves, a high neckline. I'll be the only girl at prom dressed like a nun.

No one wants to dance with the striped girl in the ugly dress, her deformed face popping out of its high neckline like some kind of grotesque balloon.

"Maisie—" Adam begins, but I shake my head.

"I've got to go," I say, getting up, relieved that I drove myself here tonight. "I think I left one of my pills at home."

"No, you didn't. I counted them."

"There's a new one," I say as I stand. "Some kind of herbal supplement my mom wants me to start taking." In any other context, the mere suggestion that my mother would want me to take an herbal supplement instead of the scientifically engineered pills my doctors prescribed would make Adam laugh.

Adam doesn't try to stop me, doesn't follow me out of the restaurant and into the parking lot, doesn't hold my car door shut when I try to open it. He's probably relieved that I'm going, relieved to finish his sandwich without my broken face staring at him from the other side of the table, the pathetically deformed girl so desperate for a date, so deluded that she thought someone might actually want her.

I stuff my key into the ignition like I'm stabbing something, ease my foot off the brake as I shift into reverse and back out of the parking spot. At a red light, I close my eyes for just a second.

I try to imagine myself at prom with Adam, what it would have looked like when I walked into the gym with my arm linked through his, the long-sleeved, high-necked dress I would have worn. Instead, I see the backless green dress I planned to wear a year ago. I see myself dancing circles around the boys, giggling in the bathroom with Serena, sneaking out to the parking lot in between songs. And it is Chirag, not Adam, that I see beside me: Chirag's arms circling my waist as we slow-dance, Chirag's lips tickling my cheek as he whispers *I love you.*

Even now, nearly a year later, whenever I am scared, or I can't sleep, or I'm in pain, I still close my eyes and imagine that I'm with Chirag at prom.

Behind me, a car honks. I open my eyes: The light is green. I press down hard on the accelerator.

Too hard. The car lurches forward. I slam on the brakes. More honking from the cars behind me.

My hands are shaking. It's dark out but I forgot to turn on my headlights.

I pull off to the side of the road and rest my head on the steering wheel. I squeeze the wheel so hard it hurts—not just my burned left hand but my normal right hand, too. I can feel my pulse, steady and strong, throbbing in my temples. Again, I see myself in the green dress, happy and carefree, dancing with the boy I loved. I can see the lights flashing on the dance floor, the press of bodies moving to the music.

No matter how hard I try, I can't tell whether that's the old or the new Maisie dancing in the green dress. I can't see whether my left arm is covered in stripes, whether the dress is revealing the scars that snake down the left side of my back. No matter how tightly I shut my eyes, how carefully I concentrate, how much I want it: I can't see my own face.

FORTY

The following Wednesday is the one-year anniversary of my accident, and I don't go to Group. I take the car and drive around in circles, careful to avoid the church and Adam's diner. I watch my left hand as I turn the steering wheel. The scars have faded but they're still there: undeniable and practically glowing in the moonlight.

I haven't skipped Group once since December and I miss it. If I go to Barnard, I'll have to find a group like ours in New York City. For now, maybe I'll have to find another meeting close by. Or maybe *Adam* will. Officially speaking, he's the one who hurt me, so he should be the one to leave, right?

But when I pull into my driveway at the end of the night, Adam is there, sitting on our stoop.

"My dad's car is in the driveway," I say instead of hello. "My parents would have let you in." In fact, there's no missing the fact that my parents are home; I can hear them fighting from here. Silly stuff again: something about gas mileage and commuting. At least they won't have to fight about that if I go to Barnard. I won't need to use my mother's car then.

That's the second time tonight that I thought *if* I go to Barnard, instead of *when*.

Adam shrugs. He doesn't seem the least bit uncomfortable with the shouts coming from the other side of our front door. "I'm not here to see your parents. I'm here to see you. And *your* car wasn't in the driveway."

"It's not really my car. It's my mom's. She just lets me drive it," I explain needlessly, and Adam nods. The silence between us is strained, worse even than the night we first met, when I didn't want to say a syllable more than was absolutely necessary. "I should go inside," I mumble finally.

As I open our front door, I think about the night when Chirag asked me to prom. My parents' shouts sound almost exactly the same, even though the subject has changed.

Now they don't stop yelling until they see that there is someone else with me, someone they've never met, someone whose scars are even worse than mine. I'm mortified by the way they stare. You'd think that they would know better. But then, like Adam and Chirag both said, it's human nature. They can't help it. When I first met him, *I* couldn't help it either.

"This is Adam," I begin. My parents are frozen on opposite sides of the living room, two boxers who've retreated to different sides of the ring. "He's my—" I hesitate. My friend? My sponsor? My almost-until-he-rejected-me boyfriend? "We're in Group together."

My mother's face twists from anger to a saccharine smile. "Adam," she says warmly, walking toward him with arms extended. "How *nice* to meet you." She hugs him. I can't remember the last time she hugged me. She closes her eyes as she squeezes; she looks exhausted, like maybe she's finally sick and tired of fighting. Or maybe like she just really needs a hug.

Adam hugs her back; he's nearly a full foot taller than she is. "Nice to meet you, too." He shakes hands with my father. My parents aren't quite staring anymore; now they're grinning. Like they're excited I have a friend who's even more deformed than I am.

Adam's gaze shifts from my father's face to the pictures on the wall behind him, seeing my old face for the first time.

"Okay, we're going to go to my room," I say quickly. I take Adam's hand—my scarred left one is closer—and pull him along behind me. My parents don't protest, even though they never let me take Chirag to my room, never let me sit with him behind closed doors. For all their talk about how they want me to have a *normal* life, they don't worry about me being behind closed doors with a boy anymore. They know I'm too hideous for anyone to want.

Or maybe, I realize with a twist in my gut, they think *Adam* is too hideous to be a threat. Maybe they can't imagine that *I* would want *him*. Somehow, that's even worse.

Adam sits on my bed while I stand by my desk, taking my pills. I've started to hate my room, to hate the plush peach carpet I picked out when I was ten; the bulletin board peppered with pictures of Serena, Ellen, and Samantha; pictures of Chirag and me; ribbons from meets that I won.

This is the old Maisie's room. The new Maisie doesn't want peach, and she doesn't want to be surrounded with relics of her old life. I'd like to paint the walls white, get a bright white carpet, a white bedspread. A blank slate.

After a few minutes of silence, Adam says, "Maisie, I want to talk about last week."

The final pill sticks in my throat. I gag, cough, then gag some more. Adam stands to help me but I shake my head and reach for my water glass. I drink every last drop of water, forcing the pill down.

"You okay?"

My throat feels like I just rubbed it with sandpaper, but I nod. I sit down on the bed beside Adam.

"We don't need to talk about it," I say softly, rubbing my neck with my hands.

"I *want* to talk about it."

I don't look at him. "Why?"

He scoots closer and puts his arm around me. "Because I owe you an explanation. I didn't handle it very well. Of course I'll go to your prom with you, if you want me to."

"You will?" I say, and Adam nods, smiling his lopsided smile.

I smile back. Maybe my first-ever-first-move wasn't a total failure after all. Maybe it led perfectly into this moment: a boy with his arm around me, smiling down at me. Before I know what I'm doing, I'm leaning closer to Adam, my face against his.

And then, I'm kissing him. The skin around my mouth feels tight. My new nose bumps into Adam's awkwardly. I tilt my head to the side but then my teeth get in the way.

Why is this so hard? I have the same mouth. Everyone said I was so lucky to keep my mouth. Marnie always says that PT for a new jaw is the hardest. And this nose is *smaller*, for crying out loud!

Gently, Adam pulls away. "Maisie," he says carefully, "I meant that I would go to your prom with you—but as a friend."

I drop my face into my hands. My hideous, disastrous, mismatched face.

"I'm sorry," I whisper. "I don't know what I was thinking."

I'm lying. I know *exactly* what I was thinking. That we could be two damaged people together, undressing in the dark, sharing our scars. But all along, he was probably only doing it for Marnie, because she asked him to look out for me and he's hopelessly in love with her. I try to remember each and every time I thought he was flirting with me—each and every time he was just being nice. Of *course* he doesn't want me. Who will ever want me when there are Marnies and Serenas in the world?

"Maisie—" Adam starts, but I shake my head.

"It must be gross, seeing my face so close up."

"No, Maisie—"

"It's okay. I need to get used to the idea—" A lump rises in my throat, so big that it's impossible to finish my sentence.

Adam puts his hands on either side of my face and pulls it toward his so that we're only inches apart. I feel his breath on my skin, feel the scars on his left palm on my cheek.

"Look at me, Maisie," he commands, and I do, even though there are tears in my eyes. But when I see his face, I blink them away. Much to my surprise, I don't see disgust in his eyes, or even pity. "Is it gross," he asks, "seeing my face this close up?"

I don't answer immediately. This close, the first thing I notice is his eyes, hazel with flecks of gold in the irises. Almost yellow, like a cat's. Next, I look at his mouth. I've come to love his crooked smile. I can't imagine him without it.

"Of course not," I say finally.

"Are you horrified, being so close to my scars?"

The first time I saw Adam, I thought the left side of his face looked like someone had chewed it up and spat it out. Now I reach out and trace his scars with my fingers like I'm reading Braille. And in a way, I am reading: Adam's scars tell a story. "No."

He lets go of my cheeks, but I don't back away. "Then why would you think that I'm disgusted by you?"

I drop my hand. An *if, then* statement, the logic so pleasantly undeniable. Still, I shake my head, and a few tears spill over. "But you don't want me—"

Adam shakes his head. "Maisie . . . I have a girlfriend."

I shake my head. "You said you broke up with your girlfriend—"

"With Caroline? Yeah, I broke up with her a long time ago. I heard she got engaged to someone she met in graduate school. She lives in L.A. now."

"But then, who?" I can still smell Adam's cologne, taste his minty breath. "Someone else from Group?"

Adam shakes his head. "Marnie."

"Marnie?" I repeat. "I mean, I knew you had a crush on her, but—"

"What do you mean you knew I had a crush on her?" Adam interrupts. "Did she say something?" He looks so embarrassed that it almost makes me smile.

"She didn't have to. It's obvious every time you say her name." I break Adam's gaze, looking at my lap instead. Quietly, ashamed of what I'm about to say, I add, "But Marnie's so—"

"So beautiful?"

I nod.

"I know," he says seriously. "She's the most beautiful girl in the world." He presses his hands to his stomach, like just thinking of her sets a swarm of butterflies flying across his belly. The romantic kind of butterflies that I thought people like us didn't get to have.

"But . . ." I wipe away what's left of my tears.

"How did I pull that off?" Adam asks for me, grinning. "How did I get a gorgeous girl like Marnie to agree to go out with a freak like me?"

"There's no nice way to ask that question, is there?"

Adam shakes his head. "Believe me, it took me a while to work up the guts to ask her out. But I figured, what do I have to lose? Worst-case scenario, she says no, right?"

"And you'd have to find a new physical therapist rather than risk the humiliation of seeing her every week after having been so harshly rejected."

"Well, that, too," Adam agrees, chuckling. "But . . . look, I know it's super cheesy, but I meant what I said at Group the other night: You have to learn to love yourself before you can love someone else. Because it's only when we love ourselves that we feel worthy of someone else's love."

"You must love yourself a lot to believe you're worthy of Marnie."

Adam laughs. "I guess I do," he agrees. "And Marnie's not scared of a little damage. Or a lot of damage, as the case may be."

"So all this time you were only being nice to me because your girlfriend asked you to?"

"Of course not. I'm nice to you because I like you."

"You mean because you feel sorry for me."

"I mean I *like* you."

"What do you like about me?" I ask, and Adam makes a face, like he thinks I'm fishing for compliments or something. "No, I mean really. I've been trying to . . . I don't know, figure out what kind of girl I am now, after everything that happened."

"That's not a question I can answer for you."

I groan. "We're not in Group now, Adam. I'm not looking for wisdom. I actually want to know. Marnie saw past your injuries to who you were, right? I guess I just need to know what's there—here—besides my injuries. What else people might see."

Adam smiles his lopsided smile. "Well, you're smart, but you know you're smart."

"My grades suck."

He shrugs like grades don't matter. "That's because you're tired. Not because you're dumb."

I sigh. "What else?"

"You're funny."

"Sick jokes that no one outside of Group understands."

He shakes his head. "No. If people outside of Group don't laugh, it's because they have crap senses of humor. You've got a sharper tongue than anyone I've ever met."

"I think my accident sharpened it a bit."

"Hey, who knows what those surgeons did to you while you were unconscious, right?"

"Gross!" I wince, imagining them reaching into my mouth and shaving my tongue into a point. "Maybe I just felt the need to cultivate more of a sense of humor now that I look like this," I add, gesturing to my face.

"Maybe now you just say what you're thinking," Adam counters.

"You don't always have to be so wise," I add, shoving Adam so hard that he falls off the bed.

"You're strong," he adds, laughing as he hits the carpet. "Did I mention strong?"

"Adam, be serious. I'm trying to figure out who I am here!"

"Okay, fine," he says, setting his mouth into a straight line and pulling himself back onto the bed beside me. "You're—I don't know, you're determined."

"Competitive." I sigh. "I've always been competitive."

Adam shakes his head.

"No," he says firmly, "not competitive. You're not trying to beat the people around you. You're just trying to do well, on your own terms."

I cock my head to the side, considering. I think Adam might be right. Maybe somewhere along the way, I stopped trying to make everything into a competition. Maybe Maisie 2.0 isn't actually a loser, like I thought.

After all, you can't *win* at having had a face transplant.

FORTY-ONE

On Monday morning, Serena is waiting for me in the school parking lot. She looks relieved to see me.

"What are you doing here so early?" I ask, closing the car door with my hip.

She nods solemnly. "I was worried that I might not get to you in time."

"In time for what?"

"I didn't want you to find out from someone else."

Before the accident, I would have thought Serena was just being dramatic (which she's always had a flair for being). But before the accident, I was just a normal girl, the kind of girl nothing enormous ever really happened to. Now that my life has been touched by an actual tragedy, the whole world seems more fragile. More *susceptible*. Serena no longer seems dramatic. Maybe she just understood what I didn't know before: Bad things happen every day, even to normal people like me.

"It's about Chirag," Serena says, and something inside of me collapses, like a balloon that's been popped. *Something happened to*

Chirag. Was this how he felt when he heard the news about me? Like he'd never be able to catch his breath again?

One thing I know for certain: Breakup or no breakup, I will take as good care of him as he took of me. I will chauffeur him around town and I'll never scold him for being grumpy or demanding or rude. And I'll be kind—I'll shower him with all the kindness I withheld every day since I got home from the hospital.

"Okay," I say. "I'm ready. Tell me what happened."

Serena takes a deep breath and she doesn't look at me when she says: "He's taking Alexis Smith to prom."

"What?"

"Don't make me say it again," Serena moans. "I know you heard me." She looks like she's actually in pain. So I say it for her.

"He's taking Alexis Smith to prom?"

"Yes." Serena nods solemnly. *"Officially,"* she adds, the same way I would.

I burst out laughing.

"What's funny?" Serena asks.

I shake my head. (Man, do I love being able to shake my head. I wonder if it will always feel like such a luxury.) I'm laughing so hard I can't talk.

"May-Day," Serena says, stomping her foot, "why is this so funny? I dragged myself out of bed at the crack of dawn to make sure I'd get here in time to tell you." She kicks the ground and mutters, "I don't think it's funny."

"I'm sorry," I say finally, catching my breath. "I'm sorry. I know you don't take getting out of bed early lightly."

"Hmmph." Serena pouts.

"It's just, I don't know. I guess—I mean, I knew they were going out, right? Of *course* he was going to take her to prom." Just like of course he was going to take me a year ago.

"I know. But I just thought . . ." Serena hesitates, biting her lip.

"What did you think?"

"I don't know. I thought you still wanted to go with him. You know, since you didn't get to last year."

Suddenly, all traces of my laughter disappear, my mouth resetting itself in a straight line. Serena's right. Part of me did want to go to prom with Chirag, the part of me that still imagines dancing with him when I'm feeling sick or sad. I tried to imagine myself with Adam, but I couldn't. I was still dreaming of going with Chirag, still hoping for that perfect night.

"You don't look so good," Serena says.

If someone said that to me in Group, it would be a joke. The whole circle would erupt into laughter. But here, in the parking lot of our high school, where some of my classmates *still* stare at me, even after all these months, even after they've had plenty of time to get used to the freak in their midst, I answer, "I don't feel so good, either."

"Do you want me to take you to the nurse's office?"

"No." I shake my head. "No, I'm okay."

As we head to homeroom, I can't help wondering: Did he hold up a sign for her, too? Did it say *I love you* the way my sign did?

I bet they're going to rent a limo. He'll wear a perfectly tailored tuxedo and she'll—I don't know what Alexis Smith will wear. She'll be one of the only juniors at the senior prom and I'm sure she'll want to show off. She'll wear something slinky and short, maybe with sparkles down the back and her hair pulled into an updo. Nothing like the matronly nun dress I'd have to wear.

If I were going. Which, obviously, I'm not.

At home later, I rifle through my desk. There it is, the picture I tore out of the magazine over a year ago, still in my top drawer. I open up my laptop and start searching. Surely some site, somewhere, still has my dress.

It takes me more than an hour, but I finally find it on an outlet site. It's on sale—more than half off—because no one wants to wear last year's dress to this year's dance. Even the matching headpiece is on sale.

I sigh. It wouldn't matter if it were free.

I close the page and check my email. There's not much there but junk, which I set about deleting so quickly that I almost delete something else.

An email from Barnard College.

Barnard probably sends an actual *letter* in an extra-thick envelope when they accept you. They probably only send out emails for rejections.

I guess the note from Dr. Boden wasn't enough to make up for my slipping grades, my long list of absences and missed classes, the fact that "track superstar" was no longer part of my application. In the fall, I typed my admissions essay with a pounding migraine and I'm not even sure I had the wherewithal to use spell check before I sent it.

Or maybe they just didn't want a broken girl like me going to their perfect school. I mean, my scars may have faded, but they're still scars. I might be able to make it through the day without need-ing a nap, but I still can't stay awake past ten p.m. and sometimes I still sleep through my alarm. Maybe Barnard knew that some morn-ings, my mother still has to shake me awake.

I stand up and back away from the computer. My heart is pound-ing and I'm flushed and hot, sweat trickling down the back of my neck. The way I felt when I woke from my coma.

Okay, Maisie, get some perspective. This is a college rejection we're talking about, not a life-altering injury.

But it is still life-altering. I mean, it could be. I open my window and let in some air. I wait until goose pimples are blossoming on my arms and legs, even in between the thick scars on my left side. Then I go back to the computer and open the email.

Instead of a note saying *thanks but no thanks*, I see fireworks. Like, cartoon fireworks. And there's music, too. The graduation song. And after the fireworks is the word *Congratulations!* and then finally a note, promising that a package will follow in the mail, but for now, they just wanted to congratulate me on being admitted to Barnard.

I got in.

I thought I would be jumping up and down for joy, but instead, I'm kind of nervous. In fact, butterflies are dancing across my stom-ach. Maybe it's because I finally have to tell my parents about Barnard, convince my mother to let me go, tell Serena I'm not going to Berkeley with her after all.

No. That's not it. I press my hands to my stomach, trying to quiet the adrenaline.

I expected it to be a no-brainer: *If I get in, I'm going.* Thousands of miles from people who know my old face, from my parents' shouts and slamming doors, from my mother's badgering and my father's sad eyes, the ones that miss his pretty little girl, that gaze at my childhood photos with longing. I wanted to be far, far away from all of it. Far away from Chirag and Alexis Smith.

But now I'm not so sure. Without my mother's badgering, who will make sure I get out of bed in the morning? Without my father's sad eyes, without those photos, without Chirag—who will remember me as I used to be?

FORTY-TWO

Early Saturday morning, Adam shows up in running clothes.

"Let's go, Winters," he orders.

I shake my head, still drowsy. "You woke my parents."

"How was I supposed to know you people weren't early risers? Come on, get dressed." He's bouncing on the balls of his feet on our stoop, blowing on his hands to keep warm.

"No one should be that perky at this hour in the morning," I complain, but I hold the door open to let him inside. I used to be a morning person, too. And the truth is, I woke up a few minutes before the doorbell rang.

"Hey!" I shout, suddenly realizing. "I slept through the night." Last night, I didn't dream about my donor. I don't remember dreaming at all.

Adam stops bouncing long enough to step over the threshold and into the living room.

"Do you think it means that I don't care about my donor as much as I used to? I mean, maybe thinking what happened to her *should* keep me up at night."

"It might just mean your body is adjusting to your meds," Adam suggests. When he sees the worried look on my face, he adds, "There are other ways to honor her, you know."

"I don't really know," I answer slowly, sitting down on our terra-cotta stairs.

"Do you think there will ever be a day that goes by that you won't think of her?"

"Of course not." Every time I look in the mirror, I see her, wonder about her. What was she like? Is her family okay? Will they ever know what they did for me?

Adam says, "Maybe that's enough. For now, at least."

"Maybe I could reach out to her family someday. Write them a letter or something." I stop myself. "Not that I could send it. They chose to be completely anonymous."

"Maybe someday they'll be ready to hear from you," he says. "You can always write the letter now and wait to send it. I could help you." Adam reaches for me and squeezes my shoulder. "Now, get dressed. I'll wait for you."

I shake my head. "I can't run."

"They told me the same thing. Didn't stop me." Before I can protest, he continues, "I'm not saying that you shouldn't listen to your doctors. But you also have to live. You have to do the things you love to do. Otherwise, what did we survive all this for?"

"Who are you, Yoda?" I ask. Chirag made me watch all six *Star Wars* movies, even though he said the first two weren't nearly as good as the rest of them. "Seriously, Adam. I tried. It's not just that I'm not supposed to. I really *can't*." Still, the bottoms of my feet itch to be out there. My feet weren't burned in the slightest. They clearly don't understand why the rest of my body is being such a bore. "I'm not a runner anymore," I add solemnly.

"What the heck does that mean? Come on." Adam grins his lopsided smile. "We'll go slow," he promises.

I hesitate. Adam is still bouncing on the balls of his feet, his calf muscles flexing with each spring. Moist air is spilling into the living room through the open front door; I inhale, smelling the early-morning scents I used to know so well: pine needles and coffee, grass and the wind off the bay. My heart starts beating just a little bit faster.

"Okay," I say finally, standing. "But if I hurt myself and get into trouble with your girlfriend I'm not above throwing you under the bus."

"Fair enough," Adam replies.

In my room, I dig through my drawers for my running clothes, then hug them to my body like they're a long-lost friend. In the bathroom, pulling my hair back into a ponytail for the first time since my accident, I catch a glimpse of my face in the mirror. Today, it doesn't surprise me. Right now, at least, it's just what I was expecting to see.

Adam sets the pace, and I follow. I don't try to run alongside him, and I don't try to pass. The fog is so thick that when he gets more than a few steps ahead of me, I can barely see him. I'm cold, my running clothes soaked through with mist and sweat. My feet feel weak. I wince with every footfall. The pain is different now, not as shocking as it was in November, but impossible to ignore. My left side is stiff, slower than my right. The muscles wrapped around my rib cage pound out a dull ache every time my left foot hits the ground. *No, Maisie,* they seem to scream.

Stop it, Maisie.

What are you thinking, Maisie?

This was a bad idea. I can't even breathe this hard through my new nose, so I'm panting through my mouth like a dog.

Turn around, Maisie. Go home.

No, Maisie. No, Maisie. No.

But out loud, in between labored breaths, I manage to whisper the word "*Yes.*"

We're less than half a mile from my house when something clicks inside of me. My body—both sides of it—*remembers* this. I know how to do this: I know how to run.

The ache in my muscles shifts. It hurts, but it's a sweet ache, familiar and warm.

I think it's called muscle memory. Like how riding a bike is supposed to come back to you after decades off two-wheels. Instead of *No, Maisie*, every step is punctuated by my body silently insisting: *I remember, I remember.* I'm not going fast, but I can feel the muscles in my legs waking up, tightening as I climb the hill, shaking beneath my skin. I can feel the breeze on my face, taste the air in my throat. *I remember, I remember.* I drop my head and pick up speed, studying the ground beneath my feet: the moist concrete, the gravel and the dirt filling in all the cracks.

I remember, I remember.

A new girl joined Group about a month ago. Amy. Amy lost both her legs in a car accident—one just below the knee, the other up by her pelvis. She's learning to walk with prosthetics and crutches.

Amy is beautiful. Like stop-on-the-street-and-stare kind of beautiful. The skin on her face is dewy and glowing, but the first time she spoke up in Group, she cried almost nonstop, sobbing that no one would ever want her now, asking all the questions it took me so long to work up the nerve to ask: *Do you have a boyfriend? Did he want you after your accident?*

Later, I told Adam that I kind of hated Amy. When she's sitting down, you can't even tell she's injured. Adam laughed, but he also suggested that there might come a time when I'd be grateful that my injuries were nothing like hers, despite her perfect face.

And Adam was right yet again, because right now, I can't stop thinking about the fact that Amy will never be able to run, not with her own legs, not like this.

I remember, I remember. I remember, I remember.

"What do you remember?" Adam asks suddenly, slowing down so that we're running side by side.

I shake my head, panting. "I didn't realize I was saying it out loud."

"What do you remember?" he repeats.

"This," I answer. "Running. I used to do it on mornings like this, in the fog."

I shake my head. I thought letting go of running was an important step on the way to acceptance. With each footfall, I wonder if I'm taking a step forward or back. I look down and see that my sports bra isn't black, like I thought, but navy blue. For the first time in months, I'm not wearing a stitch of black.

This feels like going forward.

"You were out running the morning of your accident, right?"

"Jeez, Marnie didn't keep much to herself, did she?" It's hard to talk, breathing this hard.

Adam shakes his head. "Not Marnie this time. It was on the news. 'Local girl burned in electrical fire.' They didn't release your name or anything, but after we met I figured it must have been you."

"Oh." I nod. Chirag had mentioned something about that, too. "So?"

"So what?"

"So was it like this that morning?"

I used to make fun of people jogging along with their friends, too busy talking to realize that their form was all wrong, going so slowly that their heart rates were barely elevated while I zipped past. Today, I don't care that I'm going every bit as slowly as those people I used to mock. Adam and I aren't racing like Chirag and I used to. Today, it's a win simply because I'm running.

"The fog wasn't this thick. Then it started to rain halfway through my run. And then—" I stop talking and look down, concen trating on putting one foot in front of the other, savoring the instant of weightlessness in between my steps.

"And then?" Adam prompts.

I shrug, panting heavily. "Thunder. Lightning. I'm sure they covered it on the news."

"But I want to know what *you* remember."

I stop, and so does Adam. The trees tower above us, and beyond them, the bay stretches out. I take a deep breath, tasting bark and salt water.

"I don't . . . I don't remember much," I say. "When I was still in the hospital, I thought maybe that was some kind of trick my brain played on me, like the same way the doctors induced my coma to get me through the pain, my brain induced some kind of amnesia so that I wouldn't remember the trauma."

I pause. "Sometimes I remember the smell. The burning smell." Even though I'm sweating, I shiver. "The neighborhood must have reeked for weeks."

Adam nods, but he doesn't say anything. I close my eyes. Before my accident I never knew what fire sounded like, the enormous *whoosh* when it moves, like the ocean; a wave crashing and receding.

"It was pretty," I say finally, almost smiling. "The sparks looked like fireworks. I love fireworks." There's a bench on the side of the road, one of those lookouts where people stop to admire the view. Adam and I sit down and he hands me a water bottle. I take a long drink.

"They told me later that I was on fire, but I don't remember that. The last thing I remember is the sparks. I thought it looked like the Fourth of July. Chirag and I were going to watch the fireworks together." I kick the ground. "Maybe this year, he'll go with Alexis Smith."

"It'll get easier, you know."

"I don't understand why it's this hard to begin with. We hadn't been close for months, not since my accident. And I'm the one who broke up with him. I *wanted* this."

"You didn't *want* it, Maisie," Adam corrects gently. "Nobody wants this."

I nod. At Group this week, I finally said my biggest fear out loud: *I'm scared that no one will ever want me again.* Everyone in the circle nodded. No one told me that I was worried about nothing; nobody tried to convince me that I was still beautiful on the inside. Adam didn't insist that if he could get a girl like Marnie, any of us could get anyone. Instead, Maureen took my hand in hers and agreed that it was a terrifying thing, to be alone.

"You wanna hear a secret?" I ask suddenly, and Adam nods. "I almost broke up with Chirag last year. Before all this."

"I thought he was the perfect boyfriend," Adam says, mock scandalized.

"So did I!" I agree, laughing. "Serena had to remind me. He used to drive me crazy. But after we'd been dating for a month or so, I guess I got sick of his seriousness and his movies, and I was going to end it."

"His movies?"

"He used to make me watch all his favorite sci-fi movies. And that was fine. I liked a lot of them, but mostly, I just liked experiencing the things he loved with him. Liked that he wanted to share them with me. But he never wanted to watch any of *my* favorite movies with me and that made me nuts."

"So why didn't you break up with him?"

I shrug. "I loved him. I mean, I was falling in love with him then, I guess. I just . . . I think I forgot that we were never perfect. Even before this," I add, gesturing to my face.

"It's not unusual to idealize our lives before."

"Another trick our brains play on us." I pass the water back to Adam. He has to concentrate to get his lips to curl around the lip of the bottle.

"What do you remember?" I ask suddenly. "From the day you were burned?"

Adam doesn't hesitate. "The heat. I mean, it was the desert and we were loaded down with all this equipment, with helmets, with boots. It was so hot. And then I just took one step too far, and there was a sound like nothing I'd ever heard before. Did you know I lost seventy percent of my hearing in my left ear?"

I shake my head.

"Acoustics are lost on me now," Adam says, and I think about all those injuries I'd wanted to understand. The wedding pictures of the surfer whose arm was bitten off by a shark, the snowboarder who went back to competition after a traumatic brain injury. On the news last night, the last story was about runners in the Paralympics. I swear my mother turned the volume up on that story to make sure I heard it. She didn't know that I already know all about the Paralympics, thanks to Michael from Group.

I tighten my ponytail and sigh. "Man, my mother would do back-flips if I were more like you."

"What do you mean?"

"You're the person she wanted me to be. You have it so together, like you're my freakin' spirit guide through this journey, or whatever it's supposed to be."

Adam laughs so loud that I jump out of my skin. "Are you kidding?"

"I'm serious," I insist, punching his arm. "You were probably so polite to your doctors. You never sat around thinking: *Why did this happen to me? It isn't fair!*" I shrug. "Things like that."

"Of *course* I did. When I first got home, I spent a lot of time shouting at the heavens." Adam tilts his head skyward. "You know: *Why me? Why me?* You might have trouble believing this, but I was kind of a jerk in high school. Everything had always come so easily to me: girls, sports, grades. All those things seemed so important before I enlisted."

I shake my head. It's impossible to imagine Adam like that.

Adam takes a deep breath. "I never told anyone this. Not Group. Not even Marnie. For a long time, I wished I'd died. Wished I hadn't been some miracle survival story. I thought it would be better to be gone than to live like this." He runs his fingers through his hair, and I see the smallest of burns on his scalp, bald patches that are normally covered by the longer strands from above. "But I never told anyone how I felt. How could I? Some of my friends died over there. Some of them died that *day*, from that same explosion. And even some of the guys who made it back home . . . some of them were in a lot worse shape than I was, inside and out, you know?"

I lean back against the bench, genuinely surprised that Adam wasn't always as wise as he is now.

"What happened that changed things?"

Sheepishly, Adam says, "I broke my brother's nose." He looks so serious that I burst out laughing.

"It's true," he insists. "I picked a fight and we got into it the way we used to when we were kids. He was careful to keep his punches on my right side, though," he adds, laughing. "My mom watched for a few minutes, letting us rip into each other, before she literally came between us."

"What took her so long?"

"I think she knew I'd been itching for a fight for months. Guess she thought that after everything my face had been through, my brother's face could take a few punches for my sake. And afterward, when she yelled at us and our dad tossed us steaks to hold over our black eyes—I don't know. I can't explain it. For months, people had been saying what would my lost friends give—what would their loved ones give—to be in my shoes, you know?" I nod. Adam continues, "I needed time to understand that myself. People said it every day but it didn't make any difference to me until I really *felt* it on my own."

A lump rises in my throat. "I know I should feel lucky. That's what everyone says—the doctors, the nurses, my parents. I'm such a lucky girl. My donor—" I shake my head.

"The doctors, the nurses, your parents—they don't have to live in there." He presses two fingers to my forehead. "They don't understand that this isn't some switch we can flip. It's more like . . ."

"A dimmer switch," I suggest, and Adam laughs.

"Yes, perfect! I'm going to steal that line next time I have a speaking engagement."

"I expect a deposit in my checking account every time you say it."

Adam nods. "Fair enough. But seriously, you're right. We come out of the darkness slowly. It takes a long time to feel lucky after something like this happens to you."

"I don't feel lucky," I whisper. "I don't even remember what it's like to feel lucky." I run my fingers along my thighs, tracing the seams of my leggings. "The old Maisie was lucky."

"The old Maisie?"

I nod. "You know, the girl I was before the accident. I told you, I've been trying to figure out who this new Maisie is. Maisie 2.0."

"Maisie 2.0?" Adam echoes. "What are you, a computer program?"

"It's not funny!" I say adamantly. "I've given this a lot of thought."

"I'm sure you have," Adam says, but he's struggling not to laugh.

"I've been trying to, I don't know, cultivate a new personality, in opposition to my old one. Like, if the old Maisie was on the track team, then the new Maisie would have to try yoga. If the old Maisie woke up early, the new Maisie would learn to sleep past noon. If the old Maisie had a boyfriend, the new Maisie would be perpetually single."

"Those aren't personality traits, Maisie. Those are just things you do."

I wiggle my toes inside my sneakers, stretch my arms over head, releasing the ache in my muscles. "I thought the new Maisie couldn't be a runner. I thought it was progress, that I'd accepted that about her."

"And now?"

"Now I think she's the kind of runner who needs to take a rest after a half a mile. Which the old Maisie would have totally laughed at."

Adam shakes his head. "How do you know what the old Maisie would have done, if she were here? The old Maisie wouldn't be here right now. *She* would never have met *me*."

Adam stands and so do I. "Look," he begins, "I'm not saying that what happened to us didn't change us. There is definitely a before and an after and a whole slew of changes in between. But you can't figure out who you are by taking inventory."

"But so much is different now. Not just my face."

"Yes," Adam concedes, "you're different. You've gone through a lot this past year and these kinds of experiences leave all sorts of scars behind. But like you said, it's a dimmer, not a switch. Your life will continue to shift and change the more time that goes by—which, by the way, it would have whether you'd been burned or not. The bottom line is that right now, in this moment, you're *this* Maisie. The girl standing in front of me. And instead of wondering what the old Maisie would have done or how the new Maisie should feel, just ask yourself two questions: What do *you* want? What will *you* do?"

I take a deep breath, filling my lungs with heavy cold air, and press my feet into the ground, imagining that I can feel the wet asphalt under the rubber of my sneakers. Maybe I'll never run the way I used to, but I *can* run. And I will, today at least.

I look at Adam and grin. "*This* Maisie is going to race you back home." I take off down the hill. I might not be able to win as often as I used to, but that doesn't mean I can't enter a race once in a while.

Later, I leave the lights on when I look in the mirror. My cheeks are rosy around my scars, still flushed from my morning run.

FORTY-THREE

I can't remember the last time we went shopping together!" Serena squeals the next afternoon. I promised to help her find a prom dress, so here I am, my arms laden with about a hundred pounds of organza and taffeta that Serena just *has* to try on.

"I was too busy avoiding reflective surfaces to risk stepping foot inside a department store," I answer, and Serena laughs her great big laugh. There are mirrors around every corner of the store, and the lighting is bright and unforgiving. Glimpses of me are everywhere.

This morning, I found a black ribbon in the closet where Mom keeps all of our Christmas detritus. I tied it around my wrist like a bracelet, a tiny symbol that I'm still mourning. I finger it now, playing with the frayed edges.

In the dressing room, there are mirrors on all four walls. I see my face from more angles than ever before. From the right side, with no scars running up my neck, my face looks almost normal, like maybe I was born with this chin and these cheeks. The scar under my chin, where they attached the chin to my neck, has nearly disappeared altogether.

I can't stop looking.

I'm so distracted that when Serena—inspecting herself in yet another perfect dress—says, "You can go by yourself, you know. I am," it takes me a second to realize what she's talking about.

Oh, right. Prom.

"That's different. You're going by yourself because you couldn't decide which boy to say yes to." Serena got asked four times by four boys, and I'm sure there were dozens more who couldn't work up the nerve to ask her. Date or no date, she'll be on someone's arm all night if she wants to be.

"It wasn't that I couldn't decide which boy to say *yes* to," Serena insists as she pays for her dress—gauzy and nearly transparent, with champagne-colored sequins down the back—"it was that I couldn't decide which boy to say *no* to."

Serena swings her shopping bag back and forth as we walk through the store. If I go to Barnard next year, I will miss her so much.

"I'm lucky that dress was on sale," she adds suddenly. "Otherwise it would have been way out of my budget. I mean, I've been making extra money babysitting ever since my dad got laid off, but—"

"Your dad got laid off?" I interrupt.

Without looking at me, Serena nods.

"When?"

"A few months ago."

"Why didn't you tell me?"

She shrugs. "I didn't want to—I don't know. You'd just broken up with Chirag and you were still so tired all the time. It's not like you had any energy left over to worry about my problems."

At once, I'm aware of another string around my rib cage, a string that's been there all along but that I've never actually felt before because it's never been pulled quite so tight. This is the string that links me with Serena: This string keeps all of our shared memories, from our first game of hide-and-seek to each of our first kisses. It's soft as silk and loose as a pair of perfect jeans because it's always just been there; even with everything that's happened, even when I imagined moving away and finding a new best friend, *this* string has never threatened to snap, not once, not even close. Because Serena and I have always been best friends, and Serena at least never doubted, not for a second, that we always would be.

Until now.

"I'm really sorry," I begin.

"For what?" Serena asks absently. She walks toward another rack of clothes, even though she's already bought her dress and isn't the least bit interested in any others.

"I haven't been a good friend since I got home."

"It wasn't your fault."

"Maybe it wasn't," I concede. "But if I don't try harder, then it will be." *If, then,* just the way I like it. I reach for Serena's hand and hold it with both of my own. I squeeze tight, and the skin of my left hand barely even aches in protest. Marnie would be thrilled.

"You can tell me," I say, "I can take it."

Serena stops and looks up. She smiles, but her eyes are bright with almost-tears. "Okay," she begins. "You were a crappy friend. For months."

I nod. "I know."

"You never asked how *I* was doing, and you never let me ask how you were doing—"

"I know."

"And now you're not even excited about Berkeley, and I've been looking forward to this for my whole life, so can't you at least be excited for *me*?"

"You're right," I agree. "And," I add slowly, "I have to tell you something. I might not be going to Berkeley." I pull her to sit beside me on a nearby bench. I tell her about Barnard. I explain that I wanted it more than I wanted anything else since my accident, but now I'm not so sure. I apologize for keeping this from her. Say that I'm sorry for keeping so much from her: that my parents are fighting again, that I go to a support group on Wednesdays, that I tried to kiss a twenty-five-year-old boy named Adam—

"What?!" she squeals. "That sounds like something I would do. Way to go, May-Day!"

And I tell her that it hurts so much that Chirag is going to prom with Alexis Smith, and I don't know what to do about it. I want him to get to be with a pretty, normal girl like Alexis, and I want to move on, too. But it also aches that he's with someone else.

"And," I say finally, "I've missed you."

"You've seen me almost every day."

"That's not what I mean. I miss hearing your stories. I miss being your friend. You've been my friend, but I haven't been yours for a long time."

Serena's tears finally overflow and there's a lump in my throat when I pull her into a tight hug. The string between us loosens gently, resuming its easy residence on my rib cage, so that once more, I can't even feel it.

But I know it's there.

"Come on," Serena says, wiping her eyes when we finally let go of each other. "I've got an idea."

———

"*This* is your idea?" I ask twenty minutes later, when Serena has planted me into one of the tall chairs at the makeup counter on the ground floor of the department store.

"You said you wanted to be a good friend to me again. And, as a good friend, you have to do whatever I say."

"I don't think that's what being a good friend means."

"Today it does."

A makeup artist is brushing tinted moisturizer all over my face. The liquid feels slick and rich soaking into my skin—the old parts and the new. It smells good.

Serena decided that I needed a total makeover. She didn't tell the makeup artist that I'd been in an accident or had a face transplant. Surely the woman can see the scars on my cheeks, can see that my forehead is dotted with freckles while the rest of my skin is clear, but she's too polite to ask questions.

The old Maisie never really wore much makeup and I almost say so out loud, but I remember what Adam said and keep my mouth shut. This Maisie, *this* girl, is getting a makeover with her best friend.

"What gave you this idea?" I ask Serena finally. The makeup artist tells me to look at the ceiling while she brushes on eyeliner. It tickles the delicate skin beneath my eyelashes and I concentrate to keep from sneezing.

"Promise you won't get mad?" Serena sounds more shy and tentative than I've ever heard her before.

"Of course."

"Well, I've been reading a lot about recovery. You know, from surgeries where you look different from the way you looked before."

"You have?" It's not a very Serena-like thing to do. Maybe what happened to me changed her, too. It changed Ellen, and she and I weren't nearly as close.

Serena nods. "Ever since Halloween. You didn't just look different. You *were* different. Things were never going to be the way they used to be. But even if you were different, I still wanted you to be my best friend." Her voice is quiet and serious. I pull away from the makeup artist and hug her again.

"I'll always be your best friend," I whisper fiercely. I mean it. I thought I wanted distance from everyone who knew my old face, but that's not worth losing Serena.

"What if you go to Barnard?"

"Wherever I go. No matter what. No matter how many new noses and cheeks I go through."

Serena laughs. Serena always laughs at my jokes, even the ones I make about my injuries, the ones I thought no one outside of Group could possibly find funny. Maybe Adam was right; maybe I really am funny and anyone who doesn't laugh—like Chirag—just doesn't get my sense of humor.

"Don't start crying. You'll mess up your makeup before it's even finished," Serena says finally, pushing me back into my chair. "So anyway, on one of the websites, someone had posted a story about taking her sister to get her makeup done after her surgery."

"Did she have a face transplant, too?"

Serena nods. "Partial. Nose and mouth. The sister said that it really seemed to help."

"I'll take all the help I can get," I say, but Serena doesn't answer. She looks like there's something she wants to ask me, but she doesn't know how.

"It's okay," I offer quietly. "You can ask me anything."

"What's it like?" she asks finally.

I shrug, cocking my head to the side so that the makeup artist brushes bronzer onto my ear instead of my cheek. She clucks her tongue at me and I straighten my neck. She corrects her work carefully, her face as close to mine as Adam's was the other night.

"It's like . . . you know when you get a new haircut? Like maybe the stylist cut your hair four inches shorter than you asked her to, and every time you look in the mirror, the new cut kind of takes you by surprise. 'Cause when you weren't looking in the mirror you'd managed to forget how short your hair was, and that you'd never wanted it to look like that? And then when you're in the shower, you still pour enough shampoo for your long hair even though you don't need nearly that much anymore?"

Serena nods.

"But eventually it surprises you less, and then less, and then less. Until sometimes—not always, but sometimes—when you look in the mirror, it's what you expect to see. It's like that, only, I don't know. That times a million, I guess."

"But with a haircut, you can tell yourself that it'll grow back."

I nod, and the makeup artist sighs heavily. I bet she can't even imagine what it's like to have your head completely immobilized.

"At first, I think part of me did think it would grow back. I mean, not actually *grow* back, but sometimes it was hard to believe that this wasn't temporary, that I wouldn't go back to the old me eventually. I knew what had happened, but I just couldn't quite *believe* that it was forever."

Maybe Chirag couldn't believe it either. Maybe that's what he meant, deep down, when I heard him say that he couldn't break up with me until I was *better*.

"But you don't believe that anymore?" Serena asks as the makeup artist coats my lashes with mascara; I wonder how closely she's following our conversation.

Before I can answer Serena's question, the makeup artist says, "Never use black mascara." She explains that gray is better for me since I'm so fair. She rubs concealer onto the pink scars on my cheeks, and finally finishes by brushing blush across my cheeks, my forehead, the bridge of my nose. I like the feel of the brush against my skin, as soft as rabbit fur.

"There you are," she says, holding a mirror up in front of me.

I never knew makeup could make such a difference. There is purple powder on my eyelids and along my lashes; my cheeks are rosy, the way they look after a run. And my skin—it's not flawless, but it's smoother somehow. You can still see where my old skin stops and my new skin starts, but the transition is fuzzy, blurred. My scars look lighter. I trace them gently, the same way I do when I'm alone in my room at night.

"I'm sorry," the makeup artist says softly. "I just couldn't cover them up completely."

"It's okay," I say. "You did a beautiful job."

"You look so pretty, Maisie," Serena says, and I shake my head. *Pretty* is beside the point, and it's not the right word for how I look anyway. Right now, I look *normal*. I don't look like the old Maisie, but like Adam said, the old Maisie has been gone for a long time now. She died, along with my nose, my cheeks, my chin. I spin the ribbon around my wrist, fingering the knot that keeps it tied tight.

I look away from the mirror and lock eyes with my best friend. "No," I say firmly, answering the question she asked a few minutes ago, "I don't believe that anymore—I know there's no going back."

Finally, officially, I know I've reached the final stage: *acceptance.*

FORTY-FOUR

n her car later, Serena says, "There's something I really want to tell you."

"Tell me."

She shakes her head. "Not here." She changes lanes, pulling onto the freeway. "Let's go for a drive."

Twenty-five minutes later, we're hiking through the tawny hills behind the Golden Gate Bridge, the ground so dry that it's hard to believe we ever had a rainy season at all. It's dusk and the fog is rolling in, bringing the temperature down at least ten degrees, but I'm sweating from the effort of climbing. This definitely qualifies as rigorous exercise.

"Will you please tell me what we're doing here?" I pant at Serena's back. She hasn't turned around since we got out of the car. Just led the way up the hills and expected me to follow. "This is ruining my makeup!" I shout, even though that's the kind of thing Serena would say, not me.

Serena finally stops walking. "I guess this is close enough," she says. "I don't know exactly where he did it."

Catching my breath, I ask, "Exactly where who did what?"

"Chirag. He didn't want me to tell you, but I think you should know."

"Know what?"

"About junior prom."

"Look, if this is going to be a story about how he danced with other girls all night, I'd rather not hear it. Or is that why you dragged me up here? So I could fling myself from the cliffs when I heard it?"

"Don't be so dramatic, Maisie, jeez," Serena says, but she doesn't laugh. In fact, maybe I've never seen her looking so serious.

"Serena," I say softly, "what are we doing here?"

"Chirag didn't go to prom last year."

"He didn't?"

"Of *course* not. Seriously, did you really think he was going to go when you were in the hospital, in a coma they'd put you in because you were in too much pain to wake up?"

I shake my head. "I don't know. Maybe." I press my fingers to my mouth, blowing on them to keep warm. "Maybe I just didn't want to think about him all alone at home, waiting for me. Waiting for the phone to ring so that my parents could tell him whether I was going to wake up again or not."

"He wasn't home."

"Where was he?"

"He was here."

"Here?"

"Well not exactly *here*, here," Serena shrugs, stomping her feet. "But around here somewhere."

"How do you know?"

"Because he got arrested."

"What?" I'm as shocked by this as I was when I first heard that there was such a thing as a face transplant. It sounds just as impossible. Just as much something that happens in movies, but not in real life.

Serena sits cross-legged on the ground and pulls me down to join her.

"After the fire, that branch that ripped up the wires on your street was chopped down by some city workers, along with the rest of the tree. They said it wasn't stable or something. They dragged the wood to the side of the road and told your parents that in a few days it would be hauled away by the sanitation department to be turned into mulch or whatever. And that drove Chirag crazy. That this branch had changed everything, but it was just being treated like regular garbage."

It's hard to imagine Chirag being driven crazy by anything at all. "What does this have to do with Chirag getting arrested?" I ask impatiently.

"I'm getting to it," Serena says, squeezing my hand. "So the night of junior prom, Chirag loaded the wood into the back of his car and drove here."

"Here? Why did he do that?"

"I asked him. He said something about the Fourth of July. I didn't know what he was talking about."

Slowly, my lips curl into a smile.

"What?" Serena asks. The sun is just beginning to set, casting pink light across my best friend's face.

"We were going to watch the fireworks together. Up here in the mountains."

Serena nods. "I guess that explains it. He brought the wood here and started a bonfire. Which is totally illegal up here, you know, because of the drought and the risk of forest fires. He said the branch had burned down to almost nothing when the rangers came for him."

I nod, trying to imagine Chirag standing up here all by himself, building a fire and watching it burn until the branches that changed my life forever—and maybe his life, too—burned down to embers, to ash, to smoke. It's difficult to imagine my rational, levelheaded ex-boyfriend doing something so over the top.

"His parents thought he was losing his mind or something," Serena continues. I nod; I probably would have thought the same thing. "They were convinced that the arrest on his record would keep him out of Stanford. They wanted him to stop calling your parents, stop asking to visit you, and they certainly weren't happy when you came home and he drove over to visit you the first chance he got. Like you were some kind of bad influence or something."

I picture Chirag, patiently explaining that I could hardly have been a bad influence when I was in a coma at the time. Using logic even after the least logical thing he'd ever done. It makes me laugh out loud. But soon, I'm crying, too.

It wasn't just a bonfire that Chirag built in these mountains. It was a funeral pyre.

Chirag understood, months before I did, that something—a part of me, a part of *us*—had died. He knew it was over, and he mourned in a big way. That's why he could be so calm, talking about us at Halloween; why he could offer me a ride even after we'd broken up; why my touch startled him at the restaurant in Sausalito. He'd already been through the messy part: the nonscientific, somewhat irrational, and maybe even melodramatic work of breaking up.

Chirag understood, months before I did, that we had to say good-bye.

Serena hands me a tissue so I can blot my tears away before I totally destroy my makeover. I wish I could have been here when Chirag set the fire. I think I would have liked seeing that branch go up in smoke. Would have liked seeing Chirag's less scientific side.

And I wish I could have figured out how to say good-bye to him sooner. Instead, I dragged it out until our beautiful relationship was messy and ugly, so that now I can't even be civil when we see each other at school. I guess I'm more my parents' daughter than I realized.

"The night we broke up, I said—" I take a deep breath. I've never told anyone exactly what I said, not even Adam. "I told him I never loved him."

Serena whistles. "Why did you say that?"

"I thought I had to. I wanted him to hate me. So that he wouldn't—I don't know. So that he'd be able to move on. So that he wouldn't feel guilty, going to prom with Alexis Smith. But now . . ." I pause.

"What now?" Serena prompts.

"Now it just feels like this terrible lie." I sigh, twisting the black ribbon around my wrist until the threads that hold it together snap. It falls to the ground and before I can pick it up, the wind blows it out of my reach, into the fog, where I can't see it anymore.

"Maybe it's time for me to tell him the truth," I say finally.

When I get home, I head straight to my computer. I don't even have to search; I remember exactly where I saw my dress. I don't hesitate before clicking the purchase button; it's so inexpensive now that my mother probably won't even notice the charge on the credit card they gave me years ago *for emergencies only.*

I have a plan, and I need the dress to carry it out. So this is kind of an emergency.

FORTY-FIVE

'm taking my evening dose when there's a knock on my door. Mom never waits for a response before barging in (and Dad never really comes in here anymore), so there are a few seconds of silence before it occurs to me to shout, "Come in."

"Your father and I need to talk to you," Mom says solemnly. She looks shy, lingering in my doorway with one leg wrapped around the other, fidgeting like a nervous middle schooler. I'm taken aback by her quiet, polite approach, as though I'm a stranger and not the daughter she bosses around twenty-four hours a day. I follow her down the stairs and into the living room, the terra-cotta tiles cool beneath my bare feet. Dad is sitting on the couch facing the television, but the TV is muted. The images cast flickering shadows across his face.

He looks every bit as serious as my mother, who sits down beside him. I sit in the chair across from them, trying to remember the last time we all three sat in the room without someone fighting—either Mom and Dad, or Mom and me. The silence is strange after all that shouting; I've heard about the calm before the storm, but no one ever talks about the calm that comes after it.

"Your father and I have something to tell you," Mom begins softly. Her voice sounds small, like we're talking on the phone with a terrible connection. In fact, all of her seems small: She's sitting with her legs folded beneath her body, curled away from my father like she wants to make sure there isn't the slightest chance they might touch each other.

Mom opens her mouth to continue, but nothing comes out. She does this three times before my father finally says, "Your mother and I are separating."

I shouldn't be surprised—not after all of this time, all of their fights—but I am. I actually gasp. They seemed so close when I was in the hospital, and then when I first got home. Maybe, after all this time, after all the years they've spent fighting, I never really believed they'd ever go through with breaking up.

Dad continues, "We wanted to wait until you were well enough before we—"

"Wait," I interrupt. "How long have you been planning this?"

Dad glances at Mom like he's asking permission. I guess he won't have to do that for very much longer. "A while," he says finally.

I look at my mother. "How long?"

Softly, she says, "Since before your accident."

So they've been waiting, all this time, waiting for me to be—what? Better? Cured?

Just like Chirag was waiting.

"Are you telling me that if I had never gotten hurt, you would have broken up a year ago?"

Almost in unison, my parents nod.

"So in the hospital, all that comforting each other—that was all an act?" Was it for my benefit? It's not like their united front made things easier for me.

"Of course not," my mother says quickly, and her voice sounds normal again. Strong. Loud. I'm surprised to discover that I prefer it that way.

"So what was that?"

"It was two parents, two people with a long history, taking care of each other in a desperate time."

"Oh," I say dumbly. I wonder if, at any point during my recovery, they actually thought their marriage could be saved. That there could be a silver lining to all this. Looking at them now, on opposite ends of the couch, I doubt it.

"Your father is moving out tonight," Mom says softly.

"Where are you going?" I look around for packed bags by the door, the way it is in the movies, in books. Some sign that he's moving out.

"To an apartment in the city," he says. "I rented it a few months ago."

Wow. I guess they really have been planning this for a while.

"I know it's late, but I'd love it if you'd drive me if you're not too tired."

"Why can't you drive yourself?"

"I'm leaving my car here for your mother. Since you use her car now."

I can't believe we're talking about cars. But then, I guess it's the logistics that hit you after a breakup. Like how I had to find my way around once Chirag wasn't there to chauffeur me. Or once I wouldn't let him chauffeur me.

"Maisie," Dad prompts. "Will you drive me?"

I glance at my mother. If I say yes, does that mean I'm taking his side?

I can't believe they kept this from me, this secret, for so many months—and then I remember that I have a secret, too.

Instead of answering Dad's question, I say: "I have something to tell you guys, too."

I tell them *my* secret: Barnard. I tell them that I'd wanted to live somewhere where no one knew my old face. I say that I'm not sure where I want to go anymore, that I need some time to think about it. I wait for my mother to insist that I'm not strong enough to move someplace so far away, that I need to be closer to my doctors, closer to home, closer to *her*. Instead she says, "I'm glad you told us. I had no idea you felt that way."

"Come on, Mom, can't you imagine how difficult it is to go to school with kids who keep looking at you like they're expecting to see your old face?" I find myself gazing at the wall of photos behind the couch. I wonder how long it will be before she takes down her wedding photo. Or the pictures of my dad's parents and grandparents. Surely she won't want those around once they're divorced.

Maybe those photographs will make her feel the way I feel when I see pictures of me from before. Maybe pictures of a face that doesn't exist anymore aren't all that different from pictures of a marriage, a family, that doesn't exist anymore.

Now Mom follows my gaze, looking at the wall behind her. When she turns back to face me, her eyes are very bright. "No," she answers finally. "I can't imagine what that's like. But I hope that someday you'll tell me."

She smiles, and I do, too.

––––––––––

It's dark when I drive my father across the bridge and into the city. The fog is so thick that I can't see the tops of the orange arches of the Golden Gate.

My father didn't load any bags into the car; no clothes, no toiletries, no mementos. When I ask him about it, he answers that he'd already brought most of what he needed to the apartment over the past few weeks.

We're coming off the bridge, driving through the Presidio and into the city. My dad's new apartment is in the Marina, my favorite neighborhood in San Francisco. I always hoped I'd move here after college, imagined Serena and me sharing a tiny apartment we could barely afford. I never thought my father would beat me here.

Now he's humming to fill the silence in the car. It takes me a second to recognize the song: It's his old lullaby.

"Stop," I say finally. "I never want to hear that song again."

"What?" he asks absently. I'm not sure he realized what he was humming.

"Maisie Rose Winters. Pretty name for a pretty girl. Maisie Rose Winters. Pretty name for a pretty girl," I sing, practically spitting the lyrics. "You're going to have to come up with something new, Dad. I'm not pretty anymore."

I catch a glimpse of myself in the rearview mirror. I'm still wearing the makeup from this afternoon: blue eyes ringed with dark liner, cheeks pink with blush, scars heavy with cover-up that's beginning to flake off.

I pull up in front of his new building, but I leave the motor running. I want him to jump out and wave from the curb so that I can drive away before I start crying, before he can see my makeup drip and smear all over my face. I keep both hands firmly on the wheel and stare straight ahead.

"Maisie," Dad says. "Look at me."

I shake my head. I'm crying. "I know you can't stand looking at me. You've worked late practically every night since I've been home from the hospital just to avoid me."

"It wasn't you I was avoiding," he explains softly. He reaches across the car and puts his hands on my shoulders, forcing me to turn.

"You wanted me to have this surgery so that you could have your daughter back."

"What are you talking about?"

"I heard you in the hospital, arguing with Mom." More words I never thought I'd say out loud make their way out of my mouth. "The other parents"—I gulp—"the ones who had their kids back after a transplant surgery. But you didn't get your daughter back. I'm still too different."

He shakes his head and presses his thumbs to my face, brushing away my tears. I can feel the ridges of his knuckles, the callus on his right fingertip, different textures, just like mine.

"Did I ever tell you the story of how your mother and I picked out your name?"

I shake my head. What does that have to do with anything?

"We weren't like the other parents at the hospital, the ones who knew their babies' names months before they were born. We didn't have a clue—sure, we'd spent the past nine months tossing names around, trying to see what would stick, but nothing sounded right. Finally, we decided that we'd wait until we met you. I still remember exactly what I said to your mom. I said, 'It's ridiculous to try and name someone we haven't even met yet.' I said, 'She'll tell us what her name is.'"

He pauses, smiling. "I have never been more scared than I was the day that you were born. Not even the day of your accident," he adds when he sees me opening my mouth to object. "What were we thinking, bringing someone into the world when we didn't even have the wherewithal to name her? But then, there you were. My god—Maisie, you were the ugliest little thing I'd ever seen."

"What?" I ask, brushing away the last of my tears. I've only ever heard him say that I'd been a beautiful baby.

"You were covered in goo and kind of purply. And your face was all smushed and flat and your head was pointy. And you were screaming—it was the most ghastly sound I'd ever heard. It was nothing like what everyone said it'd be, all magic and butterflies." He's laughing, and soon I am, too.

"I thought *What have I gotten myself into?* Then they handed you to me, and you struggled and squirmed in my arms. You were so tiny but somehow you felt so heavy, so solid, so *strong*. I thought: *This girl is stronger than anything. Stronger than me. Stronger than her mother. She'll take on the world someday.* And I thought, *A girl this strong needs a pretty name.*"

"Why?"

He smiles at the memory. "So that people wouldn't see you coming."

"But what about that song?"

He shrugs. "Do you know how many different things I used to sing to you to get you to fall asleep?" He holds his hands out like a conductor in front of a symphony. "*Maisie Rose Winters, singsong* name for a singsong girl. *Maisie Rose Winters, dreamy name for a dreaming girl.*" He shrugs. "Pretty is just the one *you* remember."

"But the way you look at me ever since I got home—like you're disappointed that I don't look the way I used to."

He shakes his head and leans forward, his face close to mine like he wants to make sure I hear every word he says. "I've never been disappointed in you a day in your life," he says firmly. "I was just sad. Sad because *you* were sad, and there was nothing I could do to fix it." I bite my lip, wondering if he'd have told me this if I'd just said what I was thinking sooner.

Dad adds, "That's why your mother and I didn't want to tell you about us any sooner. We didn't want to make you any unhappier than you already were."

They weren't in denial, they were protecting me. Maybe that was Chirag's plan all along, too: He knew it was over and said good-bye to us a long time ago. To him, *better* didn't mean that I had to go back to being who I was before. Instead, he was waiting for me to be ready to say good-bye myself.

I take a deep breath. "So why tell me now?"

He loosens his grip on me so that we're facing each other, our foreheads almost touching. "Well," he says quietly, "you seemed like you weren't so sad anymore."

FORTY-SIX

A dam is the one person who knows my plan for prom, and I only told him so that he'd stop offering to go with me if I wanted him to. He's become so much like a big brother that when I think about it, it's actually pretty gross that I tried to kiss him.

"I want a full report," he insists. I promise to tell him everything.

It takes me a long time to put on my makeup, and not just because I'm carefully following the instructions the makeup artist at the mall gave me. I stare at my face in the mirror, trying to decide whether to layer concealer over the scars on my cheeks the way that she did. No matter how much cover-up I use, the scars will still be visible. There's no hiding the fact that my face has been through trauma.

I pull my hair back, twisting it into a bun. Serena will be here any minute. I told her I wanted her to stop here on her way to the school so I could see her in her dress. The last thing she'll expect is to see me all dressed up like this.

I decide not to use any concealer.

I pull the green dress from my closet. It arrived a few weeks ago, and I quickly stuck it in the back of my closet, where it's been waiting ever since. I never even tried it on. Now the material is soft beneath my fingers, the softest thing I think I've ever touched. I shiver as it slides down my body, rippling like liquid over my scars.

After Halloween, I said I'd never go to a Highlands High party again. But this Maisie knows better than to ever say *never*.

I can't reach the zipper that snakes up the side. I try as hard as I can, even twisting a hanger into a hook, but nothing works.

"Mom!" I shout, opening my door and hurrying downstairs.

My mother is sitting on the couch, staring at the TV, which isn't even on. The house feels empty since my father moved out, emptier than it should from just one person's departure. It's so quiet without my parents' shouts echoing through the rooms. Now the click of my high heels coming down the stairs sounds like thunder. I don't think I've ever seen my mother look more surprised.

"What are you all dressed up for?" she asks, getting up from the couch and joining me at the foot of the stairs.

"Prom is tonight."

"You're going to the prom?"

I nod. "But I can't zip my dress," I explain, turning around.

"Is Chirag taking you?" she asks as she slowly, slowly zips me up. I walk to the mirror by the front door and stand on my tippy-toes to get a better look.

Even zipped, the dress shows a lot of skin. The scars running down my neck and onto my left arm are completely visible. In the back, along the edge of the dress, the rough scars on my left side stick out when I move. The silk is so thin that even where my scars are covered, they show through, creating ripples and ridges beneath the material.

And I'm not wearing a stitch of black. Not even black mascara.

"No," I answer. "Chirag is taking another girl."

"I'm sorry." Mom's standing behind me and I can see the reflection of her face in the mirror beside my own. I don't have her nose anymore, but somehow, we still look related. There is something else, something about the way that I focus my gaze, something in the way that I square my shoulders and lift my chin that reminds me of her.

I shake my head. "Don't be. I broke up with him, remember?"

"That doesn't make it any easier," she says, and I don't argue. "Do you still love him?" she asks. It's been so long since we had a real conversation, just the two of us, about anything other than my pills and my physical therapy, my grades and my teachers.

I turn around to face her. "Not the way I used to."

She smiles, and for a second I think she's going to cry. Instead she shakes her head and rolls her shoulders onto her back like I used to do before a race.

Unlike with Dad or Serena or Chirag, it doesn't feel like there are so many things that I haven't said to my mom. Until Group, she was the only person I didn't worry would hate me if I actually said what I was thinking.

But maybe it wasn't because I didn't care what she thought of me.

Maybe it was because I always knew, deep down, that she would love me no matter what I said or thought or did.

And suddenly, I know that there *is* something that I haven't said to her.

"Thank you."

"What for?"

"For making me go to school, and take my medicine, and go to Group, and—" I pause. "For letting me get the transplant. I know it wasn't your first choice."

Mom shakes her head. Finally, I understand why she wished they had more time to make the decision, instead of pushing things forward the way she always has with absolutely everything else. She was frightened.

"It wasn't my choice to make," she says. Now tears do spring up in her eyes. "The other night, when you drove your father into the city, I wasn't sure if you'd come back home. I thought you might decide to stay with him."

"I thought about it," I admit. "Sometimes—for a long time, before my accident even—I wished you two would split up just so that I could live with him. With him, it's just . . . easier, I guess."

She nods, looking pained. "I know."

"But the night he moved out, it didn't even occur to me to stay with him," I say honestly. "And if you'd asked me, I would have chosen you," I finish finally, a lump rising in my throat.

Mom's tears spill over, and I put my arms around her. It's the first time since all of this happened that she's actually cried in front of me. With my heels on, I'm about five inches taller than she is and it feels, just for a second, with my arms wrapped around her and her head no higher than my neck, like I'm the one taking care of her.

"Don't make me cry," I say, swallowing the lump in my throat. "I don't want to have to do my makeup all over again."

Mom pulls away, wiping her tears. "I wouldn't want to ruin it. You did a beautiful job. I'm so proud of you."

"For finally learning how to use makeup?" Mom laughs, and I shake my head. "I know you're disappointed with the way I've handled all this."

"How can you say that?"

"You wanted a daughter who could get up in front of the school and speak about her experience. Someone who'd never even consider going a day off her meds. Someone who'd come out of this stronger than she was before."

"Maisie," Mom says solemnly, "I am so proud of you. And you *are* strong. Stronger than I could have imagined. Stronger than I would have been, had this happened to me."

I feel myself blushing. "Maybe I should get dressed up more often," I say.

"Maybe you should," Mom agrees.

Serena cheers when she sees me, a high-pitched screech that makes me grin.

"Ohmygodohmygod. May-Day, you're *coming* tonight?" The nickname sounds like spring and sunshine for the first time in months.

I nod, spinning around so Serena can see everything.

"Chirag is going to pass out when he sees you looking like that," she says, and I don't argue. Instead, I ask her to clip the matching headpiece into my hair. Last year, I thought I might not wear it because people would stare. Tonight, they're going to stare no matter what. So I may as well be the best-dressed girl there.

Serena and I are walking out the door when my mother stops us.

"Just let me take a picture," she pleads, and Serena and I turn and face her obediently, putting our arms around each other, grinning broadly.

Click. The first picture anyone besides the doctors, tracking my progress, has taken of me since my surgery.

"Perfect," Mom says. "This one's going up on the wall," she adds, turning to face the collage of photographs on the wall behind her, all those framed pictures of our family. Her old marriage. My old face.

"The wall is already packed," I point out. "There's no room for a new picture."

She shakes her head. "I'll just have to take one of the old ones down to make room for something new," she answers, and I hug her once more before Serena and I run out into the fog.

FORTY-SEVEN

Our school has been transformed into a Winter Wonderland. Like most kids who live where the temperature rarely drops below freezing, every student at Highlands High is fascinated by snow, so my class picked a prom theme that gave us an excuse to get a snow machine. They've coated the hills outside the building and people are racing down on sleds in their formal wear. Serena holds my hand as she makes a dash for the sleds, but I pull away.

"I'm going inside," I explain.

Serena hesitates. "Do you want me to come?"

I listen to the shouts of my classmates flying down the hills and shake my head.

"Good luck."

I shrug, trying to look calmer than I feel. "Piece of cake, right?"

Serena leans in to kiss my cheek and then runs off toward the sleds.

The music in the gym is almost deafeningly loud. I'm shaking so hard that I can feel the headpiece teetering on top of my head, threatening to fall off. No, Serena secured that thing with about a zillion bobby pins. It's not going anywhere.

No one is staring at me. Maybe it's too dark in here—under the paper snowflakes and twinkle lights—to see the pink lines on my cheeks, the rippling scars peeking out from the side of my dress. Or maybe they simply don't care, too caught up in their own prom nights to notice mine.

Or maybe they've finally all just gotten used to me.

I spot Alexis and Chirag in the center of the dance floor. Even though the music is upbeat and fast, Alexis is clinging to Chirag like they're slow-dancing. Is it just my imagination, or is she hanging on a little more tightly than he is? Is she staring into his eyes while he glances around the room like he's looking for something?

Or someone.

Our eyes lock. It's officially too late for me to turn around. Too late to beg one of the limo drivers waiting in the school parking lot to take me home, where I could take off this dress, change back into long sleeves and pants, wash off my makeup, and climb into bed.

Instead, I take a step forward, into the press of bodies moving in time with the beat. I struggle to steady my shaking hand as I tap Alexis on the shoulder. Her dress is strapless, black and shiny. I feel sweat on her bare skin when I touch her.

Shouting to be heard over the music, I ask, "Can I cut in?" even though that sounds like a line from an old movie, something no one would actually say in real life.

For a split second, I think she's going to say no. But before she can say anything at all, Chirag peels himself away from her, wrapping his long fingers around her wrists and pulling her arms down from around his neck.

"Of course," he answers. The music shifts into a slow song and Chirag holds his arms out for me. I step toward him, my left hand on his shoulder, my right hand in his. But I don't stand nearly as close to him as Alexis did.

We dance in silence, Chirag leading in time to the music. His right hand rests on my left hip, over my scars.

"You're a good dancer," I say, surprised. I never knew that about him. "I guess we never actually danced together."

Chirag shakes his head. "Never had the chance."

I want to tell him that I know what he did the night of last year's prom, to give him credit for mourning before I did, like it was another one of our races and this time, he won.

But instead I lean into him, willing my muscles to relax, begging my body to stop shaking. Silently, I repeat the words Marnie has told me a thousand times during therapy: *Talk to your muscles, teach them to do what you want them to.* Chirag bends his left arm, bringing me closer. Despite the paper snowflakes hanging from the ceiling and the snow on the ground outside, I don't think I've ever been so pleasantly warm. I'm finally living the picture in my head: the girl in the green dress, slow-dancing with Chirag.

Before my accident, I thought we'd play on the beach all summer long, then spend senior year walking through the halls with our hands in each other's back pockets. But maybe, even if my face hadn't changed, *we* still would have. Maybe all those little things that bothered me would have made me erupt one day, or maybe we just would have fallen out of love, the way people do from time to time.

But whatever might have happened, there is one thing I know for sure: If I'd never gotten hurt, I'd have had the chance to say *I love you, too,* just like I said in my head a thousand times.

And so I say it now, because Chirag deserves to hear it: "I love you, too."

"What?"

I shake my head. This isn't how I planned it. First, I was going to say *I'm sorry*. I was going to apologize for being a bad girlfriend and a bad friend, for making everything awkward and awful between us. I was going to explain that I'd handled things all wrong, that I should have broken up with him immediately after my accident. It would have been so much better that way: He'd still have driven me to school and PT and anywhere else I'd asked him to. He'd have been a good friend at a time when it was impossible for anyone to be a good boyfriend to me. *Then* I was going to tell him that I'd been lying when I said I never loved him.

And not because I'm trying to re-create something that's gone. But because I owe it to the people we used to be. To the old Maisie. The girl who never got to say it. The girl who wanted to say it. Who *deserves* to say it.

"I never got to say I love you, too," I say, louder this time. "I couldn't stand the idea that you might go the rest of your life without hearing me say that."

Chirag shakes his head. "You didn't have to say it, May," he says, and my mouth is filled with the taste of him: clean sheets and Ivory soap and cumin.

"But I never should've said—"

Chirag interrupts me. "I know why you said what you did the night we broke up," he says, swallowing so that I can see his Adam's apple bobbing up and down beneath his bow tie.

"You do?"

He nods. "I always knew." He smiles. "Do you remember when I said I had about a million things to tell you that night?" Now it's my turn to nod. "Well, that wasn't entirely true. I mean, yes, a lot of things have happened since your accident, and someday I'm going to tell you every single one of them, but mostly, that night, I just wanted to tell you that I loved you—even though it was over, even though so much had changed. You know what I mean?"

I know exactly what he means. I open my mouth to begin my apologies, but Chirag speaks first, anticipating my thoughts just the way he used to. "You have nothing to apologize for," he says softly. "Say you're sorry to everyone else if you have to. But you never have to say it to me."

I look up at his face—his perfect, unmarred face. I guess there are some things that I don't have to say out loud. I press my cheek against his chest and we sway back and forth to the music.

"You know," I begin with a smile, "you never really *said* it. You just wrote it on a piece of paper, like that was enough to make it official. *I* actually said it out loud: *I love you, too.*"

Chirag grins. We're competing again, just like we used to. I guess my competitive side didn't vanish completely. Maybe I'm only competitive about a few select things now.

Like teasing Chirag.

"I literally *just* said it," Chirag protests.

"No," I counter. "You said that you *wanted* to say it. That's not the same thing."

Chirag cocks his head to the side, considering. "So really, when you said it, you didn't need the *too*, right?"

I shrug. "Maybe not."

Out of the corner of my eye, I see Alexis Smith standing at the edge of the dance floor, her hands folded across her chest. Ellen and Erica are standing on either side of her. They look like bodyguards, ready to take me down the instant I make a wrong move. Ellen leans over and whispers in Alexis's ear, maybe something about how Alexis doesn't have to worry about a freak like me stealing her man.

No, Ellen wouldn't be that mean. Not anymore.

"I think we're pissing off your girlfriend," I say softly.

"She's not my girlfriend," Chirag says. "I mean, we've been hanging out a lot lately, but tonight, she's just my prom date."

"I'm not sure anyone told her that."

"Well, I'll make sure she gets the memo," he says, and slowly, he leans down until his lips are just above mine. His right hand still rests on my left hip, and he begins tracing my scars, his fingers curling over the edge of my dress, touching the broken parts of me. It doesn't feel anything like I imagined it would. His touch is warm, gentle, and insistent, like he could go on forever.

So I stand on my tiptoes and press my lips to his. Chirag opens his mouth slightly, then closes it. For half a heartbeat, I think he's having second thoughts, but then I realize it's something else entirely: He's scared that he might hurt me. So I press against him, guiding his lips to follow mine. I want him to know that it's okay. *I'm* okay.

The kiss is warm, and my knees feel wobbly, just the way they used to. And I discover that there are butterflies, even for someone like me.

The music changes. A fast song comes on, and Chirag and I pull apart, grinning sheepishly, like two kids whose parents have just caught them making out.

I don't know if falling in love a second time, like Michael and his girlfriend did, is in the cards for Chirag and me. But I do know that what we had before was real. He was the first boy I loved, the first boy to love me. And nothing will ever change that.

And I know that *this* is the way things should have ended between us, not with me slamming his car door shut behind me.

It should have ended with a kiss good-bye.

"I better go," I shout over the music. Chirag nods. We glance at Alexis Smith, who appears to have turned fuchsia in the last two and a half minutes. I spot Serena at the edge of the dance floor and make my way toward her, taking her hands in mine. Her skin is icy from the snow outside and I press her fingers to my cheeks, which are flushed and warm. I don't care that she is touching my scars. I don't even care that Alexis is dragging poor Chirag out the door and to the parking lot, where I'm pretty sure they'll have a fight every bit as epic as the fights my parents used to have.

I can't stay much longer. Adrenaline kept me wide-awake tonight—I could taste it—but it's beginning to fade now, and exhaustion is taking its place. I'll call my mother, ask her to come and get me. I have an appointment in the morning with Dr. Boden, one in a long list of appointments I will have with doctors and psychologists and physical therapists for the rest of my life, whether I move to New York or stay in California. I will always carry around a box of pills so that my bag jingles when I move. I will always wish this hadn't happened to me.

I'll never look the way I did before. No amount of makeup will turn me into the pretty girl I used to be—despite the pale skin, the freckles, and the big nose that I hated. Years from now, even after I've spent more time with *this* nose, *this* chin, *these* cheeks than the sixteen years I spent wearing the features I was born with, sometimes I will still be surprised when I see my reflection in the mirror. Maybe I'll never be able to sleep through a thunderstorm. And even though I danced with a prince at the ball tonight—even though I'm leaving early just like Cinderella—I don't feel like a fairy-tale princess about to find her happy ending.

But I know who I am. I'm a girl with a sharp tongue and wicked sense of humor, just like Adam said. I'm a girl who fell in love for the first time when she was sixteen, who's had the same best friend since she was five, who fights with the mother she loves fiercely and whose father sang her to sleep every night when she was small.

I also understand that who I am is fluid, ever-changing, impossible to pin down—no matter how much I'd like to make a list and stick to it. And who I am would be ever-changing even if I hadn't been out running that morning, even if that tree had never been struck by lightning, even if I'd never heard the words *electrical fire* or *face transplant*.

But I'd like to think that I will always feel this grateful: to my doctors, to my friends and my parents, and especially to the donor whose skin I live in. Whose skin has become my own.

Finally, I feel lucky, just like everyone said I was. And I hope that will never change.

Acknowledgments

I learned so much as I researched and wrote this novel, and so many friends and colleagues helped me along the way. Tremendous thanks to Emily Seife for giving me the chance to tell this story, and for all of her extraordinary help and encouragement as I navigated my way through it.

Enormous thanks to David Levithan and the entire team at Scholastic. Thanks to Elizabeth Parisi for the lovely cover and to Abby Dening for the book design; to Rebekah Wallin in production and to Jessica White, my fantastic copy editor; and thanks to Veronica Grijalva and Caite Panzer and the sub-rights department. Thanks also to the entire sales, marketing, and publicity teams, especially Tracy van Straaten, Saraciea Fennell, Bess Braswell, and Emily Morrow.

Enormous gratitude to the inimitable Mollie Glick and the wonderful team at Foundry for their unwavering support and guidance, especially to Joy Fowlkes and Deirdre Smerillo.

Thanks to the many resources online and in-print that helped me as I researched this novel, starting with an article written by Raffi Khatchadourian and published by *The New Yorker* in February 2012. Many thanks to Amy Li, Shoshana Woo, and special thanks to Dr. Bill Losquadro for answering my many questions (no matter how absurd they must have seemed to him!)—and thanks to my sister Courtney for putting us in touch.

Thanks to my teachers, colleagues, family, and friends for their advice and support: thanks for reading and for listening.

And, as always, thanks to JP Gravitt, for everything.

"It's funny how dogs and cats know the inside of folks better than other folks do, isn't it?"   —Eleanor H. Porter, *Pollyanna*

About the Author

Alyssa Sheinmel is the *New York Times* bestselling author of several novels for young adults, including *A Danger to Herself and Others*, *R.I.P. Eliza Hart*, and *What Kind of Girl*. She is the coauthor of *The Haunting of Sunshine Girl*. Alyssa grew up in Northern California and New York, and currently lives and writes in New York. Follow Alyssa on Instagram and Twitter at @AlyssaSheinmel or visit her online at alyssasheinmel.com.

Books about Love.
Books about Life.
Books about You.

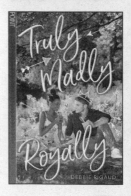

POINT PAPERBACKS
THIS IS YOUR LIFE IN FICTION
IreadYA.com

POINTSUMMER19